MORE GROOVY GUMSHOES

Private Eyes in the Psychedelic Sixties

Michael Bracken, Editor

MORE GROOVY GUMSHOES

Private Eyes in the Psychedelic Sixties

Down & Out Books
3959 Van Dyke Road, Suite 265
Lutz, FL 33558
DownAndOutBooks.com

Cover design by Zach McCain

ISBN: 1-64396-306-6
ISBN-13: 978-1-64396-306-8

For Temple
My Love, My Muse, My Everything

TABLE OF CONTENTS

BY THE BAY

Wendy Harrison

From my desk, I could read my name backward on the opaque glass panel in the door. Looking at it from the hallway, it read "P.J. Sampson, Private Investigator." Spelling out Penelope Juniper Sampson would've cost more, and I thought it might scare off clients. A girl PI? Not the thing in 1961, especially not in a small city in Southwest Florida. When I first opened, I had a speech ready in case whoever walked in assumed I was P.J. Sampson's secretary. I was a former cop, I'd explain, who left the force after being injured but wanted to use my skills to help people. No need to add that I was badly beaten by a john in a prostitution sting. Charlie, my so-called backup, decided to slow-walk coming to my rescue when the john didn't respond well to the handcuffs I was hooking onto his wrists. Charlie figured I had it coming, scoring higher than he did on the sergeant's exam. When finally released from the hospital, I knew I'd have to find another way to make a living. It was enough to have to watch my back with the perps. I was tired of being the lone woman on the force and having to defend myself against guys like Charlie. Most of the officers were all right, but there were enough like him to wear me down. The new gig had worked out. There were lots of cheating husbands with suspicious wives, even in Porta Larga. Word had spread I was a ticket to a bigger divorce settlement, and being a woman turned out to be a plus.

The open window let in a taste of sunshine and an April breeze. It was Friday, I had paid the rent the previous week, and life tasted like spring. The radio kept me company, but when the news came on, I switched from reports of Castro's latest tirade against the dirty American capitalists to a music station that was playing Elvis Presley. I was singing along to "Are You Lonesome Tonight?" when I saw a silhouette outside the office door, followed by a tentative knock.

"It's open."

A woman flowed gracefully through the doorway and reached back to close it. "Are you P.J. Sampson?" The wide skirt of her pastel print dress swung as she turned toward me, but the fabric didn't disguise her generous figure. Long dark hair framed her face, and her voice was low and sweet.

I nodded and pointed to one of the two chairs in front of my desk. "Please." When she settled down, she had a death grip on the purse on her lap, the only sign of stress. "How can I help you?"

She hesitated and then looked directly into my eyes. "It is my husband. I think he is seeing another woman." There was a hint of an accent in the rhythm of her words.

Pulling a pad toward me, I started by asking my basic client questions. Name: Elena Fernandez. Husband's name: Roberto Fernandez. Address: 405 Wisteria Lane, Porta Larga. Phone: ED5-8209. When I asked about children, she showed the first sign of emotion. "None," she said, her voice quivering, "but we want to." She explained that they met on a blind date in Miami two years earlier. He was a doctor in Cuba but escaped before Castro took power in the beginning of 1959. She was a nurse, second-generation Cuban, and they fell in love. They married three months after they met and moved to Porta Larga, where friends helped him get work at the local hospital.

"We were so happy," she said. "But then he started going out at night. With friends from work, he told me. But I never got to meet them. And now he is going away for a weekend with them." She shook her head. "He has been different. He does not talk to me. I knew something was wrong, but this? It is too much. I have to know."

I told her my usual rates, and she pulled an envelope filled with cash out of her purse. "I have been putting money aside. He did not even notice."

I counted the money and wrote a receipt. I arranged to be outside her house early Saturday morning so I could follow him. "I'll let you know what I find out," I assured her. "It could be just what he said." We both knew I was probably wrong.

At sunrise on Saturday morning, I pulled up in my sweet silver-and-blue '55 Ford Fairlane, half a block from Elena's house. It was a small wooden structure with an actual white picket fence and a garden that had been carefully tended. I settled in to wait, wishing I had a cup of coffee to help pass the time. Unfortunately, coffee and stakeouts didn't work out well when you were a woman and couldn't take care of things behind a handy tree. Two hours went by, and the door of the house opened right at 8:00 a.m., just when Elena said her husband was planning to leave. He was tall and dark with close-cropped hair and perfect posture, and he carried a duffel bag in one hand. Elena stood in the doorway, watching him walk to the curb and get into their car—a dark green sedan with plates from Miami. She looked around but didn't spot me before she gave up and went back inside.

Before I pulled out, I gave her husband a chance to reach the corner. Heading across town, he made three stops to pick up passengers, men who also carried small overnight bags. This didn't look anything like a cheating husband on the move. My curiosity grew as I maintained my distance but kept Roberto's car in sight. After the third stop, he headed west to the Porta Larga marina and pulled into the parking lot. Finding a space on the street only took a moment, so I was able to find them again as they walked to the dock. A high-powered motorboat waited for them. It was frustrating to watch as they settled in with several other men and the boat began to move. As it entered the widest part of the river, the engines roared, and they were quickly out of sight. This was getting interesting.

Back at my office, I called Brady Ledford. Brady was a retired cop who had been enraged but not surprised by the story about why I left the force. Adopting me as a special project, he helped me get my PI license. A good guy with a big heart. I told Brady what I was up to and asked if he could take the first shift surveilling the marina on Sunday morning in case Roberto returned early. We agreed I'd relieve him around two o'clock and stick it out until the boat came back.

I drove to the marina on Sunday afternoon. Pulling into the parking lot, I spotted Brady's car. The windows were closed, which seemed strange since the weather was mild. As I approached the driver's side, I saw Brady slouched down, head resting back against the top of the seat. I knew before I knocked on the window that he was dead. There wasn't any way Brady would be sleeping on the job, especially not one he was doing for me.

I tried the door handle, and as the door swung open, Brady's body fell sideways toward me. I grabbed at his shoulder and pushed his lifeless body back inside and closed the door. No one was inside the marina office, so I went to the desk and used the phone to call the police. I told the operator I was reporting a death and gave her my details and location. As I put the receiver back, I heard a voice behind me.

"Can I help you?" I turned and saw a short, middle-aged woman in jeans that probably fit her ten years ago and a gray T-shirt with the name of the marina on it. "I'm Margaret Webster. I'm the manager here."

"I needed to use your phone," I told her as I motioned toward the parking lot. "My friend is dead." I couldn't think of any other way to say it, but her shocked expression made me a little sorry I hadn't sugarcoated it for her.

"Take me there?" she asked.

As we walked through the lot, I explained I was meeting a friend, but he had died in his car while waiting for me. She touched my arm and told me she was sorry. Not nearly as sorry as I was. Brady was getting on in years, but this didn't make sense. As far as I knew, he didn't have any medical issues, and he would've told me if he had. We were that close. I wasn't ready to let myself think about the possibility there was a connection between the mysterious gathering of men and his death. It seemed unlikely, I reassured myself. I couldn't be responsible for him dying like this.

We waited together near the car, my new friend Margaret and me. "I lost my Douglas last year." She sighed. "Just like this. One minute he was here, tying up a boat, and the next, gone. His heart, you know."

I murmured something sympathetic, but she seemed to understand I wasn't in the mood to talk.

A police car and an ambulance pulled into the lot. Two cops walked toward us, and I explained what had happened. Fortunately, no one thought to ask me what Brady and I had been doing here. "Heart attack," Margaret told the police. "Just like my Douglas."

We were joined by EMTs who opened the car door and performed a perfunctory examination of the body. One of them turned to me. "That's what it looks like, but we should wait for the ME."

I gave the officers my information and described how I had to push the body back into the car. They had already taken Brady's wallet and had his ID confirmed. "Is it okay if I leave now?" I asked. "I'm not feeling well. This has been a shock." To emphasize my weakened condition, I swayed a bit.

They exchanged glances and the older one nodded. "That's okay, ma'am. We can contact you for a statement if we need it." It was clear he didn't think they would. This looked like a no-brainer. I hoped they were right.

After I made it home, I called Elena but there was no answer.

I had a lot more questions for her but decided to wait until morning before trying again. I was wiped out by the death of my friend and the waves of guilt that left me stunned.

When I woke the next morning, it felt like I was waking from a nightmare until I realized the nightmare was real. Brady was dead, and it was my fault. After a cup of coffee and a stale doughnut, I drove to Elena's house. She answered the door, showed me into the living room, and gestured toward a chintz-covered armchair. Perching on a couch across from me, she was stiff with anxiety.

"Was I right?" Unconsciously, she twisted the gold band on her ring finger.

Shaking my head, I said, "I don't think so, Elena." I described what I had seen but left out the part about Brady. "Do you know why he would be traveling somewhere by boat with these men?"

"No. When he came home late last night, he said nothing about boats. I kept asking, and he told me they had gone to Naples to talk about starting a second hospital. You would not take a boat to Naples, would you?"

Not personally, I wouldn't. Driving down Route 41 would be my choice. Looking around the room, I saw a group of framed photos on a bookshelf. One caught my interest, so I picked it up and turned to her. "Is this Roberto?"

She took it from me, and tears began to fall. "This was him in Cuba. He was in Batista's Guardia Nacional. The National Guard."

That explained the uniforms. I pointed to a soldier standing next to Roberto. "Who is this?"

"His friend Andres. Andres Guardron. They came here together to escape Castro."

I knew that face. It belonged to one of the men on the boat with Roberto. I told her that and wrote down Andres's address and phone number. "Do you know anyone else Roberto might have been with this weekend?"

She shook her head. "I don't know any of the other people he works with. He did have a visitor once. He said his name was Edouardo, but he was an American, so that might not be true. He came once, and Roberto was angry and told him never to come to the house again. But he would not explain to me who he was."

"Any idea what they were doing?"

"No. But as long as Roberto was with Andres this weekend, I am not going to worry." She had a beautiful smile. It was the first time I had seen it. Her whole body relaxed, a weight lifted. "Andres has no one. We are his family. If they were together, it was nothing bad." Holding out her hand for me to shake, she said, "I am sorry for taking up your time. I did not think Roberto would have another woman. We love each other so much. You have given me a great gift." I was glad I had a satisfied customer, but I wasn't about to walk away from this until I found out what happened to Brady.

The only clues I had led to the marina. It was late in the afternoon by the time I returned. My plan was to wait there to see if Roberto had gone out again without telling Elena. I settled in, uncomfortably aware that I was in the same position in my car that Brady had been in his. I thought I was probably in for a long wait if Roberto returned as late as he had the night before. But I got lucky. I was there only an hour when a van filled with men pulled into the lot. The passengers headed for the dock and then waited. This time, I didn't recognize any of their faces. Ducking out of the car, I made my way to the marina office with its "Boats for Rent" sign in the window. Margaret wasn't there, which saved me from having to explain why I was going for a boat ride right after my friend had dropped dead.

The man behind the counter was tall, tan, and middle-aged. He had the look of a cop, an attitude I recognized off the bat. It was in his eyes, coldly assessing me, and where his hands went, ready to reach for a weapon. Ignoring his unwelcoming stare, I told him I wanted a small boat with a motor that was ready to go right away. "I don't want to miss another minute of this beautiful day on the water," I babbled. When I spotted a display of small binoculars on a shelf behind the desk, I bought a pair, telling him how much I loved watching the seabirds. When he began to pay closer attention than my rantings deserved, I quickly filled out the paperwork. He pointed me to a small Chris-Craft gray runabout not far from where the men were waiting to be picked up. I thanked him, assured him I had grown up around boats—which fortunately was the truth—and headed out. As soon as I was around the corner of the building, I stopped and waited out of sight as a large boat pulled up to the dock. It was identical to the one that had taken Roberto out the day before. My little rental would've fit neatly on the rear deck. As soon as the new group of men settled aboard and the boat headed into the river, I ran to where my boat was waiting, started the motor, and followed them from as far a distance as I could while still keeping them in sight.

The sun was sliding lower toward the water, but I couldn't take the time to enjoy the view, afraid I'd lose them in the fading light. There were other boats on the water, so I wouldn't be conspicuous. I knew the river well, and soon saw they were heading for Useppa Island. The beautiful island had a fascinating history that included Calusa Indians, a pirate named José Gaspar, and a plush resort for the rich and famous, although not all at the same time. Many of the buildings still stood, but the island hadn't been used for decades except by boaters who wanted a place to picnic.

I stayed well offshore, but I could still see the men disembarking and walking inland. Slowly, I circled the island, grateful for the binoculars. As the boat bobbed gently on the waves, I trained the binoculars on the wooded areas without seeing any signs of life. Then, as I panned to the small beach, I could see a group of men lined up in military formation. As I watched, some of them marched out of sight into the woods. The rest of them continued close-order drills with rifles.

I had a bad feeling that if I didn't get out of there in a hurry, it might not end well. I turned the boat back the way I had come. As soon as I was out of hearing distance from the island, I revved the motor and headed back to the marina. I knew I wasn't one for imagining things, but I couldn't make sense out of it. I began to think that if this group had become aware that Brady was watching them. Was it possible Brady had seen too much and had to be silenced?

Back at the marina, I returned the boat keys to the office. The man who had rented it to me wasn't there, and I avoided any conversation with the young man who had replaced him. I regretted having given my real name and address when I filled out the rental form, but they would've had it from my driver's license. As I walked through the parking lot, I looked around to see if anyone was paying attention to me. I didn't see anyone worrisome, and I was happy to get to my car. Reaching into the glove compartment, I pulled out my Colt. No one had pushed me to return it when I left the force. They wanted me out as quickly and quietly as they could manage, and I figured it was the least they owed me. I made sure it was loaded and left it next to me on the seat as I drove out of the lot and turned toward home. It was already dark, and I decided I would try to talk to Andres the next day. Thanks to Elena, I knew where I could find him.

I was a mile from home when I realized I was being followed. The car behind me had been keeping a steady pace, a little too far back to see the driver or read the license plate in the darkening night, but it had stayed with me all the way from the marina. I hadn't noticed at first because traffic had been heavy, but the passenger side headlight wasn't working, and now that the traffic had thinned out, it was unmistakable.

I ran through my options. Stop and confront the driver. Head for the nearest police station. Try to put distance between us. I was saved from choosing when the other car pulled next to me at high speed and bumped the left side of my bumper, spinning me off the road. A pit maneuver. I had used it myself to stop a fleeing car. This was someone who knew what he was doing. Not a good sign.

I slammed on the brakes, and my car screeched to a stop in front of a large oak tree. The engine was still running, but before I could back up, my door was wrenched open and the man who had rented me the boat reached in and grabbed my throat. "Nosy, aren't you?" I assumed that was a rhetorical question. "What were you doing at Useppa? Who knew you were there? Who sent you?" The best I could do was gurgle at him.

He must have realized he wasn't going to learn anything until I could breathe again, and he eased up on my throat. Enough for me to gasp out a few words. "Don't know what you're talking about. Who are you?"

"You first," he growled. "Who're you?"

"Just a local birdwatcher." He wasn't amused or convinced. I choked out the words. "Your turn."

"I don't have time to waste on you." He let go of my neck and stepped back, pulling a small aerosol can from his jacket and aiming it at my face. I assumed it wasn't going to be shaving cream. "Another heart attack, coming up," he growled.

Not so fast, I thought as I grabbed my revolver from the seat next to me and pointed it at him. He looked surprised as the shot caught him between the eyes. As the can dropped from his hand, he fell backward onto the ground. I slid out of the car and retrieved the can. After storing it gently in my glove compartment, I turned to take a closer look at my attacker.

What was left of the back of his head reassured me he wasn't going to hurt anyone else. Searching his pockets, I found a wallet with a driver's license belonging to Edward Howard. Maybe this was the mysterious Edouardo? The address on the license was the same as the marina where he had been working. I emptied the contents of the wallet on the ground and discovered a slip of paper under a flap where his paper money was. In the light from his car's headlight, I saw a handwritten phone number.

I left him there but kept the phone number and returned to my car. I backed up, away from the tree and out to the road. At a closed gas station, I used a pay phone near the pumps and dialed the police. "I want to report an abandoned car on Victoria Road near Palmetto," I said. "It's blocking traffic." I hung up and headed home, this time making sure there was no one behind me.

Once in my apartment, I took a long hot shower and, with regret, cut up the clothes I had been wearing and buried them in my kitchen garbage can under the remains of several pizza boxes and beer cans. After stirring the mess around, I removed the bag and put it next to the door, so I'd remember to take it outside when I left the apartment, in time for the city garbage man to pick it up. I figured I was overreacting. There was no reason for anyone to connect me to the body on Victoria Road, but I wasn't taking chances. The next problem was the gun. If everything went wrong and the police found it on me, ballistics could tie it to the murder. At least, they would call it murder. It was a clear case of self-defense, but I hadn't yet figured out what to do about the mystery canister. Reluctantly, I decided the gun had to go. I still had a backup piece, a smaller revolver than the one I used on the mysterious Mr. Howard, but it wouldn't be the same. I had killed him with the gun I had used during my years on the force, and even though I had never fired it outside the shooting range, it had sentimental value—admittedly a strange concept for a killing machine.

I drove across the Peace River Bridge, slowing down when I reached the highest part of the slope. There were no other cars on the bridge and no sounds from the river below. I threw the gun out the window, waiting until I heard the plopping sound as it hit the water, and then headed home to face a sleepless night.

First thing in the morning, I dialed the number on the piece of paper. The call didn't go through, so I dialed zero and asked the operator to dial it for me.

She asked, "Are you sure?"

That seemed like an odd question. "Why wouldn't I be?"

"If I put the call through for you, honey, it's going to cost you a bundle. It's long distance, to Washington."

"Washington? The state?"

She giggled. "No. Washington, DC. Where the government is."

I thanked her and hung up. Why did Edouardo, or Edward, have a direct phone number to a government office? I wondered if Andres might know. He was next on my list.

Andres lived in a neighborhood much like Elena's, with small, neat houses. I was glad Elena had told me he wasn't married. Not too many wives would understand an early morning visit from another woman, especially one Andres wouldn't be able to explain easily.

I knocked on the front door. "Yes?" The voice through the door was low, cautious, and accented.

"Mr. Guardron? Elena sent me." The door swung open and the man from the photo stood in front of me.

"Elena? Has something happened to Roberto?"

"May I come in?" I didn't wait for an answer but pushed my way in, feeling happy that my backup revolver was safely tucked into the holster under my loose shirt.

He followed my eyes to the coffee table in front of the couch. It was covered with newspaper, and a disassembled rifle was spread across it. We both chose not to mention what I saw. I sat in a chair at the small round table in front of the window, and he sat across from me.

"Why are you here?" he asked. He had a soldier's bearing and a calm voice, but his eyes weren't calm at all. He sat with one hand on the table and the other on his lap, where I couldn't see it. I mimicked his pose, with my left hand resting casually on the table and my right hand down by my side. His eyes went to my right side and his mouth curved slightly upward. We silently acknowledged the stalemate. I didn't know what he had under the table, but I was guessing it made us even.

"Elena gave me your name," I said. I hesitated and decided

the truth wasn't going to hurt anyone at this point. "She hired me to follow Roberto to find out if he was seeing another woman."

His eyes widened. He wasn't expecting that. "Roberto?" Shaking his head, he opened the hand that was visible as if to show he wasn't hiding anything, on this subject at least. "Elena is his life. Ever since they first met."

"And Cuba? Is Cuba also his life?" I wasn't an idiot. If Roberto wasn't spending his free time with another woman, he was spending it in secret military training. Elena had made it clear that Roberto fled Cuba to save himself from Castro, not because he didn't love his country. When he didn't answer, I asked another question. "Where does Edouardo come in?"

He became still. "What do you know of Edouardo?"

"I know he was working at the marina, watching for anyone who showed an interest in the men being ferried back and forth from Useppa Island. And I know he had a Washington, DC phone number in his wallet." I paused for breath and hurried on. "And I know he killed my friend who was watching Roberto as a favor to me." I decided to leave out the part where I had shot Edouardo. Andres already looked as if he had heard more than he could deal with.

Suddenly, he pushed back from the table and started to stand. I pulled out my gun and aimed it at his stomach. "Don't," I said.

He slowly raised his hands. His hidden right hand came up empty.

"I'm not going to hurt you," he said.

"That isn't reassuring." I slowly stood, keeping my revolver trained on him.

"You don't know what you're getting into," he told me. "There are some very dangerous men who would harm you if they heard what you are saying. Edouardo is one of them. There are very important people who would do anything to keep this a secret. But I am an honorable man. I won't kill a woman civilian, not even for Cuba."

I was at a loss to figure my way out of this unless I took him at his word. "Why should I believe you?"

"In less than a week, you will know. Please. I beg of you. Do not tell anyone what you have seen before then. After that, it won't matter."

I did the math. Edouardo, or whoever he was, had been the only one who had used force on me. He was dead, which was my way of bringing justice to Brady. Whatever Roberto and Andres were up to, it was way above my pay grade and either no one would believe me or, worse, they would, and I'd be up to my neck in a pit of gators.

I lowered my sidearm. "One week, Andres."

He nodded. "One week. Thank you." His eyes glittered but I figured it was a trick of the light and not the unshed tears it looked like. He held out his hand, and I took it. We shook on my promise, something I believed we both would take seriously.

I turned to leave. In case I was wrong, if he meant me harm, now would be the time. I was quick with a gun and was gambling that even if he went after me, I'd be able to defend myself. But nothing happened as I walked out the door and down the walk to my car.

The next day, I was in my office when the phone rang. It was Elena. "I wanted you to know that Roberto has convinced me he does not have another woman. I need you to forget I ever came to you."

"Your secret is safe with me," I told her. "And Elena, please take care of yourself."

Her voice was soft with resignation. "I will be fine, P.J."

"And Roberto?"

She hung up the phone.

Three days later, I was sitting in my office when a radio news bulletin interrupted Elvis crooning that it was now or never. "An invasion by former Cuban soldiers has begun at the Bay of Pigs in an attempt to rally Cubans to overthrow Fidel Castro." I wondered if Roberto and Andres would survive the battle. The answer came four days later when the morning paper had a grainy photograph of a dozen ragged men under armed guard in Cuba. Roberto and Andres were in the front of the group. I couldn't help but wonder what might have happened if I hadn't listened to Andres and made that call. Would I have changed history?

"Get over yourself," I said out loud and tossed the paper in the kitchen trash can.

POODLES ARE OUT— PANTS ARE IN

gay toltl kinman

What's great about this day and age—I'm talking January 21, 1965—is being able to wear slacks, now called long pants, without being arrested. Women were. You guys won't get it because you've always been able to wear them. So much more comfortable. Although I don't envy you your stiff collars and tie tight against your Adam's apple.

Thanks to Marlene Dietrich and Katharine Hepburn for starting the trend way back before the sixties. They took the brunt of the scorn by wearing slacks.

I'm a PI for a few insurance defense firms. When I investigate claims, sometimes I have to slog around mucky places. That's why I started off praising the current fashion. On some big claims, the insurance companies might smell something fishy and deny the claim. The law firms must defend them and need evidence to justify the refusal to pay. That's where I come in.

Today I went to meet Gavin, a lawyer in a midsize law firm on Wilshire Boulevard. Almost at his office door, I ran into one of the two senior partners. I knew who he was— his stomach precedeth him. Old white guy.

"Who are you, young lady?" Big scowl. I couldn't imagine what he was on a rampage about. I explained who I was.

"If you ever come in here dressed like that again, don't expect any business from us."

"Dressed like what, sir?" I didn't point out his rumpled, off-the-cheap-rack suit and the cigar ash on his stained forties tie.

"Like...like that." He pointed to my long pants.

"Oh, these." I pulled the fabric away from my thigh as though I was about to curtsy. "They cover up my prostheses. But if you wish, I'll wear a miniskirt next time," I said, flaunting my most innocent look. At that moment, Gavin came out of his office, sized up the situation, and grabbed my elbow. As he propelled me down the hallway, he said loudly, "Need to hear your report."

I didn't get to see the old guy's expression, but I did hear him sputtering. Old guys like that are prone to heart attacks. I could only hope.

Under any other circumstance, I would have sat him down and explained the facts of life to him—because, obviously, he didn't know them. "Think about it," I'd say. "Was I supposed to go to an old junkyard in stilettos and a mini to check out a wrecked car that may have been sabotaged?" When stilettos and a mini work better, I wear them—and pantyhose.

Now that's the best reason for wearing long pants—no need to wear pantyhose. If I had to toss anything in the protest bonfire of feminine accoutrements, it wouldn't be my bra.

But to continue with him, I'd tell him I know a lot about cars, which is why most of my cases have to do with them. And that's why I traipse around junkyards and police impound lots. And sometimes ravines and other not-so-handy places.

Because I wear long pants and heavy, steel-toed work shoes, a few guys have called me a dyke and worse. Let 'em. That saves me from having to explain my hands-off policy. Occasionally, I do have to go into an explanation. If the guy still doesn't understand what untouchable means and thinks "no" means "Come On-a My House," then I do a ballet exercise or two with my work shoes. Jeté! And I yell it at the same time. Message delivered.

The reason I mentioned the song is that I just heard Julie London sing it. Still like Rosemary Clooney's rendition the best.

Gavin took me to a nearby restaurant on Wilshire. He always picks white-tablecloth-and-napkin places. "Okay, talk," he said after we had ordered.

I told him about the VW I'd seen the previous day with its nose up against a sturdy pine tree, about fifteen feet off the edge of a mountain road in San Bernardino County. It could have missed the tree and disintegrated about two thousand feet below. That looked to me to be the murderer's plan, and that's the case we were building.

So, slipping down the side of a hill in stilettos and a mini did not happen. Instead, I slid down in sturdy work shoes and pants, carrying my magnifying glass and a roll of tape. No deer-stalker hat, though. I save that for Halloween.

The deputy sheriff had finished his investigation and had arranged for the body to be transported. Now it was my turn.

Even with my unaided eye, I saw the scratches on the black engine cover and the bumper at the back. No one would notice them, but I was looking for them—one of the items on my checklist.

Fresh scratches. No dirt or dust on them. Where the primer paint showed through was clean. Ditto for the bumper. I used the tape to pick up paint and chrome flakes from the VW and hopefully, from the car that pushed it over. I was able to look at everything thoroughly, take pictures, and write up my notes before the tow truck cranked it up roadside.

Snow doesn't usually last long below three thousand feet, and this was a tad above that, so there were a few piles of the stuff around, nothing to hamper anything, nor any good tire tracks. Too many vehicles had been in the small pull-off area of this mountain road. No matter, I had what I needed.

I pushed everything I had—my report, pictures, and an evidence envelope with the tape inside—across the table to Gavin. We both knew the old scenario that would play out in this case.

* * *

Next, I would check out the bereaved widow. Find Mr. Lover—in particular, find his car. Goodbye, big insurance payoff. Fine with me; I get paid a percentage of what I save the insurance company plus the fee for my investigative hours.

You and me—there's always someone we'd like to murder. Do we do it? No. But there are others who aren't you and me—and that's what keeps me in business.

Two days later, I learned from Gavin that the body in the VW—Mr. Husband—had a long contusion on the back of his head. Something that a tire iron would make. No way could that happen in the fifteen feet over the side, even if the body had bounced around inside the VW—which it hadn't.

This case was fitting like a well-worn leather glove.

Next—a visit to the weepy widow, and if she's following the scenario, I'll learn who Mr. Lover is. Find him and perhaps find the car with some scratches and a few flakes of black VW paint. People who want to do away with their significant others haven't read the manual. The Significant Other Is Suspect Number One. Always.

Who profits? The Significant Other. Money is suspected of being the root of all evil. It's the root of a lot of evil, but not all of it. There are other motives just as evil. But money is a great motive for killing someone, and that's evil in my book. Traipsing around a cemetery of dead cars for a living has made me philosophical.

Because I'm a solo PI, I can't cover everything. There's a women's PI group. We call ourselves the Crime Sisters. You won't see any billboards inviting you to join. You must be in the business and network. That's what we're all about.

Another PI and I made the visit. Mr. Senior Partner would approve—we wore dresses and kitten heels. I told Mrs. Bereaved Widow that we're working for the insurance company, and we have a form to fill out to request liquidation of the policy on her behalf. Don't ask me what it means, but it sounds insurancey enough. The form is meaningless, but we do pick up some info. Anyhow, it's a long form, and after I ask a few questions, would she mind if I used her bathroom while my partner continues?

My partner for this meeting, Chatty Cathy, aka Nannette, adds her condolences to the Bereaved Widow and talks about her husband's death and how she handled it. When you take the oath to be a PI, you don't swear on the Bible that you will always tell the truth. Being a part-time actress, which Nannette is, she loves taking on parts like this—becoming the character—and she's good at it. Real good.

I hear her going at it as I walk down the hallway. I'm checking the place out. First of all, I want to find Mrs. Bereaved Widow's purse. The bedroom is the most likely place. I don't expect to find Mr. Lover's name and address on a piece of paper with a neon arrow pointing to it. Not likely there's anything evidentiary hidden in her nightstand—after all, she was sharing it with Mr. Husband. I just snoop around a little. Anything that will give me a lead on who the boyfriend is. And I'm not ruling out a girlfriend, either. Anyhow, I don't find her purse.

I slip out the side door to check out her car. I rummage around in the glove box and under the seats but can't get into the trunk. Damn, she's a neatnik.

The kitchen is visible from the living room, so I don't check it out. No purse in sight. Dang.

Back to the living room. I shake my head so Nannette can tell my foraging around was a bust. She finishes up. We all chat for a bit, not asking questions. That's too obvious. More condolences, then we take our leave. We drive around the corner, I get out and into my car. Nannette drives on. I go back and park up the street. Luckily, there are a lot of cars.

This part of the waiting isn't productive—but necessary. The lovers are not going to get together until they think the coast is clear. But somehow, the longing, the loneliness, and the lust get to them, and one of them makes a move. Usually, it takes about four days. Meanwhile, the Sisters and I each take a shift and watch her place.

Day four, I was on watch when she backed out of the driveway. I followed. We were in the south part of Pasadena on Catalina. She made a left on California, then drove due north on Lake, a right on New York, a left on Hill, and a left on Boston. We were almost to the border of Altadena and across from the golf course.

Somebody up there likes me because a guy came out of a house, walked across the street, and slipped into Mrs. Bereaved Widow's car. Which meant—and before I got any further in my thoughts about where his wheels were—I saw his car.

I fell in love. High, wide, and handsome. A dazzling red convertible Mustang that looked like it had just rolled off the showroom floor. Not cheap—about twenty-five hundred bucks—but not expensive either. Add a racing engine and a few other bells and whistles, and it came to about four grand. I mentally wiped the drool off my chin.

Then I remembered what I wanted the car for. It was parked in the driveway, so I sauntered up as though I had every right to be there. I looked admiringly all the way up one side to the front. I squatted down and checked it for scratches. Bingo! A match! I took my camera out and snapped a few pictures. Used some tape. I saw the scratches but didn't know if I had picked up any chrome or paint flakes from the black VW. I needed a tangible connect between the two cars.

The bumper was higher than the VW's, so it had to go over it. The license plate was dented in a horizontal line where it had pushed against the VW's bumper. That was my scenario.

By this time, if there was anyone in the house, I expected them to have come out all cylinders firing. But nobody did. I took for granted I was being watched by neighbors, so I continued to walk around admiring the car. Then I got bold and rang the doorbell. Nada. If there was anyone home, they didn't come to the door. I didn't sense any movement inside.

I called Gavin and told him what I had. With the license number, he could find out the owner's name. When I had that, I'd do a little research: find out where he worked—if he did—where his favorite watering hole was, and where else he hung out. Then I would "accidentally" meet him. Have to wear the stilettos then and a mini and the cursed pantyhose. Size him up, find what his game was—was he really in love with the lady or looking for a life-support system?

As I said, I know a lot about cars, but I also know a lot about people. I'd be able to figure him out after a few drinks on his part—not mine. All I needed was the opportunity.

Imagine my surprise when Gavin called two days later to tell me about a 1964 Ford Mustang red convertible going off the road in Rubio Canyon. It was just north of where the car had been in the driveway. The top had been down and the driver thrown out, so no surprise he was found dead. The body had been there for about twenty-four hours—a feast for the denizens of the woods. We have bears, coyotes, cougars—and other nibbling creatures.

A little irony here: Mr. Lover had met the death he had planned for Mr. Husband.

Which meant—back to the drawing board.

Now I had to rethink the scenario. No question that the red Mustang was the murder weapon for the husband. But did the weepy widow have another boyfriend? Gavin read me the police report. The person who wrote it would never be accepted in journalism school.

I met with some Sisters to brainstorm.

I had underestimated Mrs. B. Widow. She'd read the manual. Did the Mrs. get rid of Mr. Lover? With the help of Mr. or Ms. Lover #2? Or was there no #2 in sight?

Dang. I hate it when I'm wrong.

I went to the junkyard where the new love of my life lay, a

shattered hunk. I could order a forensic on the car—fingerprints, hair, fibers—but I didn't think it was worth the expense. Traces of her would be in the car, but she could explain that.

At the yard, the Ford Motor Company was about to transport the remains back to the factory to study how their product had survived—not well.

I stared at the car. It was late afternoon, and a ray of sun hit the back of it like a spotlight. Okay, I'd look for push-into-the-canyon marks.

They were there. Magnifying glass and tape in hand, I knew it was a long shot that I'd get some paint and chrome flakes from the pushing car—Mrs. Bereaved Widow's nondescript tan one. I got something. The lab the law firm uses could suss it out as they would with the other pieces of tape I'd given Gavin.

Long shot, because rolling down into a canyon sort of shakes things off—like incriminating paint and chrome flakes.

Gavin was keeping in touch with the coroner's office about what Mr. Lover might have had in his system so that Mrs. B. Widow could get him to sit still while she or someone else nudged the car into the canyon. No tire iron-type contusion this time.

If I was a betting woman, I'd wager my percentage of the payoff that she did it. Which meant I had to get a closer look at her nondescript car. The scratches wouldn't be fresh, but the pattern would tell me what I wanted to know.

What to do? First was to check her car, but that was a little late. Like closing the barn door after the horse had escaped. Three days had elapsed. She had time to get the car shampooed, manicured, and pedicured.

If there was Lover #2, I'd look for that person after checking out Mrs. B. Widow's car. I needed someone to watch my back. No, no, not Nannette, as the Mrs. would recognize her. I had to get another Sister.

How to work this? What was our scenario? Who were we, and why were we checking out her car? Then I had a brilliant idea. We didn't have to do it at her place. When she went to the supermarket, we could park beside her. My partner could keep her busy, if necessary, while I inspected the car.

Only—only, she had a new car.

Dang.

Mrs. B. Widow was a step ahead of me. I didn't like that. Gavin gave me the information from the DMV—the new owner was a scrap metal dealer. When he told me, he added, "The car's probably on its way to San Pedro to be shipped to China and come back reincarnated."

I knew the car hadn't been inoperable, so it would be cannibalized for its parts, which scrap metal dealers also sold. All I wanted to do was look at the front, so if there was even a scintilla of a scratch, that would give me a clue.

I expressed all this to Gavin.

"Can't use that in court. No way, José," Gavin said. He was such an upright, buttoned-down guy, the very image of a lawyer, that I had to laugh when he street-talked.

Yeah, they had the car. It was about to be crushed. Talk about the nick of time. I hotfooted in my heavy work shoes over to the scene. The guys were taking a break, but the vehicle I wanted was about to be flattened—the usual way the cars were shipped.

The look at the front puzzled me. Want scratches? I got 'em. The bumper and the front part of the car had a crosshatch of scratches, gouges, and abrasions. And relatively fresh. Which meant somebody had done a number on it to cover up what I was looking for. I don't get paid big bucks for nothing, so down on my knees I went, into the cold muck. Out came my trusty magnifying glass and tape. My stilettos would have been up to their shanks. I mentally flipped the bird to Mr. Senior Partner.

I could tell the new ones from the old ones, only because I was looking for the difference. The pattern was there but definitely a no-way-José piece of evidence. I used the tape to pick off what looked like a flake of red paint and then took flakes of the paint from the car too.

I wondered what sort of tool could cause that. Find the tool with some of this car's paint on it and maybe have courtroom evidence. Big sigh from me on that issue.

I asked the guy in the office if he could look at the scratches and tell me what might have made them. The tow truck? Preliminary crushing equipment? The only scratches I learned about was him digging into his thin-haired scalp with his dirty fingernails, as if that would give him an answer. Eventually, he shook his head.

The law firm had a tool-mark expert. I thought about calling Gavin and asking for the expert to come out, but the crusher guys were walking back to their posts. I decided not to get in their way.

I had another pair of work pants in the trunk of my car, so I could change out of the mucky ones. Very annoying. I scrubbed my knees with a paper towel and soap in the ladies during my stop at a drive-in. Back at my car, strong, hot coffee was waiting for me on the tray attached to my car door. A few sips and all was right with the world.

Since the Mrs. was a woman and her kitchen looked like it was used, maybe the tool was some sort of appliance. My next stop was Williams-Sonoma, an upscale store that catered to up-scale folk. I might mention it was my first visit.

I walked around, but no neon sign here pointed to the tool. I certainly couldn't ask what gadget would make scratches on a car. I stopped at the knife case. Next to it was the new electric knives' display. Hey, I liked that. I asked for a demonstration. Then asked what sort of marks it might leave on metal. Bingo!

I called Gavin and brought him up to date with my findings and theory. My job was done if there was a link joining all three cars. The insurance company would have enough to deny the claim, and Gavin would have enough to justify the denial.

When the lab results came out, the police would be the ones to get a search warrant and find the electric knife with evidence of chrome and tan car paint. But what did that prove? You can mar your car if you want.

What if she had thrown the knife away like she had the car and bought a new one?

Think positive.

The red paint flakes I took from the front of Bereaved Widow's tan car matched the Mustang. Tan paint flakes from the rear of the Mustang matched her car. Red paint on the back of the black VW and black paint on the front of the Mustang. The connection had been made.

Things sort of fell apart for her. She learned the Mustang owner was not a one-woman man—no surprise there—and he had bragged to one of his girlfriends that he was coming into big bucks—and he didn't mean a herd of deer.

Then the insurance company looked through the paperwork and the circumstances with the agent who wrote the policy. A little funny business there, apparently. Although I wasn't given the assignment to work further on the case, I got my bonus, and I was going to spend it on the new love in my life.

A 1964 Ford Mustang convertible in dazzling red.

And just to make my day even better, Gavin told me about the latest dress edict of Mr. Senior Partner. We met for lunch near the office—the café in the Carnation Building on Wilshire Boulevard. The clam chowder was to die for—whoops—maybe not a good analogy.

"After your visit, he"—meaning Mr. Senior Partner—"sent out a memo to all the women in the office."

"I bet he said 'girls.'"

Gavin choked a bit on that, then went on. "That's all the secretaries, the office manager and our one female attorney. The memo stated that if anyone came to work in long pants, they would immediately be terminated."

It got better.

"The memo went out on Friday afternoon. Monday morning, every woman wore long pants—even the women who'd been with the firm since the ark docked. I heard they had to go shopping to buy a pair of slacks to wear. And it wasn't that they wanted to wear them to work—it was because of the memo saying they couldn't."

"So, he fired everyone, and there was no one to run the office?" I said, with a big grin.

"No way, José. He saw the light. Was so upset he took the rest of the day off—and that's a first. Next day everyone came in dressed as usual. No long pants. But the lawyers, us guys, talked about wearing dresses one day, but we couldn't get a consensus."

We laughed. What a great day this was. Plus, I got a new assignment. Then I slid into my new convertible with the top down, and at every red light a lotta guys waved to me.

Cool!

CROCODILE TEARS

Bev Vincent

Cassandra Parker was only twenty in December 1963, still trying to find her way in the world, when the murder of Selma Chesterton rocked Bellaire, a tiny city embedded in Houston. For four years, Sandy had been a popular member of the cheer squad at Robert E. Lee Senior High School, rising to head cheerleader for her final two years.

It came as a rude awakening to her to discover that the real world didn't place much stock in former cheerleaders. She'd spent a year at TCU studying accounting, but Fort Worth wasn't her style—too many cowboys and religious types—so she'd returned to Houston and found a cheap apartment on the west side, supporting herself with a variety of waiting and secretarial jobs while she figured out what to do with her life. She'd read *The Feminine Mystique* in a women's study class at university and, though she would never have declared herself a feminist or burned her bra—although there were some long days waiting tables when she was sorely tempted to do so—she gave much thought to the unfulfilling life her stay-at-home mother must have endured. Not that she could ever have raised that subject with her.

The murder would have made the front page of the city's two newspapers—the *Post* and the *Chronicle*—no matter when it happened. Bellaire was a ritzy community where people were supposed to feel safe in their cushy mansions. Selma Chesterton was wealthy in a way Sandy could only ever dream of. She was in her mid-sixties when an intruder broke into the house and shot her while she slept, like something out of an episode of *Perry Mason*, a show Sandy never missed. She liked Perry and Della well enough, but it was Paul Drake, the private investigator, who fascinated her. He was ruggedly handsome, although far too old for her, but the things he got to do—that was the best part of the show for her.

That Selma Chesterton's ten-year-old granddaughter was awakened by the shots and rushed from a guest room down the hall to find her grandma dead in her bed added a level of pathos to the story no reporter could resist milking for all it was worth. The nation was still in a collective state of mourning after President Kennedy's assassination just a few weeks earlier. Sandy sometimes wondered whether she would have gone out to see the motorcade on that fateful day in Dallas if she'd stayed in college. Probably not, she decided. Kennedy had been in Houston the day before, and she hadn't bothered to go see him then.

To top it off, Selma Chesterton was killed just two weeks before Christmas, so it was no wonder newspapers carried stories on the front page above the fold for days on end. There were regular televised news conferences where the chief of police reassured the public that they were doing everything within their power to bring the perpetrator of this heinous crime to justice.

However, when there weren't any new developments to report, the police briefings stopped, the headline fonts grew smaller, the news stories briefer, and the articles slipped down the front page until one day—as if by mutual consent—they disappeared into the inner pages of both newspapers. By early spring the following year, there was barely a mention of Selma Chesterton in the media, and the world moved on.

That's not to say the people of Houston forgot about the case. Anywhere drinks were served in the city, there was a good chance the subject would come up at some point in the evening.

Sandy Parker was working at a bar in the Shamrock Hilton one evening when a young woman struck up a conversation with her. At first, Sandy wondered if her customer was trying to flirt with her, but gradually she relaxed and became interested when the woman told her she worked for a private investigation firm as an agent.

Sandy asked so many questions about the job that she ignored her other customers. Finally, the woman told her she should come by the office and meet her boss, Wilson Bennett, if she was serious about a possible change in career. Sandy tucked the detective's business card into her purse behind the bar and assured the woman she would do just that.

After a year on the job, Sandy was constantly begging Bennett for meatier assignments. She was ready to tackle anything and had already demonstrated her aptitude as an investigator with the ability to think on her feet in tense situations.

One morning in early March, Bennett called Sandy into his office. He was smoking a cigar and looked like he was just getting home from a three-day bender. "Are you familiar with the Chesterton case?" he asked.

She nodded, although she was a little hazy on the details.

"Look," he said. "I know who did it. The cops know who did it. Trouble is, we don't have any evidence, and after this long, we aren't likely to find any."

"We?" Sandy asked.

"The victim's daughter hired us to reopen the investigation. Now, I coulda told her that the case was as cold as my ex-wife and deader than..."

"Selma Chesterton?" Sandy suggested.

"Well, yeah. Coulda said something like that. But she wants to pay us good money, and I'll never turn up my nose at that."

"So, what's the plan?"

"The guy who pulled the trigger is named Tony Francone."

"That rhymes."

Bennett gave her a look. She shut up. "He's buddies with...well, you're so smart, why don't you tell me?"

Sandy shrugged.

"The victim's son. Christopher Chesterton. Chesterton paid Francone to kill his mother."

This revelation took Sandy by surprise. "Why on earth would he do that?"

"Money," Bennett said. "Why else? He inherited his share of the estate. Selma Chesterton was old, but she coulda lived another ten, twenty years—even more. Her son decided to speed her along."

"That's insane."

"One thing I learned early on in this job—if a VIP gets whacked, there's a pretty good chance there's another VIP at the other end of the equation. Selma Chesterton was a VIP, no doubt about it. High society and all that. And Christopher Chesterton is now, too. Complicates things for the cops. They can't just go barging around like they normally do. People get upset and make calls to the mayor or their congressman. The governor, even."

Sandy nodded.

"But we can sniff around wherever the hell we want," Bennett said.

Sandy produced a notepad. "Where do I start digging?"

"Put that thing away. Like I said, this case is both cold and dead. There's only one way we're going to solve it."

Sandy raised an eyebrow.

"We have to get him to confess."

"Why would he do that? After all this time. He's free and clear."

"That's where someone smart and beautiful like you comes in. You're going undercover, and you're going to get him to talk."

Sandy sat back in her chair as she let that sink in. She could end up cracking one of the city's great unsolved crimes. All she had to do was get a total stranger to reveal his darkest secret. "How do I do that, boss?"

"That's easy. Just make him fall in love with you."

Bennett and his operatives gave Sandy a crash course in undercover detection. Guys like Francone loved to talk, they told her. He was vain and might already have spilled the beans to a friend. "Although, we probably would have heard about that by now if he did. There's a big reward, and people don't mind selling out their friends if there's cold hard cash on the line."

Sandy thought her undercover character needed a new identity. She wanted to use a name from fiction—she was an avid reader—but the obvious ones didn't suit her. She liked the Tommy and Tuppence stories by Agatha Christie, but she couldn't pull off Tuppence with her Texas drawl, nor Prudence, the character's real name. She finally settled on Nora from the *Thin Man* movies. Nora Charles had a nice ring to it.

She went shopping for a new wardrobe for Nora. She'd never had enough money before to buy nice clothes, but Bennett was footing the bill now. She loved the bright pastel colors of the latest fashions, and they looked good on her lithe body, showing off her long, muscular legs. She tried on a minidress with metallic tights and silver shoes. Although the shop clerk assured her that she looked spectacular in it, it was too risqué for this kind of operation. She wanted the guy to get ideas, but not that kind of idea.

She settled for a patterned blue minidress and a sleeveless red cocktail dress she could use for formal occasions. She also found a knitted yellow top that clung to her body and matched it with blue bell-bottoms with buttons studded across the waist. That would be good for casual wear but sure to catch a man's eye.

Before orchestrating her first meeting with Tony Francone, Sandy memorized every detail in his file. He was an ex-Marine who'd served in Korea and had had a couple of run-ins with the law, although nothing too serious. He knew his way around guns, worked out regularly at the gym—that was where he first crossed paths with Selma Chesterton's son—and liked expensive cars. Chances were he'd already burned through most of what he'd been paid for the hit because he was currently working as a mechanic at a garage on Gessner and not living the life of Riley. Christopher Chesterton, on the other hand, had received half of his mother's estate and had become a well-known man-about-town. Not only did his sister want Francone and her brother convicted of her mother's murder, but she also planned to sue to get his share of the inheritance—whatever was left of it after over a year of high living.

Francone also thought of himself as an intellectual, according to the file. He loved arguing about current affairs, philosophy, and religion, so Sandy made sure she read the newspapers every morning for a week to bring herself up to date with current affairs.

Sandy met him for the first time by simply showing up at his apartment. Bennett had instructed her to be aggressive, and so she was. Francone answered the door wearing an open-fronted shirt with a couple of gold chains dangling around his neck and tight jeans. He was at least three inches taller than Sandy, which put him at six foot two or more, with a close-cropped haircut and a mustache. He was, in fact, quite handsome.

"Is Linda here?" she asked.

His mouth fell open as he looked her over. "No one by that name here," he said. "Are you lost, gorgeous?"

Sandy put her hand to her mouth. "My friend took a call from her, but her writing's a mess. She said she really needed to talk to me—Linda, that is—but now I don't know how to find her." Then she put into play one of her superpowers—crying on demand. It wasn't quite as impressive as the ones in her younger brother's comic books—she was particularly fond of the *Fantastic Four* because that one had a female superhero—but it had served her well. As a teenager, she turned on the faucet whenever she got into trouble with her parents, and, in recent years, she'd gotten out of several traffic tickets thanks to her sobbing abilities.

When Sandy turned on the tears at Francone's door, the object of their investigation invited her inside. He offered the use of his telephone to straighten things out while he fetched her a glass of water. By the time he returned, Sandy had regained her composure. She thanked him profusely for being such a nice guy. Naturally, he asked her out to dinner, but Sandy knew better than to seem too eager. He'd have no reason to suspect she was playing him, but she turned him down just the same, although she did agree to give him her phone number.

He called the next day. Sandy played a little hard to get—but not *too* hard—because, as her grandma used to say, there were plenty of fish in the sea. If she didn't encourage him a little, he might give up on her.

She met him that evening at a bar on Westheimer. Francone was with a few of his friends, strapping young men who also worked at the garage. If it was a test to see if she'd be distracted by the other possibilities on offer, Sandy passed with flying colors. She had eyes only for Francone, giving him her brightest smile and plying him with questions about himself, listening to his answers with wide-eyed fascination.

They arranged to go out for dinner the very next night. Sandy said she would meet him at the restaurant, not wanting to get trapped in his car, where he'd be completely in control. When he walked her out to her car that evening, he pointed out a robin's-egg blue Mercury Park Lane Marauder, the 1964 model, she later learned. "Sure you wouldn't rather I pick you up in that baby?" he asked.

"Another time," she said, giving him a peck on the cheek before slipping away.

It was a delicate operation. She had to get close to him but not so close that it might jeopardize the case. Besides, she had her scruples. They might be experimenting with free love out on the left coast, but there was no way she was going to sleep with a murderer.

And she had to keep reminding herself that was what he was. He was a little rough around the edges, coarse on occasion, but for the most part, he seemed like a nice enough guy. A little dumb and vain beyond belief but otherwise harmless, she would have thought. At times, she wondered if Bennett had made a mistake and they were after the wrong guy. It wasn't lost on her, though, that Lee Harvey Oswald had also been a Marine.

Then, one night at dinner—after a free-ranging discussion about the Kennedy assassination, the war overseas, the Civil Rights Movement, what kind of president Goldwater might have been, and whether a man would ever walk on the moon—Francone turned serious. "I know it's only been a few weeks, baby, but I have a good feeling about us, don't you?"

Sandy—known to Francone as Nora—nodded.

"And I respect that you want to wait until you're married before we...you know."

She nodded again. *Oh, God*, she thought. *He's going to propose.*

"It's just that...there are things you don't know about me that I figure you should know before we get hitched."

Sandy tried to keep her breathing in check. Was this it? Was he about to confess...with no one else around to confirm it?

"Do you like baseball?" he asked.

"Do I like what?"

"The Astros."

The unexpected shift left Sandy a little disoriented. Why was he talking about baseball all of a sudden? "Sure."

"I have a pair of tickets to the exhibition game at the new Harris County Domed Stadium. We can go out for a nice dinner after we watch the Yankees get their asses handed to them. It'll be the first indoor baseball game ever. Historic. A friend got me the tickets."

Sandy wondered if the friend was Christopher Chesterton. "Sounds like fun."

"Great," Francone said. "I'll book us a table at Brenner's Steakhouse. I have something I need to tell you and then something I need to ask you."

"So mysterious," Sandy said. But she had a good idea what he meant.

She convened with the team at Bennett's, and they came up with a plan. Bennett had a connection who knew someone at Brenner's. "We're going to wire up your table," he told Sandy.

"Wire it? With electricity?"

"With this," an operative named Oscar said, showing her a beige box about a foot on each side, with dials, knobs, and jacks on the front panel. There was a little plastic window in the middle that revealed a couple of discs inside. "The smallest tape recorder on the market," he said with pride. "A Mercury TR-3500. Five-inch reels, records for about forty-five minutes, so you'll have to get him talking soon after you arrive. We'll strap it to the bottom of the table, and the microphone..." He showed her a large plastic tube. "This'll be hidden among the flowers on the table. Don't worry about talking into the vase. As long as you use a normal voice, it'll pick you up. We'll make sure the tables nearby are clear to cut down on noise."

"Would you look at that?" Sandy said. "You could carry that with you. Listen to music just about anywhere."

Oscar nodded. "Wave of the future. Weighs less than nine pounds. Runs on four D batteries."

"Just get him talking fast," Bennett said. "We don't want to have to figure out how to swap out reels if he takes too long."

Sandy was duly impressed by the new domed stadium, doubly so when she found out the president and his wife were going to be there, along with many other Texas dignitaries. She'd voted for LBJ, although she hadn't shared that fact with Francone, who'd supported Goldwater.

The dome was spectacular, a feat of modern engineering.

Eighteen stories high and made of translucent panes to allow enough light through to keep the grass alive. Governor Connally, who'd been seriously injured during the assassination, threw out the ceremonial first pitch in front of a sold-out crowd of nearly forty-eight thousand people. Sandy never did get to see LBJ and his wife, who were reportedly watching the game from the owners' box high above them, but the crowd roared when the announcer said their names.

Sandy didn't know much about baseball. "Where are the cheerleaders?" she asked Francone, who chuckled as if she had been joking. She did recognize Mickey Mantle's name. He scored the first run of the game for the Yankees with a solo homer that just made it into the first row of seats. By then, it was the sixth inning, and Sandy was starting to get nervous about dinner. This was going to be their best chance—perhaps their last chance—to close the case. If Francone proposed tonight and they didn't have his confession on tape, that would be the end of it. She'd have to turn him down, and they wouldn't get another shot at him.

Houston tied the score in their half of the sixth, but the game went into extra innings. Sandy kept looking at her watch, but Francone told her not to worry. The restaurant would hold their reservations. Sandy caught the eye of Oscar, who was undercover selling peanuts, and gave him the sign that everything was under control.

Finally, Houston scored in the bottom of the twelfth inning to end the game. Francone took Sandy by her arm and led her through the crowd to the parking lot. Soon they were on their way to Brenner's.

Half the restaurant seemed to be staffed with Bennett operatives, from the maître d' to their waiter, to the guy bussing tables. The woman who had recruited her in the bar that night over a year ago pretended to be cleaning up something under their table, but Sandy knew she'd activated the recording device. The clock was now running.

They took their seats, and Francone ordered for both without consulting her. After the wine was poured, he reached across the table and took her by the hand. Sandy tried not to look at the vase of flowers between them in case she inadvertently drew his attention to the hidden microphone.

"I told you I was in Korea, right?"

"The Marines."

"Exactly. On the ground—like what's going on over in Vietnam right now. That one is going to be bad, let me tell you. Worse than Korea. Anyway, when we were over there...well, it was a war, right? And in wars, you have to shoot at the enemy. Sometimes you kill them."

Sandy took a deep breath. Was this his big confession? That he'd killed people during a war? She covered her distress by taking a swallow of wine.

"I know," he said. "But that's what the country asked of me. What I was drafted to do."

Sandy nodded and gave him a smile, though it felt false and weak. "I understand."

He gave her wrist a squeeze. "I knew you would." He took a swig of his wine, swishing it around like mouthwash. "When I got back, I had a hard time for a while. Getting a job was easy but holding onto one...not so easy. I had a bit of a temper back then. That's why I started going to this gym. Working out my aggressions." He flexed his other arm to show her his bicep. "So, I met this guy, and we became workout buddies. We started going out to bars and clubs around town, too. He always had plenty of cash and a ton of friends."

Sandy was almost holding her breath, waiting for him to get to the point. She risked a glance at her watch. They'd been here for at least twenty minutes.

Francone paused before plunging ahead. "One night, he asked me to do something for him. He knew I'd been in the war and that I knew how to use guns." He grimaced. "Okay, I'm going to come right out and say it: He paid me to shoot someone."

Sandy gasped, covering her mouth with her hand.

Francone's grip on her wrist tightened. "It was a one-time thing, baby. I promise you that. Never again. I've been real torn up about it ever since, and I just had to get it off my chest. It doesn't change anything between us. Right?"

Sandy wasn't sure how to respond. She inhaled and exhaled slowly. "What happened to the person you shot?" she said at last.

"It was some old broad. She was on her last legs anyway. I was just helping her along. Doing her a favor, if you want to look at it that way. But it was all over the news. I had no idea she was famous."

"Selma Chesterton," Sandy said.

Francone looked surprised, then recovered. "Yeah, that's right. Of course, you'd know. You read up on all these things. One of the things I love about you. Anyway, that's all behind me now, and thanks to that, I can get some more money, and we can set ourselves up in a new house. After we get married, that is."

He got up from the table and dropped to one knee. For a minute, Sandy thought he was going to look under the table and see the recorder strapped to the bottom, but he had other plans. He pulled out a small jewelry box. "Nora Charles, would you be my wife?"

Sandy stared at him. Time was ticking by, and she had to get away from him. She summoned up her superpower and burst into tears. "Oh, Tony. This is so unexpected." She sobbed like never before, heaving and panting as the tears ran down her cheeks. "Oh," she said between gasps, wiping her eyes and smearing her makeup. "I must look a frightful mess. Let me go to the powder room and fix myself up." She stood and stumbled backward, almost knocking over her chair, before heading quickly in the direction of the restrooms. On the way, she patted the back of her head to let her colleagues know they had the goods.

Once she was far enough away, the restaurant erupted into

bedlam. Three Houston police officers emerged from the kitchen, weapons at the ready, catching Francone by surprise. They threw him to the ground and restrained him. Once the situation was under control, Oscar emerged from the kitchen and checked the recording device under the table. He rewound the tape and listened to the conversation using an earphone. He fast-forwarded and listened again, then gave the thumbs up. "We got it," he said.

By then, Francone had figured out what had happened. He glowered at Sandy as they led him away. Bennett arose from one of the nearby tables and congratulated Sandy on a job well done. "He'll flip on Chesterton. They always do."

"Didn't you say something about a reward?" she asked.

"We have a strict policy against accepting rewards," Bennett told her.

Tears started streaming down Sandy's face, and her upper lip began to tremble.

Bennett laughed. "Okay, okay. Stop that. There'll be something nice in your next paycheck. Just turn off those damned tears!"

ONE NIGHT IN 1965
Stacy Woodson

The date was August 26, 1965, the day I took the case that changed my life forever—at least my perspective of it, anyway.

I sat in my PI office, two blocks from the Vegas strip, eating a Swanson TV dinner, watching the *CBS Evening News*. Cronkite, the most trusted man in America, was at the news desk. A soda straw view of the Vietnam War rolled through the screen. The audio faded in and out, too.

Someone pounded on my door.

I ignored it, my focus still on the TV. I pushed up from the couch. Looked for my cane. Gave up. Limped over to the Magnavox. Adjusted the rabbit ears. Then smacked the box for good measure.

The sound finally kicked in.

Cronkite was talking about President Johnson, how he needed more men to fight the war against communism. Which wasn't news.

The change Johnson planned to make to the draft—*this* was news.

Hours ago, Johnson announced deferments would still be granted to men who married before midnight. Tomorrow, however, men could no longer get married to avoid military service.

Good, I thought. Fewer opportunities for men to shirk their duty. I had stepped up to the plate. It was time others did, too.

More pounding.

"Jack—" Lou called. I recognized my friend's voice through the door. He was a big-deal defense attorney and a pal I'd served with in the Marine Corps. He sometimes threw me a job. Usually, to look through police reports, copies of evidence, photographs, witness statements for inconsistencies, so he could get a guilty client off on a technicality.

"Come back during office hours," I yelled.

"Damn it, Jack!"

I groaned. "Fine." I clicked off the TV, made my way to the door, flipped the dead bolt, eased it open. Lou was dressed to the nines—shirt starched, suit perfectly pressed. A sharp contrast to my boxers and T-shirt.

"Nice threads," Lou said.

"Hey—it's *me* time."

Lou eyed my stomach. "A whole lot of it, apparently."

He wasn't wrong. My belly was round. Definitely not the six-pack I had before Korea.

Before I was shot.

"Do you need something?" I asked. "Or did you come here to bust my balls?"

"Both." Lou handed me my cane. "Found this in the hall."

"Christ. I was looking for that." My mind went back to the previous night, one too many bourbons, stumbling home from The Atomic.

Lou followed me to my desk—the transition smoother with the cane. My pants and shirt were draped across my chair. I tossed them aside and took a seat.

"You know, it's only a matter of time before the landlord catches you living in your office."

I shrugged.

"He could bounce you, Jack."

"I'm not worried." I offered him a cigarette and the couch. He waved away both. I lipped a cigarette from the box, lit the tip, inhaled. "What gives? Must be something big if you're declining a smoke and a seat."

"You're going to be getting a call."

"Ain't that mysterious."

"Don't screw with me, Jack. It's a big client. Work that needs the utmost discretion."

I smiled.

Lou didn't. "I'm serious."

I could tell he was serious and nervous, too. Which was unusual. During the Battle of Chosin Reservoir, I watched him charge the enemy. He didn't hesitate. The man was fearless. This whole anxious thing I'd never seen before.

"Jack…"

"I get it," I said.

"Good." He folded his arms. "You do this job, you do it right, the firm will offer you a permanent position. More money—maybe enough to afford a roof over your head. At least enough for some real food."

"I have a roof over my head. And don't knock the Salisbury steak. It's better than those C-Rats we used to eat."

"That doesn't say much." Lou looked like he was about to say more, but my phone rang. He pointed at it, bug-eyed, like I didn't hear it. And I couldn't resist the opportunity to screw with him again. I grabbed an ashtray, crushed out the cigarette, my movements slow and deliberate.

"Pick it up, Jack."

"I'm working on it."

"I swear to God—" He yanked the phone from the receiver and pushed it at me.

I grinned.

Asshole—he mouthed.

I cleared my throat. "Vegas Investigations."

"Please hold for the senator from Nevada."

I frowned, covered the mouthpiece. "Senator?"

But Lou wouldn't look at me, his eyes laser-focused on the phone.

A man came on the line. "Is this Jack Taylor?"

"Speaking."

"Senator Wilkerson here. Calling from Washington. There's a bill on the Senate floor that needs my attention. So, I'll be brief. Lou tells me you're the best. I have a family matter that I'd like you to handle."

The senator told me about his son. That he'd been drafted to serve in Vietnam. How he'd left for Vegas for an I-do-and-dash.

"At least that's what the wife thinks," the senator continued. "Thomas has an old flame who lives in Vegas. This afternoon, he cleared out his checking account, took my Ford Fairlane, left Carson City. The wife found an address for the Clark County District Courthouse in his bedroom."

In true Sin City fashion, the county's license bureau offered same-day-marriage licenses and no-wait weddings until midnight daily. Odds were the senator's wife was right.

"Even if he's planning a quick wedding, it isn't illegal," I reminded the senator.

"True. But here's the thing. The policy change, the one President Johnson announced today, I'm the one who wrote it. You can imagine how this will look for me, politically, if my son marries to secure a deferment after this announcement."

"Yeah." He'll look like every other self-entitled kid who had dodged the draft.

"I fought in World War II," the senator continued. "I understand you served in the Korean conflict. We all have a duty to our country. Don't you think? I want my son to honor his. The Selective Service board requested Thomas report for induction tomorrow. I want him to be there."

Even though the senator's motives were self-serving, he wanted to hold his son accountable, and I respected this. "What would you like me to do?"

Twenty minutes later, I was showered, dressed, and in my Buick Riviera, driving to the Clark County District Courthouse. The senator wanted me to stop Thomas's wedding and convince him to return to Carson City. If the kid refused, I was supposed to detain him until someone from the senator's staff arrived. Lou would handle things for the senator moving forward. He gave me a picture of the couple and details on the Fairlane.

My first task was to locate Thomas.

When I arrived at the courthouse, couples spilled out of the license bureau, down the sidewalk, and onto the lawn. They were young—some dressed like they were going to church, others to a protest rally.

All had anxious faces.

I tried to feel some empathy for them. But I couldn't do it. Kids who didn't have money, kids who couldn't afford to run away to Vegas and get hitched—they would be drafted and forced to take their place.

Someone always took their place.

I tightened my grip on my cane, pulled out the picture from Lou—a prom shot of Thomas and Lilly. It was a few years old. But it didn't matter. Their likeness was all I needed.

I worked my way up the line, comparing faces—one after the other.

No Lilly. No Thomas.

I continued into the license bureau.

No luck.

At the counter, the sign said the clerk's name was Betty. She looked as young as the people she served. She seemed stressed, haggard. The pace she processed paperwork determined who would make the deferment deadline, and the responsibility clearly weighed upon her. I needed to question Betty and find out if Thomas and Lilly had been here.

I elbowed my way to the front.

"Hey, pal," a kid with a flattop whined. "There's a line here."

I ignored him and tried to get Betty's attention. "Excuse me, miss."

"Ms." She corrected me, her hands still working—typing,

stapling, processing. "You need to move to the back of the line. When it's your turn, I can assist you."

"I'm not here for a marriage license."

"Then you're in the wrong place." Betty looked at Flattop. "That'll be eight dollars."

Flattop elbowed me out of the way and handed Betty the money. She pushed a ledger toward him. He signed it. Then, she handed him a license. "Go through the double doors on the right. The justice of the peace will see you in the back."

"I don't know if I can do this," the girl with Flattop whispered.

His eyes went wide. "Don't you love me?"

"It's not that." She visibly swallowed. "It's just...we've only been dating for three weeks."

"Do you want me to die in Vietnam?"

The girl's breath caught. "God, no."

"Make up your mind!" someone in line yelled.

She started to cry.

"Tick. Tock." A man in a sports coat chimed in. "We are running out of time. Your indecisiveness is going to get the rest of us killed."

The yelling seemed to prompt a security guard to emerge from the judge's chambers. He stood near the doors, arms folded.

"Here's the thing," the girl started again, "I just applied to be a stewardess."

"You'll be married," Flattop said. "You won't need to work."

"But I want to travel."

"Do you want to save his life or not?" Betty demanded.

"Well, since you put it that way..."

"We'll sort it out later, okay?" Flattop grabbed the girl's hand and tugged her toward the judge's chambers.

"Excuse me," I tried to get Betty's attention again, my mind on the ledger. I needed to see it. If Thomas had picked up a license, his or Lilly's name would be inside.

Betty still ignored me.

I walked behind the counter.

"You're not allowed back here." She motioned to the security guard.

"It's my leg," I said, gripping it dramatically. "Sometimes the pain is too much, and I need to sit. There are no chairs in the reception area. Please forgive the breach of protocol."

She looked at my leg. Then, at my cane. Her face flushed. "I didn't know."

The security guard hovered over me now, so close I could smell the tuna and rye he had for dinner. "Is there a problem here, Betty?"

"I'm good, Tom."

"You sure?"

"Yeah." She nodded.

He walked away, his eyes still on me. I flashed Betty a grateful smile.

She continued to work. "How did you get injured?"

"Korea."

"Damn wars." She shook her head. "They take something from everyone, don't they?"

The conviction in her voice, the anger. I could tell this ran deeper than politics. It was personal. "Did you lose someone?"

"My brother." She pointed to a picture on her desk, a snapshot from a huge family gathering—at least fifteen faces. "Teddy is on the bottom right."

He looked young.

They always did.

"I'm sorry for your loss," I told her. And I meant it. I waited for her to finish with another couple before I said, "There're a lot of people here to manage by yourself."

"Normally, two of us process marriage licenses, but my coworker didn't come back from her break today."

"She picked a hell of a day to play hooky."

"Tell me about it."

I eyed the ledger on her desk, watched Betty work, considered my next move. If I told her my purpose, to stop a wedding and a deferment, she wouldn't help me. Hell, she may even try to stop me. I needed to take another approach, find the right angle. Something that would resonate with her. And then, I got it—the picture on her desk. Family was important to her.

This was my way in.

"Look, I know you're busy, and you've been so kind. It's just—I'm looking for my little sister. She's getting married today, and my mother is beside herself."

Betty frowned.

Crap. She thinks I'm trying to stop them.

"My mother," I paused, reworking my approach, "she can't imagine her baby taking such a big step without someone from the family being there. I'm here to support my sister, of course. I didn't see her in your line. I'm worried I may be too late. That she's already married."

"Of course." Betty glanced at the picture on her desk and nodded knowingly. "I can't imagine getting married without my family." She wheeled an application into her typewriter. "If your sister picked up a marriage license, she or her fiancé signed for it." She motioned to the ledger. "Feel free to take a look."

"Thank you." I reached for the book, flipped through the pages—nearly one hundred entries today, so far.

None for Thomas and Lilly.

"Any luck?" Betty asked.

I shook my head. "Maybe they haven't arrived yet, or maybe one of them changed their mind."

"We've had a few of those today."

"I know you're swamped. But will you take a quick look at a picture for me? Just in case they came through your line but didn't finalize their license. I need to tell my mother something."

Betty glanced at the line of people, which didn't seem to end.

"Please," I pressed.

"Fine." She exhaled the word. "Put the picture on the desk. I'll look while I work."

"Thank you." I smiled. "I feel like I'm saying that a lot to you today." I slid the picture over.

She took money from another applicant and directed them to the judge's chambers before she finally looked. "Lilly Miller? Seriously? *She's* your sister?"

"You know her?"

"You're sitting at her desk."

"What?" I said, surprised.

"Lilly took her break. Left here with that guy in the picture. She left and never came back."

Lilly Miller's *brother* should have known she worked at the courthouse. Thankfully, Betty was too busy with applicants to notice. I quickly disappeared before she got wise to me.

I located a phone booth outside, flipped through the White Pages, found Lilly's address, and headed to her apartment.

On the drive, I considered my latest development—that there was no evidence Lilly and Thomas applied for a marriage license. The assumption that Thomas had come to Vegas to marry Lilly for a deferment seemed less likely.

So, why would Thomas come here the night before his induction? Maybe he wanted one last night with Lilly in Sin City before Vietnam? I suppose this could be true. But then why not tell his parents? Why leave Carson City in such a hurry?

The Grecian was a Mediterranean-style apartment complex with open-air units that horseshoed around a pool. Lilly lived on the third floor. Navigating the stairs was an event. When I reached her apartment, sweat pooled under my arms, and my leg screamed.

I sucked in a breath. Then, another. Tried to steady my ragged breathing before I finally knocked on her door.

No one answered.

There was a light on inside. I pressed my face to the window.

But there were curtains—thick, like cotton. I could only make out shapes, no details.

I went back to the door.

Knocked again.

Still, nothing.

I reached into my pocket, pulled out my knife to jimmy the lock. Reconsidered it. Tried the knob instead. It turned in my hand.

"Hello?" I eased the door open. "Lilly?"

Her studio apartment looked like it had been tossed—drawers half open, clothes strewn on the bed, costume jewelry scattered on the floor. I continued to the bathroom. The medicine cabinet was empty. Lilly's toiletries were gone. In the closet—empty hangers. No suitcase.

If Thomas had come to Vegas to party with Lilly, she'd have no reason to pack, no reason to leave her apartment in a hurry.

None of this made sense.

I raked a hand through my hair, circled the room again, found nothing. I needed to figure out my next steps. I tried to sort through the facts and the assumptions I'd made.

I knew Lilly and Thomas were together—thanks to Betty. Thomas picked her up at the courthouse. Lilly had her suitcase with her, or they came back to her apartment and packed. The order didn't really matter. They planned to disappear together— at least, that's what it looked like. But where? Canada, maybe?

This would make sense if Thomas was dodging the draft. But why become a fugitive if there were a legal way to gain a defer- ment?

Desperate for answers, I went to her trash cans. The bath- room one was empty. But the kitchen can was full. I pulled the bin from under the sink, the contents nearly spilling over the sides, and dumped it onto a table. Food leftovers, wrappers, bottles—everything you'd expect in a kitchen can was there.

Nothing useful.

Which meant I would need to question Lilly's neighbors. See

if they knew anything. Interviews like these took time, time I didn't have.

I had to call Lou. I washed my hands. Found Lilly's phone, dialed his number.

"Jack?"

"Yeah."

"Any luck?"

"No dice."

"What do you mean no dice?"

I told him about my trip to the courthouse, going to Lilly's apartment, how I had nothing.

"I can't go to the senator with nothing."

"I hear ya, Lou. I'm not happy about it either."

"You need to give me something, Jack."

"I'll continue to look for leads. But it could take some time. If you want to move things along, have the senator call Vegas PD, report the car stolen. I know he wants to keep this a private matter, but this may be the quickest way to locate his son."

"I don't know." Lou blew out a breath. Ice dropped into a tumbler. A splash of liquor—whiskey, maybe? That's what it sounded like over the phone. Lou took a long sip and sighed. "I'll suggest it to the senator."

"Good." I pulled out a chair, collapsed into the seat, my leg still sore from the stairs. I leaned back, my eyes rested on the space under the kitchen sink, the spot where I'd yanked out the trash can. Then, I saw it—the newspaper. It must have tumbled out, and that's why I'd missed it.

"Did you hear me, Jack?"

I ignored Lou, put the receiver on the table. Made my way to the sink. Reached for the newspaper. An issue of *The Rebel Yell*—UNLV's student newspaper.

On the front, pictures of antiwar protests, students burning draft cards, an editorial encouraging students to join the campus resistance movement. It mentioned the Student Union for Peace Action, the Committee to Aid American War Objectors, and the

Anti-Draft Programme—all Canadian groups willing to help resisters once they crossed the border. The name of the person who wrote the piece was circled: Arlo Stanley. His picture was included as part of his byline.

Did Lilly and Thomas plan to connect with Arlo and use his connections to make a run for the Canadian border?

I walked out the door and was halfway to UNLV before I remembered that when I'd left Lilly's apartment, Lou was still on the phone.

It was only the second week of the fall semester, and UNLV's Student Union was busier than I expected. Still, I managed to find a parking space next to the building. I walked through double glass doors that opened to a common area. Students sat at tables drinking coffee, talking, studying. I walked to the Student Union's directory, located the newspaper, and followed the signs to their office on the first floor.

When I arrived, *The Rebel Yell* was in full swing—students at desks typing copy, others proofreading—everyone seemed to be working to put the newspaper to bed.

No one matched Arlo's picture.

A pimple-faced kid saw me at the reception desk and walked over. I told him I was looking for Arlo Stanley. He turned to a group of students gathered by a desk. They were debating the placement of an article.

"The piece about Johnson's new policy should be above the fold," someone in the group said. "I know UNLV seniors that had college deferments who got married today because they didn't want to be drafted when they graduated in the spring."

"I still think the piece on substandard housing conditions is more wide-reaching for our student body," another person argued.

"Anyone seen Arlo?" The pimple-faced kid asked before the group could wind up again. "There's an old guy here looking for him."

A blonde seemed to study me. Her eyes narrowed. Maybe it was the haircut or maybe it was because I still carried myself like a soldier that set her off. But it didn't take a genius to see she didn't trust me.

"You just missed him," she said, her voice tight.

"Really?" A kid with Buddy Holly glasses thumbed toward a row of closed office doors. "I could've sworn I just saw him in the—"

"Shut up, Walter," she hissed, her eyes still on me. "He's gone for the night."

I considered pressing Walter. But the way he clammed up when the blonde yelled at him, I knew he wouldn't tell me anything in front of her.

The pimple-faced kid returned to the reception desk. "Sorry for the confusion, man." He handed me a business card. "If you want to call tomorrow, Arlo's usually here between classes."

That wasn't going to work for me. I took the card anyway and thanked the kid.

Arlo was clearly nearby. The question was where.

Outside the Student Union, I followed the sidewalk that looped behind the building until I was on the back side of the newspaper office. My plan was to peer in the windows and see if Arlo was in one of the offices.

But I didn't get that far.

Along the sidewalk, at the curb in a no parking zone, was the senator's Ford Fairlane.

I stood there stunned. "I'll be damned."

I walked closer.

A parking ticket from campus security was clipped under a windshield wiper. I looked inside the car. There was a suitcase in the back seat. I didn't know where Thomas and Lilly were on campus, but I did know one way to slow them down.

I glanced around, confirmed I was still alone. Pulled out my knife. Slashed a tire. In case there was a spare, I slashed another. I waited until both tires were flat before I turned to the Student Union and peered through the windows.

The newspaper offices were empty.

I walked up the sidewalk, looking for Thomas. Maybe he and Lilly were at a table in the Student Union with Arlo, and I'd somehow missed them. I went through the common area again.

They weren't there.

I continued through the rear doors of the Student Union which opened onto the quad, a wide-open space that connected one side of the campus to the other. That's when I saw them, huddled under a cluster of palm trees.

Three people—two men, one woman.

At least, I thought it was them.

Despite the lights that ran along the sidewalk and the full moon overhead, the trees still cast shadows on their faces making their features difficult to distinguish.

I dropped behind a group of kids walking across the quad, a cloud of pot wafting behind them. I did my best to stay upwind while I made my approach. When I was closer to the trees, I shortened my gait and confirmed their faces.

Arlo was talking. His afro was big, probably the biggest I'd ever seen, and I fought the urge to stare. He tapped an envelope against his hand. "Everything you need, man—passport, driver's license, credit cards—it's all here." He stopped talking and looked at me.

My stomach tightened. I glanced away, pretended to struggle with my cane.

"Everything okay?" Thomas asked Arlo.

I walked toward a bench. It was close enough that I could still hear while I pretended to nurse my leg.

"Sorry." Arlo shook his head and laughed. "I've been doing this for a year now. I'm still a little paranoid. Guess I still expect the feds to rush in and arrest us."

He handed the envelope to Lilly.

She looked inside, seemed to confirm the contents before she dropped the envelope into a leather shoulder bag.

Thomas handed Arlo a wad of cash. "You sure this will work? I don't want any issues at the border."

"No issues so far," Arlo said.

"None that you know about," Thomas muttered.

"There is a list of addresses in the envelope," Arlo continued. "Sympathizers, safe houses, places where you can stop if you get jammed up."

Guess I was right. Thomas was making a run for the border. The kid couldn't commit to the military or a woman. Why get married when you can buy a new identity and disappear instead?

They continued to talk. But I didn't need to hear anymore. I pushed up from the bench and walked back toward the Fairlane. My job was to ensure Thomas made it to his induction. And that's what I planned to do.

I leaned on the hood of the Fairlane and waited for Thomas and Lilly. It was secluded behind the Student Union. If I was going to honor the senator's request for discretion, this was the best place to confront them. It wasn't long before they were walking toward me. When Thomas saw me, he stepped in front of Lilly.

Kid was chivalrous. Certainly not what I expected.

"Can I help you?" Thomas asked.

"No." I folded my arms. "But you can help yourself."

"I don't understand."

"Friday, June 1, 1949."

"I'm sorry, sir. I'm not into riddles. We are in a hurry. So, if you could get off my car—"

"That was my induction date for the Korean conflict," I continued, unwavering. "I watched rich kids like you avoid the draft. While kids like me, kids with working-class parents, took your place. What makes your lives more valuable than ours?"

Thomas frowned. "What are you talking about?"

"I did my duty. Your father sent me to make sure you do yours. You have an induction date in Carson City tomorrow morning. It's my job to make sure you're there."

Thomas blinked. Then, his eyes went wide. "Wait. My dad thinks I'm dodging the draft?"

"Aren't you? I saw you with Arlo—the documents."

"Thomas." Lilly tugged on his arm. "This has gone too far. We need to tell him."

"It's not safe, Lilly."

"If he worked for them, I'd already be dead."

Thomas shook his head. "You don't have to do this."

"I'm not going to cause a rift between you and your father." Lilly stepped forward. She looked petite, smaller somehow than when I first saw her in the quad. "The documents aren't for Thomas. They're for me."

She told me about her job at the license bureau. How she also worked as a stenographer in the courts. The bribes she'd witnessed. Cops, judges, government officials—all connected to the mob. "I didn't know what to do. It wasn't like I could look the other way. So, I collected evidence, contacted the FBI. And—" Her voice cracked.

Thomas put his arm over her shoulders.

She sucked in a breath, tried again. Her eyes started to mist.

"The agent Lilly was supposed to meet was murdered," Thomas filled in. He handed her a handkerchief.

She dabbed her eyes and nodded. "I knew I needed to run. But I had no money. No car. No resources. I called Thomas."

They both stopped talking and looked at me now like they were waiting for me to say something.

"It's the truth, sir," Thomas added.

I thought about what they'd told me, compared it to what I knew. The rush to the courthouse but no marriage license. The meet with Arlo—he'd handed Lilly the documents, not Thomas. There was only one suitcase in the back seat of the Fairlane.

Thomas was never running to Vegas to avoid the draft.

He was running to Vegas to help a friend.

"Maybe if you explained things to the senator," I tried. "He could help you."

"We considered that," Thomas said. "But political circles in Nevada are small. If this leaked, if something was said in my father's office in front of the wrong person, it wouldn't take much for them to find Lilly."

Sirens.

My eyes went to the ticket still under the Fairlane's windshield, and my stomach tightened. "You need to get out of here."

"You think they're coming for Lilly?" Thomas asked.

"No, they're coming for you." I told him how I'd advised the senator to report the car stolen. How when campus security filed their parking ticket with the local precinct, it alerted the Vegas police department the Fairlane was here.

"If the police find me," Lilly said, panicked, "you may as well hand me over to the mob. Give me the keys, Thomas. If I leave now, I'll be gone before they get here. You can tell them it was a misunderstanding."

"That won't work," I told her. "The Fairlane has two flat tires."

"What?" Thomas asked.

"Take mine." I tossed him my keys. "It's the Buick Riviera in the Student Union parking lot. I'd take Lilly myself, but you'll be faster without me. I'll smooth things over with the police."

The sirens were louder.

Thomas locked eyes with Lilly. Some silent exchange I didn't understand.

"What are you waiting for?" I pressed.

She reached into her shoulder bag, pulled out a large manila envelope, handed it to me. "I trust you'll know what to do with this."

And then, just like that, they were gone.

* * *

Two weeks later, I sat on my couch in my PI office wearing my boxers and T-shirt, another Swanson TV dinner in front of me, waiting for the *CBS Evening News* to start. I wondered if Cronkite had received the envelope yet. The one with Lilly's recordings—evidence that connected Vegas officials to the mob.

After I left Thomas and Lilly that night, on the cab ride back to my office, I'd contemplated what to do with the tapes. I thought about going back to the feds, even giving the recordings to Lou. But in the end, I decided to send them to Cronkite. He was the most trusted man in America, after all. If anyone could shed light on the truth and hold people accountable, it would be him.

Lou wasn't happy when I told him that I'd found the senator's car but had no luck detaining the kid.

The next morning, I received a telegram from Thomas telling me where I could find the Buick. The kid must have used the registration paperwork in my glove box to find my address. He could have a future in the PI business if he survived Vietnam.

Truth was, I didn't know if Thomas made it back to Carson City in time for his induction date. And for the first time since I started this case, I didn't care.

During the Battle of Chosin Reservoir, Lou had charged the enemy not because of some obligation to our nation. He did it to protect the people who served by his side—his friends. No different than when Thomas risked everything and rushed to Vegas to help Lilly.

Meeting Thomas made me realize my hang-up with deferments had nothing to do with dodging the draft. It wasn't a person's lack of service that bothered me. It was their lack of character.

And just like Lou, Thomas had it in spades.

Cronkite started to speak. The audio faded in and out on my TV. A picture of the Clark County District Courthouse filled the screen. "Corruption and the mob. Early today, CBS News broke a story—"

"Jack." Lou pounded on my door. "It's me. Open up."

"Come back during office hours."

More pounding. "Damn it, Jack!"

I limped over to the door, flipped the dead bolt, turned the knob.

Lou pushed past me. "Are you watching the news? I've got a job. It's a big client. Work that needs the utmost discretion. It's about the tapes that went to Cronkite's office."

My eyes went wide.

"I need you to track down the whistleblower. You do this, Jack. And you do it right. The firm will offer you a permanent position..."

I looked past Lou at my TV dinner, the smell of Salisbury steak wafting in the air, and I couldn't help but think that I'd be eating them for a while.

DEVIL IN DISGUISE
David H. Hendrickson

August 7, 1966
Lynn, Massachusetts

I'd never billed a client for hours spent attending church. This was a first. And holy shit, I wasn't charging damned near enough. This was Hell.

The New Testament Church of Holiness was filled, about two hundred of us trying to keep our elbows out of each other's ribs while sweating our asses off in the dozen rows of white-pine pews. Fans whirring in the three windows on each side tried unsuccessfully to cool the heavy, humid air. I was downwind of the scrawny elderly man seated on my left whose body odor made my eyes water, yet I still caught cross drafts from the stout middle-aged woman on my right who must have fallen in a vat of cheap perfume. I wondered if they detected remnants of the grass I smoked last night on my clothes or the Jack Daniel's leaking out of my pores.

I stuck out like the proverbial sore thumb. Or perhaps a middle finger. I'm of average height and weight, but I was the only male with a shaggy, Beatles-style mop-top haircut. I was surrounded by military-style crew cuts and short, clean-cut hair, neatly matted in place with "a little dab'll do ya" Brylcreem. My low-slung white pants, light blue shirt, and sandals stood in stark contrast to the dark suits, white shirts, thin ties, and freshly shined shoes all around me. The women, including the perfume vat on my right, all wore conservative dresses in suitably boring colors appropriate for this Sunday morning service. There were no pantsuits and certainly no bright-colored miniskirts like the ones I'd enjoyed viewing at the bar last night. No flashy jewelry or makeup. All of that was "worldly."

I'd considered trying to maintain cover by wearing the one rarely used suit I owned, but no way was I getting my hair cut. No freaking way. If a pretty, young thing had even a fighting chance of confusing me with Paul McCartney, I wasn't going to sacrifice that. Not for any case, no matter how lucrative. And this one would pay only my minimum fee, if that, because I was helping my friend Gordo.

So, I was the lone unabashed sinner in the crowd, plain for all to see. I could not have been more conspicuous if I were naked. I certainly had been getting the disapproving "we'll have to pray for you" looks from all who glanced my way, especially the woman on my right, who I'd come to think of as Perfume Vat Pauline.

Reverend Charles Dinsmore was half an hour into his hellfire-and-brimstone sermon and gave all the appearance of just warming up. A short, squat, fiery man with black-rimmed glasses, he paced back and forth on the elevated stage, waving his well-worn Bible for emphasis and pushing his glasses back up to the bridge of his nose when they slid down.

He'd begun the sermon attacking that demon woman, Madalyn Murray O'Hair, whose lawsuit had recently gotten prayer removed from the schools, and as a result, we were now going to Hell in a handbasket.

"In the words of Reverend Billy Graham," Dinsmore proclaimed, "If God doesn't soon bring judgment upon America, He'll have to go back and apologize to Sodom and Gomorrah!"

Amens sounded from much of the congregation, including from Perfume Vat Pauline, who glanced sideways at me with a grim look. My prodigious detective skills told me her glance was not meant to be flirtatious. Just in case, though, I gave her a wink.

"Young men are protesting in the streets and burning their draft cards in defiance of our once-great country," Dinsmore bellowed. "Like their cowardly heavyweight boxing champion Muhammad Ali, who cast aside his Christian name to take on one of a blasphemous religion, these young men refuse to fight godless communism and its spread across the world. Instead, they stomp their feet like spoiled children and chant, 'No, we won't go!' They want nothing more than to stay here where they can live in sin, smoking marijuana, getting drunk, and fornicating with loose women."

Dinsmore had me there. Especially the fornicating.

"Communists like Martin Luther King break the law while they protest the treatment of their race, a race that the Bible tells us God has cursed since the days of Noah and Ham."

I sat up straight on that one, no longer content to crack silent jokes for my own amusement. Taking on Dr. King and the Civil Rights Movement was treading on my own sacred ground. Little more than a year ago, I'd driven to Alabama with my friend, Lincoln Bingham, to join the march from Selma to Montgomery to support voting rights. We'd both taken billy clubs to the head, the back, and the ribs for that privilege, and we have the scars to prove it. Some days, I'd swear there were remnants of tear gas in my lungs.

So Dinsmore had entered my own don't-fuck-with-me zone. And so had the righteous racists in the all-white congregation who were giving him amens and cries of "Preach it, brother!" in response to his attacks on Dr. King.

For me, this was war. I had no idea what the hell Noah had to do with the Civil Rights Movement but made a mental note to figure it out.

Dinsmore barreled on.

"'In God We Trust' may be what's printed on our money," he proclaimed, "but the sad reality is that it's the atheists, the depraved hedonists, and the secular humanists who our morally bankrupt government has come to trust!" Dinsmore stopped his pacing and stood behind the pulpit. He leaned on it and glared down with righteous fury from one side of the congregation to the other. His jaw clenched and unclenched. "Nowhere is this more pervasive and insidious than in the depravity of rock and roll, the Devil's music."

Resounding amens rang out.

"Preach it!" Perfume Vat Pauline called out, raising her arms ostensibly to praise the Lord, but in the process elbowing me in the temple. Seeing stars and shaking my head, I wondered if it had been accidental or if the woman had felt God guiding her elbow to His desired destination.

She tried to apologize, but I waved her away. I wasn't going to be distracted now. This part of Dinsmore's sermon was why I was here. My friend Charlie Gordon—known to his friends as Gordo—owned Gordo's Records here in the city known as "Lynn, Lynn, City of Sin," ten miles north of Boston. He'd hired me a few days ago to get something on Dinsmore, figuring it would be no different than the steady diet of cheating-spouse surveillances I was always bitching about while scouring his record bins. Dinsmore had been killing Gordo's business by directing his parishioners to picket the store ever since John Lennon opened his big mouth and said that the Beatles were more popular than Christ.

The words poured gasoline on Dinsmore's hellfire and brimstone. You could almost smell the sulfur. The words confirmed everything he'd already been preaching about rock and roll. What more proof was needed that this was the Devil's music and Lennon was Satan's handmaiden?

For Gordo, all Holy Hell broke loose. Only his most loyal customers would cross Dinsmore's righteous picket line, populated with adults and teenagers chanting and shaking placards that bore messages like "Jesus is More Popular to Me!" and "Down with Lennon, Up with Christ!" and then appalling ones that said, "Jesus Lives, Death to John Lennon!" and "Jesus Died for my Sins! John Lennon should Die for His!"

With the Stones touring to support their new album, *Aftermath*—including an appearance here in Lynn's decrepit Manning Bowl—and the Beatles less than two weeks from hitting Boston to support *Revolver*, Charlie had copies of the two albums stacked high in his store.

Which was where they were staying and would stay if I couldn't get Dinsmore to call off his dogs.

Getting dirt on Dinsmore, however, proved tougher than my typical cheating-spouse cases. As far as I could tell, he wasn't cheating on his wife, either with a horny parishioner or with the prostitutes working Lynn's downtown streets after dark. Dinsmore didn't even sneak a peek at the *Playboy* and *Penthouse* magazines in the third aisle of the Shop Qwik convenience store.

He appeared to be that most annoying of adversaries. He was a world-class asshole, but he was a genuine world-class asshole. One who practiced what he preached. So here I was, still looking for dirt while paying special attention to his attacks on the music I loved and that kept Gordo in business.

"Just weeks ago, Michael Jagger and his so-called Rolling Stones came to this very city and instigated a riot," Dinsmore said, butchering Mick Jagger's name along with the truth.

Lynn's crumbling Manning Bowl had been an odd site to kick off the Stones' US tour instead of Boston itself or any of the other surrounding cities. Even so, everything had gone fine from host Arnie "Woo Woo" Ginsburg, to the opening acts, to the Stones themselves. Ten thousand people having a great time.

Until the thunderstorms hit.

The Stones had just finished their tenth song, "(I Can't Get No) Satisfaction," when the heavy rain turned into a deluge, and the thunder struck. Mick and the boys ran for cover. Fans rushed the stage and broke through the police barriers. Next thing you know, the police were firing tear gas, the Stones were leaving in their limos, and wooden chairs were flying all about the infield.

The Stones said they'd never return, the newspapers reported the "riot," and "Lynn, Lynn, City of Sin" had once again lived up to its name. And given more ammo to Dinsmore, a self-appointed missionary intent on converting our City of Sin.

"John Lennon thinks you love his Beatles more than you love your Lord and Savior who died on the cross to save you from your sins!" Dinsmore bellowed. "But we know better! The Beatles have come, and they will go, but our Lord God is eternal! John Lennon will burn in Hell for his sins! Do not follow him to eternal damnation!"

After the service, the bonfire in the large gravel parking lot behind the church leaped high into the sky, as if symbolizing John Lennon roasting like a marshmallow in Hell. The acrid smell of burning vinyl filled my nostrils. Ashes from the paperboard album covers wafted lazily through the heavy air toward the cars parked on the perimeter.

The congregation circled the bonfire, six or seven deep, fifteen feet from the bright orange flames. I stood with the adults and little children on the outer edges looking in, them approvingly at the teenagers holding their albums and waiting their turn, me in silent horror. I wondered if any of the teenagers felt fenced in by their elders, unable to escape, forced to follow the commands of Dinsmore, who stood on a folding metal chair on the far side of the circle with the shittiest of shit-eating grins.

I wanted to slap him.

One after another teenager, and more than a few adults, took their turn and stepped forward to add their sacrifice to the bright orange flame. Always one album at a time, never more than one, not even a brown-haired girl who couldn't have been more than fourteen yet had a stack of close to thirty albums. I cried for her as she flung each album in and watched it warp and burn.

I wanted to call out, "*What are you doing?*" and probably should have. Was I worried that I'd blow my cover, a cover that had been blown as soon as I showed up here without a haircut? Even so, I couldn't flaunt my disapproval of and actual disgust for what was happening. I had to remain within striking distance.

So, I just watched. And felt a silent scream build up inside me as if I were watching a Hitchcock film. This was worse than *The Birds* or even Norman Bates in *Psycho*.

The event turned from quiet and reverential to raucous. A bit like a rock concert.

A few boys took to stomping their albums into pieces before flinging them into the fire. The crowd cheered lustily. So, a few girls followed suit. Then they all began to hold their albums up for all to see, showcasing their sacrifice before the stomping.

The crowd chanted, "Let it burn! Let it burn!"

A tall, thin, acne-pocked boy of about sixteen held aloft a copy of *Beatles for Sale*. I almost cried out in pain. The title had only been released in the UK and was a priceless collector's item in the US. But it went crunch underneath the kid's shoe, and the crowd joyfully chanted, "Let it burn! Let it burn!"

I felt sick to my stomach. This was depravity. Not careless words by John Lennon. This!

I couldn't help thinking of Ray Bradbury's novel about book burning, *Fahrenheit 451*. Supposedly, François Truffaut would be coming out with the movie version later this year, but I doubted if anyone here but me would go to see it. Hollywood, after all, like rock and roll, was the Devil's playground. Off limits, a temptation that would steal your soul. Besides, would anyone here even recognize themselves as the books burned?

Finally, the sickening event began to wind down. Only the reluctant stragglers were left. A teenage boy or girl would look longingly at an album that had no doubt been a favorite. They loved the music. They loved the Beatles, or the Stones, or Bob Dylan, or whoever the artist was. But then the crowd urged them on even louder.

"Let it burn! Let it burn! Let it burn!"

Off to the right, a tear streaked down a plump teenage girl's cheek. She was probably about sixteen or so with short, drab hair. She stared longingly at the cover of *Meet the Beatles!* I wondered if her crush was on Paul or John.

"Don't be like Lot's wife," Reverend Dinsmore commanded.

The girl's head shot up. She stared at Dinsmore and visibly gulped.

"Lot's wife was turned to a pillar of salt when she looked back on the flames devouring Sodom and Gomorrah."

The girl's eyes widened. Her hands trembled.

"Let it burn! Let it burn! Let it burn!"

The girl flung the album into the fire as if it had been diseased. Her eyes blinked back the tears.

Gordo was fucked.

He was going against the most ardent of the true believers. Unless Dinsmore went down in flames, his parishioners were going to picket Gordo's Records into bankruptcy.

Perhaps some, or even many, of those who had burned their albums would be replacing them, especially after they left home for college, where they'd no longer be under the thumb of their parents. And for the boys, unless they had a medical deferment like me, they'd be going to college, or else they'd be packing off to Vietnam.

College would be a whole new world. Many of them would be delivering a hidden fuck you to Dinsmore and their parents as they rolled a joint and sang along with Bob Dylan, "Everybody must get stoned!"

But Gordo's Records would be long gone by then. Unless I could get something on Dinsmore.

And I still had nothing. Dinsmore was an asshole, but he did all his assholery in public. He had no secrets that I could detect to expose or leverage.

I felt powerless.

One thing did nag at me, however: Dinsmore's comment about Noah and Ham. I knew Noah. Everyone does. But who the hell was Ham? Or Nam, or something like that. And whatever could Ham, Nam, or for that matter, Damn, have to do with Martin Luther King and the Civil Rights Movement?

I'd been born with the most Irish Catholic name possible— Brendan Shamus O'Donnell—and I'd gone to St. Pius and gotten my knuckles rapped by the nuns like everyone else. But all I could remember about Noah was the flood and the animals in the ark. That was it.

I was lost. No one would ever confuse me with a Biblical scholar, and none of my cases had ever involved theology. I didn't have the first idea of where to look.

So, the next morning, I hit the public library. I struck out within the card catalog. Not a single relevant index card. But there was still the librarian, a sweet elderly woman named Miss Emily McLeod, who I'd known from Mass at St. Pius back when I was, in her words, "knee-high to a grasshopper." I'd gotten to know her quite well since. Frail with white hair, bony, liver-spotted hands, and granny glasses, she was still sharp as a tack, loaded with information that couldn't be found in the stacks, and a bit of a pistol in her own way. She'd provided useful information for me in several cases, and each time I'd come back to thank her, she'd taken me up on payment via a Guinness or two or three at Casey's.

Usually three.

"Brendan O'Donnell, what can I do for you this fine day?" she asked. "And would it, by chance, involve something *legal* this time?"

I asked her about Noah and Ham, Nam, Damn, or even "Rama Lama Ding Dong," the last one tossed in for levity because Miss McLeod was a doo-wop fan.

"By The Edsels," she said without even the blink of an eye. "Their biggest hit."

"Sharp as ever," I said. "Had to look that one up myself."

"Clearly, you're better at music than theology. Not surprising since you haven't been to Mass in, oh, about a decade." She lifted her eyebrows in silent accusation.

I was about to defend myself by saying that I'd been to church just yesterday but wasn't sure if going to a hellfire-and-brimstone Protestant church would be considered a greater evil for an Irish Catholic boy than staying home and getting drunk by noon. So, I spread my hands in a gesture of pleading the fifth.

"I do remember Noah," I said. "It's the other guy I'm not sure about. And what the he—um...what the heck does he have to do with Martin Luther King?"

"You don't remember that from catechism?" Miss McLeod asked with a sly grin.

All I remembered from catechism was that I should feel guilty about everything, but I didn't say that. I just shrugged sheepishly.

"That's because they don't cover it in catechism," she said with a grin and a wink. "One of those dirty secrets left undiscovered."

"I'm all about dirty secrets," I said. "Especially the undiscovered ones."

"So, I've heard," she replied. "I'm getting thirsty for a Guinness already."

"You're on!"

"Ham was one of Noah's sons, and it says in Genesis that Noah got drunk one day, and Ham saw Noah's nakedness. Whatever that's supposed to mean." Miss McLeod gave me the eye but continued. "As a result, Noah cursed Ham and his descendants, some of whom supposedly populated Egypt and Africa. Hence, God cursed all Negroes."

"*What?*"

Miss McLeod pursed her lips and raised her eyebrows. "The Curse of Ham has been used to excuse slavery. God's will for a cursed race."

I stood there in stunned silence. I didn't even know what the hell "seeing Noah's nakedness" meant, much less make sense of all the rest.

"Not exactly Christianity's finest moment," Miss McLeod said. "I could, of course, be distorting it just a bit based on my recollections. It's not something Father O'Sullivan brings up often in his homilies.

"You could get a less-biased view—or perhaps it would be an equally or even more biased view, in *favor* of the curse—by going to the library at Gordon College," she said, referring to an evangelical school ten miles away. "It's the Winn Library, I believe. It may only be open to students, but I can place a call and perhaps get you in."

My confusion was far more basic than getting both sides of the issue. I wasn't sure I even wanted both sides of the issue.

"Why was it Ham's fault that Noah got drunk and got naked?" I asked.

Miss McLeod glanced about to make sure no one could overhear.

"Some say that 'seeing Noah's nakedness' is a euphemism." She widened her eyes and craned her head forward, leading me on. "For...you know what."

My eyes bugged out. I could not have been more floored if Muhammad Ali had nailed me with a roundhouse hook.

"And Noah is the *righteous* guy God supposedly saved in the flood? Because everyone else was wicked?" I asked, incredulous. "That's supposed to make sense? And his curse is a justification for slavery?"

"Like I said, a dirty secret."

The next afternoon, having called and scheduled an appointment, I met with Reverend Dinsmore in his office in the back of the church. Dressed in a dark suit and tie as if it were still Sunday, he sat behind a huge desk cluttered with papers. The wall behind him was a floor-to-ceiling bookcase made of white pine and filled with reference books and theological texts. Sunlight and a light breeze streamed in the large, open window on my left. The wall on my right held framed photographs of Dinsmore with apparently important people that I didn't recognize, along with a cover each from *Christianity Today* and *Guideposts* magazines.

Dinsmore pointed me to a chair, and I sat down, a Bible in my lap.

"What can I help you with, my son?" he asked. Before I could respond, he said, "I could recommend a good barber." He flashed his shit-eating grin.

I ignored the quip about my hair and said that I was confused about a few things in the scriptures and needed his help to understand. I softened him up with some easy questions until he visibly relaxed, then slipped in a tough one I remembered from my youth.

It got the predictable "God works in mysterious ways."

More softies, then a tough one from Miss McLeod got another predictable response: "Our finite minds cannot pretend to know the infinite."

One last softie. Then the question I'd come here for.

"You mentioned the Curse of Ham in your sermon on Sunday," I said. "I've read that part of Genesis so many times, but I still don't understand it. Could you explain that to me?"

I was afraid I'd get the kind of non-answer I'd gotten to previous tough questions, but Dinsmore felt no need for evasive action here. He jumped right in.

"Sure," he said. "The Old Testament says quite clearly and in several places that the sins of the father are carried on to the third and fourth generations. Now that may sound harsh, but Deuteronomy 24:16 also says that fathers shall not be put to death because of their children, nor shall children be put to death for their fathers. So, there are limits. But without question, our children do inherit our sins.

"In the case of Ham, he disrespected his father, Noah, and as a result, God has punished Ham's descendants. They are not put to death, but they bear that curse. The people of Africa and Egypt are descendants of Ham, and they bear God's curse."

He leaned forward.

"Anyone can see that the Negro man is inferior to the white. I'm sure that even Martin Luther King would agree that his own followers, however loyal and sincere as they may be, fail to measure up intellectually and morally to those in this congregation. It's God's will that we lead those who have not been blessed with the same talents as have we.

"Sometimes, it's even a burden. As it says in the Gospel of Luke, 'To whom much is given, much will be required.'"

I blinked. So, there it was. I hardly needed anything more.

Dinsmore was no benign, lonely Father McKenzie from the Beatles' "Eleanor Rigby." Dinsmore was evil, even if he didn't think so. And I had the words to bury him.

Perhaps though, I thought, he could add an exclamation point to his statement of bald bigotry.

"That's so much clearer than what you said on Sunday," I said. "Thank you."

Dinsmore smiled and shrugged.

"In private, I can be a little more blunt and speak the plain truth," he said. "At times, from the pulpit, I must be a bit more tactful and circumspect. I'm sure you understand."

The next Sunday, I was back to the concrete steps of the New Testament Church of Holiness, but I was not alone.

Protests cut both ways.

I was joined by Lincoln Bingham, my fellow veteran of billy clubs on the Selma March, and almost a hundred members of the African Full Gospel Church.

I also had an edited tape with the highlights of my conversation with Dinsmore recorded by the cassette player I'd hidden inside my hollowed-out Bible the day I'd met with him.

Also, a bullhorn.

I pressed play and held the recorder up to the bullhorn's microphone. The tape was distorted and scratchy, but Dinsmore's words were clear, repeated in a loop, and amplified through my bullhorn.

"The people of Africa and Egypt are descendants of Ham, and they bear God's curse. Anyone can see that the Negro man is inferior to the white. I'm sure that even Martin Luther King would agree that his own followers, however loyal and sincere as they may be, fail to measure up intellectually and morally to those in this congregation. It's God's will that we lead those who have not been blessed with the same talents as have we."

Over and over.

Now, on the steps of his church with his congregation slowly spilling outside as they heard his recorded words, Dinsmore took two strides toward me, and our chests thumped. Our faces were inches apart. I could smell onions on his breath.

"What do you want?" he asked, his eyes narrowed, burning fiery.

Originally, I had hoped to trade the ceasing of one protest for another. But Dinsmore's grotesque words and beliefs demanded more now.

"Nothing short of your resignation."

That first Sunday, the two congregations almost came to blows. Police arrived and forced us to move back to the sidewalks, twenty feet from the church steps. Dinsmore commanded them to arrest us, and for a moment, they appeared ready to do so. Lincoln and I, however, countered that the sidewalks in front of the church were every bit as much public property as those in front of Gordo's Records. We had the right of lawful assembly.

Dinsmore did not resign. The protests that next week in front of Gordo's continued.

The following Sunday, our protest returned in full force, this time joined by Gordo himself, short and thin with thick curly black hair, and even more importantly, photographers and reporters from the city's newspaper, the *Daily Evening Item*, along with a few other suburban papers. And once again, a police presence to keep the peace.

The third Sunday, the *Boston Globe* arrived. Dinsmore called off the pickets of Gordo's Records and claimed to be misunderstood. But the true Devil had been exposed.

The fourth Sunday, Dinsmore submitted his resignation. He would leave immediately for a more "hospitable" location for his ministry. I took that to mean somewhere near Selma, Alabama. Ideologically, if not geographically.

Sadly, though, there were all too many locations like that, places that would welcome him with open arms. Too many people here who had embraced his ideas even to the point of accepting the Curse of Ham.

We'd saved Gordo's business, but that seemed secondary now. We'd won this battle, but the fight that really mattered was just beginning.

I needed a Guinness. Or three.

HAMMER

Robert Petyo

I perked up when I heard Frank Sinatra's voice coming through the radio that tottered on the edge of my desk with its antenna poked up like a flagpole. While Jackie, "the Hammer," was more interested in that rock 'n' roll garbage, I idolized the Chairman of the Board. That was real music.

"Hey, cool it," Jackie said. He sat at a small table against the wall, his back to me. He was typing the final report on the accident investigation that I had just finished for Goldberg Insurance.

"This is real music," I said as I upped the volume. Frank's voice was just what I needed to bulk me up to face another boring day sitting in my office hoping for a phone call or a client to stop in, anything to take my mind off the fact the rent was due, and I only had a few bucks left in my account.

Jackie pressed his hands to his ears. Finally, he leaned down to the transistor radio on the floor beside his table. He turned it on and cranked up the volume.

I cringed at the noise that blared from the tiny box and turned my radio up even louder. Another one of our music battles. It was a good thing Jackie was a Mickey Spillane fan or this partnership would never have gotten past the first day. In fact, his nickname was the Hammer. I never liked calling him that—I considered it unprofessional—but he insisted I do so. All his hippie friends had nicknames. His being a Spillane fan is what brought us together in the first place. I met him in a bookstore shortly after I took over my father's business. I thought I could handle it myself. I couldn't. The Hammer," who could type sixty words a minute and wasn't afraid to run errands, was an ideal assistant. Even if I hated his taste in music.

Maybe I could win him over to the Chairman of the Board.

Someone rapped on the office door.

"Great," I said. "Just what we need. Noise complaints. It's probably the boys down the hall." Goldberg Insurance had a suite of offices while we were crammed into a tiny room. But I couldn't complain. Their proximity got a few cases tossed my way.

We lowered our volumes as the door opened and in stepped a thin young woman wearing a string of beads that hung to her waist. A thick, multicolored headband hugged her wide skull over brown hair that cascaded down to her waist.

Jackie scrambled out of his chair. "Cherry, my girl. How goes it?"

She glared at him. "Where were you, Hammer? You missed the protest."

Like an embarrassed child, Jackie kept his distance from her and bowed his head.

"J.J. was pretty pissed you weren't there," she said.

"Wait," I cut in. "What protest?"

"Just down the street," Jackie said, still staring at Cherry. "I was going to go."

"You what?" I started to rise from my chair as I felt my chest tighten with anger. I didn't want my assistant hanging out with hippie protesters.

He thrust a palm toward me. "Cool it, man. I didn't go. You had a couple things for me to do."

I forced myself back into the chair. "Don't get mixed up with those antiwar kids."

"The war's a—" But he choked off the budding argument. He knew I had done a tour in Nam, and it was a sensitive subject.

"Is that Sinatra's daughter?" Cherry asked.

"Huh?" I saw her pointing at my radio. I hadn't realized which song was playing. It was a duet with Frank and his daughter, "Something Stupid." I never liked that song. Nancy couldn't sing, and clearly, she was using her father to get into the business. That song also gave me uncomfortable thoughts about my own beautiful twenty-five-year-old sister. She was always my father's favorite.

I shut off the radio.

"That song gives me the creeps," Cherry said.

"I'm surprised you even know it," I said with a glance at Jackie. "Jackie, here, says people under thirty only dig rock and roll."

"I appreciate the older generation's music," she said with a pitying glance that made me cringe. I was only twenty-nine, yet she was treating me like a member of the older generation. "A father and his daughter singing a love song together?" She shivered as she stroked the beads across her chest. "That's the kind of thing the cops should be watching out for, don't you think? Instead of hassling us. We just want to bring our boys home."

"I love Frank," I said, ignoring the politics. "But not her. She's just riding his coattails, trying to be a singer. But still, it's better than the garbage Jackie listens to."

Her eyes darkened. Another rock 'n' roll fan.

"How did the protest go?" Jackie asked. "Everybody show up?"

"That's why I'm here. I need your help."

"Why?"

"Well, you guys are cops, right?" She spread her arms, pointing a finger at each of us. "You gotta help us out. They arrested four of the boys."

"Did things get that out of hand?"

"No." She kept swinging her eyes between Jackie and me. "We were peaceful. You know that's what J.J. says. Don't give the man a chance to come down on us."

"What happened?" I asked in my sternest schoolteacher

voice. I was getting tired of their hippie chatter.

With each hand, she gripped the beads as she looked down. "Well, things were okay until they found that dead guy."

The protesters had gathered at 5th and Carlton, just a few blocks from our office. When we arrived, only two youths stood near the intersection, waving cardboard signs with illegible crayon scrawl. Cherry led us toward them.

"Not much of a protest," I said.

Cherry said, "The cops chased everybody else away, but Gilly and Mailman hung around."

"Who'd they arrest?" I asked.

Gilly looked at Jackie, not wanting to directly address me. "J.J., Anvil, Steinway, and Gigs. They just chased the rest of us out of here." He puffed out his chest. "But I ain't going to let them push me around."

"Why did they get arrested?"

"The pigs said they were blocking traffic." He rested his sign on the ground and leaned toward Jackie as he shook his head. "But we know the real reason. They're going to go after them because of the dead guy. I know how they operate. They're probably putting a beatin' on J.J. right now. Pigs."

"Where was the body?" I asked, trying to keep the young punk focused.

"Back there." He pointed toward an abandoned mini market that was blocked by yellow tape. Steps led down to the entrance. "Body was in front of the door. Guy's name was Albert Saliviano."

"How do you know all that?"

"I got ears, man. The cops tried to chase us, but I told you, I hung around. The man ain't gonna push me around."

"What else did you hear?"

"Cops think he got into a fight about this protest and was beaten to death. No way. We're lovers, not fighters."

"What about the dead guy?" I cut in before he went off on another hippie rant.

"Beat up bad. Bruises around the neck and one eye blackened shut. Blood from the back of his head on the pavement."

"Wow. You don't miss much." Maybe I should hire another hippie. He had good ears. "Any weapons used?"

"The cops think maybe a hammer delivered the fatal blows."

"A hammer?" The Hammer perked up like he was suddenly on a Broadway stage.

"The cops looked around, but they couldn't find anything."

"A fight takes place a few yards behind you, and you didn't see or hear anything?"

"Nope. We were facing the street. Standing right on the curb and waving our signs. We were noisy. Cars were honking their horns, but we weren't blocking traffic. J.J. knows better. It was a good protest. Everything was fine until those construction workers showed up."

"What construction workers?"

"They started singing," said the first construction worker I approached. He had a stubble-covered chin and held a hard hat against his hip like a trophy. We stood on the sidewalk in front of a building that was still a hollow shell. "That's what got us worked up. We could hear them all the way down here."

We were a block away from where the protest had been. "What were they singing?"

"That commie thing. 'Eve of Destruction.'" He glared at Jackie, who stood a bit behind me, then tilted his head like he was going to spit on the street. He thought better of it and straightened. "Like I told the police, Billy was really worked up, so I decided to head down there with him. A few of the other guys, too. We were going to stand up for our country."

"What did you do?"

"We didn't really want no trouble, but we had to let them

know how we felt, right?"

I agreed with him. The protesters were probably a bunch of crybabies who just wanted to cut class, but now wasn't the time for a political discussion. "Did you see anybody fighting behind them? In front of that store?"

"I didn't see nobody. But that place is deserted. And that awning makes it dark. The front porch is sunken below the street. You can't really see it."

"But you would have heard a fight."

"I don't know. Maybe."

"How about the protesters? Any fighting? Punches thrown?"

"Nope."

"Did you see anybody standing behind them?"

"No. But I didn't really look. I just saw those kids with their stupid signs. We started yelling at them, and they kept singing."

"And when the patrolmen arrived?"

He straightened and hefted the helmet in front of his waist like he was before a four-star general posing for a picture. I saw his tool belt sagging from his broad hips. "Once the police stepped in, we backed off. We respect authority." Again, he glared at Jackie.

"And you didn't notice the victim back there?"

"Well, I didn't see him then, but we saw him before. He was at our building before the commie kids started their whining. We all know Al. He hangs around the construction site occasionally. Helps us out a little, but mainly we just send him to get sandwiches. In fact, that's what I did right when those kids showed up. Al's a bit of a hothead, and he was in the Army. I figured he might snap out at those kids and start throwing punches. I'm all for confronting the pinkos, but I don't want a riot. So, even though it was a little early, I sent him to the deli to get us lunch."

"Which deli?"

"Gonda's. That's where he works."

I knew Gonda's. Had lunch there quite a bit. And if Saliviano worked there, I was pretty sure I knew him. He was a veteran, like I was, but of the Korean War.

"What's happening?" asked the waitress when we sat at the counter. She held up an order pad like it was a rare jewel. "What can I get for you guys?"

"Sandy, I want to talk to Bert," I said. "Is he back there?"

She pouted for a moment, then smiled when I put a dollar bill on the counter. "Sure. I'll get him."

Bert was a big bald man with an apron stained brown and gray. "Man alive," he whined. "I just finished talking to the cops. What do you want now?"

"Tell me about Albert Saliviano."

Sandy made clucking noises with her tongue and shook her head. "Poor Al."

Bert told Sandy to get back to work and watch the register. He shooed us outside. "What do you want to know?"

"Albert Saliviano," I said. "That's your dishwasher, right? The thin guy always chewing a toothpick."

He nodded.

"What else can you tell me about him?"

"Works here part-time. Hangs out at the construction site the rest of the time. I know money's tight for him."

"He told me once he's divorced."

"Yeah. Divorced and remarried. Second wife passed away a few months ago. That was tough for him. He has two teenage daughters from his first marriage. He feels guilty about the divorce and sends them money. That's why money's a big problem for him." Out of breath, he stroked his forehead.

A crazy world, I thought. Protests. Rock 'n' roll. Divorces. Step kids. If I ever married, it would be forever.

"You tell the cops anything else?" I asked.

"Why do you care? You taking the case?"

I gestured toward Jackie, who stood slightly behind me. "A

couple of his friends are under suspicion."

"Really?" He looked at Jackie like he just realized he was there. "You're not one of them protesters, are you?"

Jackie didn't answer.

He jabbed a finger at him. "I'm telling you, one of your friends must have bashed Al's skull in. He wouldn't take too kindly to kids protesting the war. He'd be itching for a fight. Me, too."

Years ago, Lieutenant Chuck Kovatch was a beat patrolman with my father. At my dad's funeral, he had taken me aside and said that I should come to him if ever I needed anything. He helped me take over my dad's business. Most of my dad's clients were reluctant to switch to a kid with no investigative experience, so Kovatch sent a few jobs my way to get me going.

And with his help, I learned fast.

We were in his office behind the squad room. "None of the construction workers saw anything," I said. Through the door behind me, I could hear someone's radio playing the Beatles while detectives clattered away on typewriters. For a moment, I listened to the drumbeat matching the clacking of the keys.

"None of the protesters saw anything either," Kovatch said. "That's what they say. The guy was killed right behind them, and nobody saw anything."

"How many protesters were there?"

"Ten. We have the names. Hold on a sec." He sifted through papers on his desk and handed one to me. "And there were two no-shows." He gestured toward the list I now held. "The two names I put checks by."

The scrawl of the detective who had written the names took a little getting used to, but I managed to read them. Chris Lucas and Jackie "the Hammer" Arcane were the two no-shows. "Most of them have nicknames," I said as I scanned the list. J.J. was Jackson Jones. Anvil was Smitty Oravitz. Steinway was Peter

Berg. As I handed back the sheet, I asked, "Where are these guys now?"

"We're keeping the head guy and three of his cohorts overnight. Disturbing the peace."

"I'm sure they've got nothing to do with Al's death."

"Why do you say that?"

"They're college kids. Wimps. They're not going to get into an argument with a veteran."

"That's exactly why I want to check them out. Saliviano was a veteran. I'm sure he hated those protesters. I'm sure they had a confrontation, and all the hippies are covering it up."

"I'm a vet, too, Chuck. I did a tour in Nam. I'm not going to waste my time with some crybaby kids who need mommy to wipe their noses." As I said that, my mind drifted to the Hammer, who waited outside in the parking lot. He had planned to go to the protest. How could I continue to work with him? "Besides," I said, "the construction guys didn't see anything."

"Victim was probably dead before they even got there." He shuffled more papers on his desk. "No. I'm sure we have the right guys. Sooner or later, one of them will break. All we have to do is find that hammer. Check it for prints. They must've ditched it somewhere."

Theresa Lucas had returned to her maiden name after her divorce from Albert Saliviano. In fact, she told me she had always used her maiden name at the school where she taught. It was easier for her grade school students to pronounce.

"Thanks for talking to us," I said. We were in a small secretary's office outside the principal's office at the school. Students were finishing up lunch in the cafeteria, and the secretary would greet her students when they returned to class.

"I can't believe that Albert is gone."

"Any enemies? Someone who might want to hurt him?"

"No," she said quickly. "Everybody loved Albert."

I choked back a sarcastic response. He was so well-loved that someone killed him. "When's the last time you spoke?"

"I don't know. Weeks." She glanced down. "We didn't really keep in touch after the divorce."

"Your children?"

"Two girls. Fifteen and seventeen." She flashed a buoyant smile. "I have full custody. Albert was—" Her smile disappeared as she stumbled over her words. "Albert was a terrible father. Not really interested in their lives."

"I understand he sends them money."

"Just a little."

"Did he see them at all after the divorce?"

"Sometimes," she said as she squirmed in the chair.

"We would like to talk to your daughters."

"Do you have to bother them?"

"Do they know what happened?" I didn't want to be the one to inform them.

"I called Mary at school. I'm waiting to tell Kristin in person."

"We would really like to talk to them."

Mary Saliviano had long blond hair that draped over one shoulder so that it cascaded across the front of her muscular torso. She wore a red blouse and a short black skirt. When she crossed her long legs, exposing creamy skin above her knees, her leather boot bounced in the air like a basketball.

"We're sorry to take you out of class," the Hammer said.

"No problem." She smacked her lips like she was chewing gum. "I'll take any excuse to get out of class."

"Are you a senior this year? Planning on college?"

I stood behind the Hammer and clamped my lips together until I thought I might draw blood. I let Hammer interview the girl because they were closer in age, figuring it would work better that way. I had nothing in common with kids nowadays. But

I wished Hammer would stick to the case. It was like he was sizing her up for a date.

After some idle chatter, Hammer asked, "Do you know anybody who would want to hurt your father?"

"Lots of people. Dad was a real bum. He cheated on my mom. Smacked her around a few times, too."

Hammer glanced back at me before saying, "Your mom didn't tell us that."

She shrugged and smacked her lips again. "Mom never says much about it. She thinks I don't know." Her eyes twirled toward the ceiling. "Like I'm some dumb little kid."

"Does your sister know?"

"Sure. It's kinda hard to keep stuff like that a secret, you know."

"But your mom tried to protect you from it."

That caught her off guard, and her foot stopped bobbing as she wiped the corner of her eye. "Tried."

"Thank you for talking to us."

Kristin Saliviano looked away and waved the back of her hand as if she were swatting flies. She had left school early, complaining of a headache, and now sat at the end of the bed, her bare feet drumming on the floor. From the way she was dressed, I was sure the "headache" was just an excuse to cut school. She looked like she had been out on a date. Theresa Lucas had returned home again when she was told Kristin had left school, but after breaking the news of the death, she waited downstairs in the den. "I'll be right here if you need me," she called up the stairs to her daughter.

"I see you're a Sinatra fan," Hammer said, pointing to some posters that dotted the walls.

Her eyebrows curled in confusion.

He gestured toward me. "My partner's a big Sinatra fan. Right, Matt?"

He was trying to loosen the girl up, just like he had with Mary. "Sure. I love the Chairman of the Board."

She gave me a twisted look, her upper lip curling in a sneer.

"I'm more rock 'n' roll," Hammer said. "Beatles and the Stones." He pointed to a poster that had both Sinatras in it. "That from a concert?"

She craned back to look at the poster. "I don't know. I guess so. They did that song 'Something Stupid,' didn't they?" The words crept past her motionless lips. "I hate that song. Creepy."

"But you like Sinatra?"

Again, she waved the back of her hand.

"'These Boots Are Made for Walkin','" I said. "That's a Nancy Sinatra song." Kristin was barefoot. "Your sister wears boots. How about you?"

"Who cares," she said, as the skin crinkled above her nose.

I moved a bit closer to her and glanced toward the open closet door. There were two pairs of boots visible on the floor. "Did you love your father?"

"Of course."

"Even though he hit your mother?"

"Who told you that?"

"Your sister."

"She's lying."

"You don't have to protect him anymore. He ever hit you?"

She started to cry, softly at first, then loud enough to attract her mother, who clambered up the stairs and appeared at the door. "What's going on?"

Kristin wiped away her tears.

Her mother stepped into the room and rushed to her. She sat on the side of the bed and stroked her daughter's arm.

I looked toward the closet. I looked at the posters on the wall. "Something Stupid." The song nagged at me. Just as I could tell it nagged at Kristin. I remembered Mary's boots, square heels, like a hammer. Two more pairs in the closet, made for walking, and one of these days, they would walk all over her abusive father.

When I started toward the closet, Theresa slipped off the edge of the bed and blocked me. For a moment, we stared like two deer with locked antlers. Finally, I stepped back. The cops would have to get a warrant. Though, since she seemed to know what I suspected, it might be too late.

I started to hum.

"Maybe it's time for you to go," she said.

I started singing softly. "These boots are made for walkin'."

Kristin curled up on the bed like someone was hitting her.

"What are you doing?" Theresa asked, her gaze ricocheting between Kristin and me.

"I'm a big Sinatra fan," I said. "The daughter, too." I started singing louder, looking toward the closet as I did.

Kristin shriveled into an even tighter ball.

"Stop it," Theresa shouted.

Hammer's blank face suddenly darkened as a wave of recognition blanketed him. He, too, began to sing softly.

"What are you doing?" Theresa demanded.

"At the office, we always have music battles." He pointed to me. "He's the boss, so I have to let him win. He starts singing Sinatra, and I have to jump in." Hammer started singing "Something Stupid" in his putrid voice.

Kristin's shoulders inched up her neck, and she squeezed her eyes shut.

"You two get out of here," Theresa shouted.

I kept singing softly, repeating the chorus as I backed toward the bedroom door. Hammer finally stopped singing as he was already out the door.

Theresa kept shouting at us.

Kristin kept crying.

When we reached the bottom of the stairs, I stopped singing. We said nothing until we were out of the house and in the car. "Glad to see you got the idea."

Hammer sat behind the wheel, stretching like he had just finished a workout. "You and those old crooners," he said with a chuckle. He moved the car down the street and parked behind a Chevy Impala so that we could keep an eye on the house without being seen.

I asked, "Do you know everybody who attended the protest?"

"No. I just told J.J. I'd be there." He bowed his head like he was expecting to get yelled at.

"Kovatch gave me a look at the list. I didn't make the connection at first because the cop had written 'Chris.' But Kristin was supposed to be at the protest. She used her mom's maiden name."

"She cut school today."

"Right. She went to the protest and ran into her father. They argued."

"He was a child abuser. That was clear."

"She ended up knocking him down and stomping on him. She was wearing boots. The thick heel must have caught him in the eye. She came home and shoved the boots in the closet. That's why she was barefoot. You think the mother suspects?"

"Yeah. I got a feeling Theresa put up with some garbage from that guy, too. That's why I did my solo. To let her know we knew. Thanks for joining in. You picked up on things up quick."

"I didn't really want to upset the girl with that song. She's suffered enough. But we had to get our point across." He pointed toward the house. "How long do we wait?"

"We'll give them some time. The two of them are probably arguing right now about what to do. If we must, I'll call Kovatch and tell him to get some cops out here to watch the place. But I think she won't waste any time."

After about five minutes of debating the qualities of the Beatles versus Frank Sinatra, Hammer said, "Look."

Theresa Lucas came out her front door and hopped into her sedan. After she pulled out and started up the street, Hammer started the car.

There was a dumpster behind the all-day Pantry Quik Market on Pelican Boulevard about a half mile from her house. The place was busy enough that no one noticed when, after parking at the entrance, Theresa Lucas carried a bag and walked along the building to the dumpster. A few seconds later, she went inside, clutching only a small wallet, to innocently make a purchase.

We remained across the boulevard until she exited the building and drove home. Then I went to the dumpster and retrieved a pair of sturdy leather boots. I tilted the boots so that Hammer could see a few drops of blood on the base of one heel.

"The cops thought it was a hammer," I said.

"If I had a hammer," Jackie started singing softly as we returned to the car.

I decided not to start another music battle.

BLUE SUEDE SHOES
Wil A. Emerson

Larry and Jimmy were on a stakeout. Parked in the third row of the Kroger lot. Their five-year-old Ford Fairlane had been idling for thirty minutes. Every few minutes, it sputtered but didn't conk out.

"Using up all the gas, Jimmy. Shut it off for a while."

"Ya, and we'll lose him if this shit of a car doesn't start."

"Gotta have faith, Jimmy. When have we had to call for a ride? When, tell me?"

"Oh, go to hell, Larry." Jimmy sank further into his seat but left his wide-brimmed Stetson high on his head. He'd fall asleep if he hid the daylight. Up all night with a sore throat and a headache, he wouldn't tell his partner that he'd caught another bug. Larry would give him the usual "you catch more diseases than cheaters; that's why we can't buy a decent car." Then hover over him for days until Jimmy felt more like his better self.

The guy they were waiting for, Cezary Kaminski, wasn't doing his weekly shopping at the big chain grocery store. The tall, stupid Polack from Hamtramck who dressed like an Elvis wannabe—bell-bottoms, pink shirts, white ankle-high shoes—had stolen two thousand dollars' worth of goods from a gun dealer who ran his business out of a grease pit on Eight Mile Road where Detroit and the suburbs parted ways. A small area of the Motor City no one cared much about. The inner-city politicians didn't have the time for a cheap punk like Cezary, who everyone knew as Izzy. Bigger fish to fry. They blamed crime in the area on the suburban whites who crossed the Eight Mile border to buy drugs. The police precinct a mile away on the Detroit side had other things to worry about. Livernois Avenue, on the west side of Detroit, was about to blow up. No one believed it could be stopped until the rioters grew tired of setting fires and breaking windows. Couldn't last long, either way, was the consensus, because the cops would run out of tear gas soon. Any way you looked at it, there were no winners in riot wars.

Back to Izzy and the stakeout, there was a good chance he'd show up at Ralph Wingate's camera shop to pick up his current girlfriend. An attractive young gal, all smiles and cherry lips, with a bustline that made babies drool. She happened to be a Polaroid girl who worked in various camera shops, taking pictures of families and selling the instant cameras to husbands with an eye for candy. The wives shook their heads and whined.

Jimmy had an eye for beautiful gals and got horny the first time he saw the camera chick in the shop where he and Larry bought supplies. A short fantasy, though. After he found out she could be an Izzy girlfriend, he backed off. No one in their right mind would mess around, even flirt, with an Izzy Kaminski chick. Reckless, fearless, and stupid, the Polack would pull a knife before you could back up two feet. Those long, spaghetti arms of his could cut close.

Things were weighted in Izzy's favor. Even if the cops were called in, there were always enough people around who dug being an Izzy fan and played eyewitness. He acted in self-defense, they said. And the cops just walked away.

Larry and Jimmy weren't foolish enough to get involved in an Izzy deal. Private detectives kept a list of who was into petty crimes. Let those bums run the streets, they thought. There'd be payback someday by smarter, meaner crooks. And then Larry and Jimmy learned that a gun dealer and Izzy's second wife knew each other, and they both wanted revenge.

It started with doing a job for the wife. Larry took that call. A babe asking for help; he said, sure, why not. A cheating husband. Dime a dozen. Easy to get a photo of him with his arm draped around a dame. Sink a fin in a motel cleaning gal's hand, and she'd unlock a door. In like lightning, flash the Kodak, and out the door. Man didn't run fast with his pants off and his wiener at half-mast. Most of the time, Larry and Jimmy took those cases for fun. Or when they were behind on rent.

Better days were ahead, they knew. More gigs, corporate crimes, or maybe some professional gone missing. It would happen when their name got out there. Only in the business three years. Plenty of time still. They circulated various police precincts that didn't have the resources to keep pushing the envelope on seemingly unsolvable cases, so Larry and Jimmy jumped in.

What Larry didn't know when the distressed woman called that she didn't go by the name Kaminski. She happened to be one of those women on the march for independence and thought she fooled everyone by using her maiden name, Betsy Krueger. Two days passed before the brothers put the pieces together. The gun dealer who got involved was her brother, Hank Krueger. But then, it was too late for the private detectives to turn back. Krueger convinced Larry and Jimmy he had a legitimate complaint. Well, in his eyes it was legitimate. If you're keeping black-marketed rifles in an unlocked storage room, you're asking for trouble. Even if you have four or five thugs greasing up crankshafts and axles ten hours a day. Rumor was he sold those rifles to the Black Panthers in California and New York. The pansy lawmakers in both states thought no honest man needed a gun. So, as logic would have it, crooks and thieves bought them. Now with the riots, the Panthers were believed to be part of Detroit's problem, too, and they wanted more guns. Krueger liked having customers that paid in advance. Thing was, Krueger's guns targeted for the Panther market went missing about the same time Betsy found out that Izzy was doing a Rolling Stones' top seller, "Let's Spend the Night Together," with pretty, perky Polaroid girl. Not liking that duet, Betsy decided to sing "You Pushed Me Too Far" and called L and J Detective Agency.

At first, it was all tears and gnashing of teeth. Two kids at home, getting low on groceries, and a cheating husband. A serious complaint. So, Larry, the softer side of L and J, said they should talk in the office. Betsy arrived with cash in hand. It should have been a clue, but Larry didn't like to jump to conclusions. No telling, the gal could have borrowed the money or got it from her parents. Five hundred dollars down, a lot of dough, and five more when she had proof by way of photos. She even had names, addresses, and numbers to help get the job done fast.

At Larry and Jimmy's usual afternoon conference, they agreed, "Why not?"

Jimmy, though, wanted a little more information on the client. So, he asked his friend at the Ferndale Police Department to do a background check on one Betsy Krueger. "Oh, you mean the Krueger clan? There's Betsy and then Hank. Fred, the oldest, is in Jackson. Minor five-year delay in his career plan." The officer laughed. Jimmy did, too, but not with the same vigor.

Larry went to the bank with Betsy's down payment, obtained a money order for the rent, another one for the electricity, then added stamps and mailed them. He kept twenty-five dollars for expenses and put the rest in the savings account. With some of the secured cash, he'd get the paint chips and rust spots fixed on the '62 Fairlane and then sell it. The agency could use a better car, one with more style and dignity. Back at the office, Larry put new film in his camera, polished his shoes, and checked his Timex several times. Two hours, Jimmy out collecting that info. He wondered what took him so long. It didn't take long to dig up dirt on a client or even a suburban housewife like Betsy Krueger.

Jimmy, after his talk with the Ferndale cop, decided he needed a beer. He didn't like the idea of dealing with anyone in Hank Krueger's family. That was crossing a red line. He'd take on shady characters for a thousand bucks—characters like Izzy

Kaminski, a small-town shyster in a shiny Elvis suit—but Krueger was known to be dark and dirty. Involved in multiple crime organizations, and if things went wrong, they cut throats in retaliation. He should tell Larry they'd need to cancel the contract with Betsy. She might be an innocent party, not knowing about her brother's nefarious life, but it still was too close for comfort.

Jimmy didn't like to burst Larry's do-gooder bubble. On the other hand, a thousand smackers for a few days of surveillance seemed doable. If the older Krueger wasn't involved, maybe they could get the job over fast, swap photos and money, and never acknowledge Betsy and Hank were connected. It would take a cold beer or two to sort out the dilemma.

After the first beer and the second being pulled by an expert bartender who knew just how much it took for a head to rise to the rim, Jimmy startled. Damn Larry. He threw a buck and a quarter on the bar and darted out the door.

"Larry, don't do anything with that money," Jimmy yelled as he pushed open the office door.

Larry was at his desk with the shoe polish can in his hand. He stood. "What's all the noise?"

"We have to give that money back."

"Are you crazy? A thousand bucks is more than money in the bank. It's food, gas, and rent." Larry sat on the edge of Jimmy's desk and smoothed the crease in his brown trousers. "What's got your ass in a twirl?"

"Krueger. Doesn't the name ring a bell? Hank Krueger. Fred Krueger. All over the headlines last year. The suspected arms dealer. Some say selling to the Black Panthers, feeding the Detroit riot. Never been caught. His waste of a brother goes in and out of Jackson like it's a vacation retreat. Robbed a liquor store and beat up the clerk for a few bucks. Doing five. Krueger. Get it?"

"Betsy's in that family?" Larry shook his head. "She's all cream and sweetness. Dresses like a Catholic school girl."

"Get your shoes on and get the money back. Hate giving it up, but it could cost us in the long run."

"Don't go apoplectic on me. Take a breath, let's think this out."

"Nothing to consider. It's a no-go. Too frigging close to a fire. We could lose our license. Worse yet, our lives. Arms dealer. Not my cup of tea."

Larry laughed, "A cheating husband is one thing, weapons another. We've only got half the story. Besides, we can't give it back."

"Don't tell me. Damn, Consumer Gas could have waited. Detroit Electric doesn't expect anyone to pay on time. What the hell, Larry. You've got to curb those impulses to be a do-gooder. Not any more perks in heaven because we paid our debts on time. Fucking A—everyone knows that."

"Take it easy. Deep breath. Yes, paid some bills. And the rest is secured. Listen, we handle this, and we could get a reliable car. Take on a few more clients. Sitting pretty. Let's think about this."

It wasn't the first time the brothers had run into a difficult situation with unsavory clients. Burned by a few of their decisions. The most recent had been a dispute between two doctors—a pair of obstetrician/gynecologists—who split up their partnership. Reliable people, you would think. Then one accused the other of stealing patients. Their contract included a clause that neither could influence a patient as to which doctor they would continue to see. The practice had been lucrative, but within a few months, one doc saw only a few patients a day, then it whittled down to a few a week. Before long, the lawsuits started, and L and J Detective Agency was recruited to provide insight into the losing physician's claims. His lawyer paid a retainer of three hundred dollars. The remainder would be paid by whoever lost the case. Larry didn't like the smell of the whole thing. Too unsavory for doctors. After three weeks of surveillance, it became evident who had broken the contract. The doc with the least number of patients had started dating patients who were single. The more he dated, the fewer patients he had. When word spread that he had seduced a few of them in the office, hoping it would improve business, the other patients got wind of it and dropped like flies. The doctor on the receiving end of more patients provided free checkups at about the same time the dating doc had made another exam-room date. Of course, the free service won out at first because it came with added benefits. The ladies loved prescriptions that improved their image—weight loss being a greater motivator than the free checkups or a toss on an exam table. It turned out that both doctors provided enough illegal, unethical services that they lost their licenses. And little money remained for the private detectives to regain their expenses. Doctors and women were generally considered risky business thereafter by L and J Detective Agency.

But men cheated on their wives more than vice versa. L and J sucked it up as needed just to stay busy. However, they didn't need to take on the likes of Hank Krueger, who would only lead to big problems if they were caught in his crossfire.

When the phone rang, Jimmy was still into deep breathing, and Larry waited patiently at his side, plotting a way to do this small, easy job and catch Cezary "Izzy" Kaminski with the Polaroid girl.

"You guys still open?" Without a hello or a who's this.

"Yes, we are. What can I help you with?"

"Stay where you are." The caller hung up. Larry didn't like to jump to conclusions, but this was a no-brainer. He didn't need to recognize the voice. It was the tone. Trouble. Hank Krueger on the other end? And fifteen minutes later, they heard about Izzy Kaminski not only cheating on his second wife, which Hank Krueger didn't give a shit about, but also about Izzy weaseling two thousand dollars' worth of Hank's precious goods from him.

"You two ever hear about the Black Panthers?"

"We read the paper, Mr. Krueger."

"Well, if you had something they paid for and it didn't get delivered like promised, then you'd feel like you're up shit's creek, right, fellas?"

Larry wanted to reply, "That's how we feel right now," but he had a knack for evading a direct question and used the time to think about a satisfactory response.

Jimmy sat up straighter. His quick replies were a nasty habit. "Mr. Krueger, if this is a family matter between you and your brother-in-law, you could find a way to resolve it without detectives. We contracted to help Mrs. Krueger in a domestic dispute. That's generally our line of business. We weren't hired by Izzy Kaminski."

"Okay, no conflict. I'm adding another thousand, and when you find Izzy Kaminski with the Polaroid gal, that domestic dispute with my brother-in-law will come to an end. You call me first. He's got the goods I sold to a very select customer. The kind that won't take sorry for an answer." He reached into his wallet and pulled out a wad of cash.

The rubber band around it was stretched so thin, Larry thought it would snap and hit one of them in the eye. Let it be me, he thought. Jimmy had enough ailments as it was.

"I'm going to settle the score both ways. Mark my word. Betsy, well, she's a good kid but dumb as dirt when it comes to men. I told her, she don't listen." He put his hands up. "Women. I'll check in again tomorrow, next day at the latest."

"It's good doing business with ya." Krueger plopped the money on the pine desk and leaned closer. "If ya need work done on that shitty Fairlane in your driveway, I've got guys who can do it."

Larry and Jimmy looked at each other for longer than usual. It wasn't the first time a stranger's remarks triggered bad memories. "I've got the guys who can do it." The lieutenant who sent Jimmy and two other soldiers out in a Nam swamp that needed more coverage than their M14s could handle had said the same thing. Jimmy's buddies, in the lead, got blown to bits. Jimmy was lucky and only lost a kidney.

Larry joined the Army in late '62, thought it would be a way to show respect for his country. Just like his father and grandfather. Those sent overseas to a place no one knew much about then were called "military advisors." He felt guilty, then, that it wasn't a real war. By the time Jimmy joined, at the end of '63, Kennedy had sent sixteen thousand boys into the muck to support the South Vietnamese Army. The bombing started, all hell broke loose, and the Gulf of Tonkin and Saigon were nightly subjects for newsmen Walter Cronkite and Chet Huntley. Suited and serious, they talked as if war was happening in another world. Then the protesters in California made trouble. Didn't take long for it all to get under your skin. Larry never wanted to hear about it again. Especially knowing his buddies might not come home because they believed in the good ole USA and didn't run to Canada.

Then Jimmy came home to lie in a hospital for three months. The brothers didn't talk much about those days. Too fresh, and some of their best friends who were drafted never did make it home. Two of them were still there: Franko DaMato, Louie Benson. Their mothers cried in Mass every Sunday.

"I've got the guys who can do it" made the brothers shudder.

Larry broke the silence, "And we thought those two doctors were lunatics. Illegal weapons, Krueger, Black Panthers? Why in the hell are we in this business?"

"You were a good military cop, that's why. And we don't know who to trust, like Nam."

"Maybe I should try again. Another city, maybe."

"Something to think about. Right now, we got to catch Izzy Kaminski in the act and get out of this mess."

They sat in the car until nine p.m., and then the lights flickered in the camera shop.

Larry said, "They're closing up. Let's see if she comes out alone."

"Could be he picks her up in the back. Nobody sees nothing."

"Maybe. If we have to do this again tomorrow, remind me to go in and buy some film. Saw an ad. Two rolls for one," Larry said.

"Look, there she is. What a goddess. Looks like Elizabeth Taylor. God, she's beautiful," Jimmy said.

"Okay, good looking. But Taylor. I don't know. Taylor's got those lavender eyes. No one looks like Taylor."

"Damn, did she spot us? I swear she looked right at me." Jimmy sank lower in the seat.

"She's digging into her purse."

Jimmy leaned forward and twisted the ignition key. They'd sat for more than an hour without it running. "Damn, it better start." He tapped his foot on the gas and cranked the key again.

"Shit," Larry said. "Give it a minute. Try again after she passes us."

Larry watched the black Chevy sedan, as old as their Fairlane but cleaner, back out and turn toward their lane. "Try again while I get the license number."

Jimmy squirmed in the driver's seat, leaned on the steering wheel as if it would help the situation. The car sputtered, and then the motor hummed. "Gotta love a Ford."

They trailed behind, trying to keep two cars between them. When her car slowed and moved into the right lane, Jimmy moved to the left. "I'll make a left if she turns right. Then make a fast U-turn."

The plan worked, and they saw the car turn on a side street about three blocks down. By the time they had her in sight again, the gal was entering a small white ranch house with a covered porch and a kid's bicycle in the walkway.

"You think she has kids?"

"Izzy's crazy if he's running around with a married woman."

Jimmy drove to the end of the street and turned again to circle back in front of the small house. There were lights in the windows of all the homes. All appeared to have been built in the same time period. Neat yards, working-class neighborhood. As they eased by the house, the front door opened. A small boy, about eight, bounced down the stairs and grabbed the bike.

"No way that's her kid," Jimmy said and smiled as if he'd

made a great discovery.

Larry jotted down the license number of the car and the street address. "We'll run this by DMV in the morning. Talk to someone in the clerk's office, see who owns the house."

The next morning the brothers were in their office at nine. By nine thirty, they had the information, and it didn't add much to the case. Nothing that got them closer to confirming Izzy Kaminski was making hay with the young gal who apparently lived with a young boy and a forty-five-year-old man by the name of Howard Clinton. Was the guy her father? Jimmy hoped so. He had a hard time letting go of his dreams.

By noon they were staked out down the block on Silman Avenue with a camera and binoculars. The Clinton house in good view, and the weather couldn't be better for comfort and keeping a low profile. The sun fought with the clouds over control of the day. Larry cracked the back window for fresh air, and it was warm enough to not have the car running.

"Fall's the best time," Jimmy said. "Could last all year for me."

"Yesterday, you were crying the blues. Too cold."

"Granted, it changes but stays close to what I like until about middle of November. Then all hell breaks loose. Yeah, fall's the best."

"Look, sharpen up. Door's opening."

"It's her. Wow, dressed to the nines," Jimmy said.

The Fairlane purred like a kitten, and Jimmy cruised slowly down the street. The man they assumed was Clinton had stepped onto the small porch and watched the Chevy as it turned on John R. He waved, then seemed to hang his head down and mutter.

"Gotta be her old man, her father. Not like a husband to do that," Jimmy offered. "Saturday, he'd have the Tigers on. They're playing the Angels today."

"You'd rather go home and watch? I can handle this. No need for both of us to sit all afternoon." Larry had a hunch nothing eventful would happen.

"Hey, not my style. With that Krueger nut in the picture and stupid Izzy Kaminski on the loose." Jimmy knew it was his duty to stay with Larry even if he wanted to watch the game.

"Looks like she's headed back to the camera shop. Yep, there she goes. Same parking space, too. The girl's got her routine."

"I think I'll save us some time. I'll go buy some film, look around. Ask how long the picture-taking gal's working. Like I'm bringing my kids back for a picture, might buy one of those instants."

"Can't hurt," Jimmy agreed.

When Larry returned to the car, he opened the back door and threw in a paper sack filled with the film he'd bought. "Good news," he said as he opened the front passenger door. "She's there till seven tonight. No sense wasting time here. Go home, watch that game."

At six thirty, Jimmy was all smiles. As they returned to the camera shop, he said, "Great game, great win. The Angels couldn't get their asses off the ground. Tigers are good this year."

He parked the blue Fairlane in the fourth row, away from the overhead lights, and eased down into his seat. Larry took out a thermos of coffee and poured himself a half cup. The rule was never full. You never knew when you might have to run.

"I'm glad the game made you happy. While you were watching, I learned more about Izzy Kaminski. Seems he's been seen late nights at Louis Benton's, that steak place on Six Mile Road. He's branching out from ole Hamtramck. Once our gal gets home, let's take a run over to Benton's."

"You gonna buy us steaks with baked potatoes?"

"Sure, after we collect our money. If he's with another woman tonight, this all could have a happy ending. Your Polaroid gal might want to dump him, too."

Jimmy looked at his watch. "It's ten after seven. You said

seven or eleven?"

"Not eleven. I said seven. She's running late. Be patient."

At seven twenty, Jimmy said, "Hell, what do you think? Go in, see what happens. Follow up on buying that instant."

"Not a bad idea." Larry opened the car door. "But, hey, start her up. Just in case."

It took all of five minutes for Larry to pass through the double glass door and then return. "Shit, she left early. About six, the clerk said. Tried to sell me a camera anyhow."

"Shit. What now? Back by her house. If the car's there, we go to Benton's just like we planned." Jimmy stepped on the gas, the wheels spun, and dust rose from the pavement.

Saturday evening traffic was slower than usual. "Good weather brings everyone out." Jimmy beeped the horn and then turned on Silman Street, where he had to ease off the gas. A regular neighborhood with kids in their yards. A ball rolled out into the street.

"Let's go home," Jimmy muttered.

"Why the foul mood?"

"I just don't like this. Something's not right." He pointed to the white ranch where the same bicycle lay on the sidewalk.

"No car," Larry said. "Off to Benton's. Maybe go in, have a drink."

Jimmy perked up. "One of them fancy martinis."

The parking lot was small and lined with cars. Both checked the rows.

"Nope, nothing that looks like her Chevy," Jimmy said.

"Couple black ones over there." Larry pointed.

"Hers is a sedan. Probably her old man's."

They were met at the door by a man in black trousers, a white shirt, and a black vest.

"Reservations, gentlemen?"

"No, just having drinks," Larry said. "At the bar, if that's good with you."

"Of course." He pointed the way to a long, sleek bar with a

mirrored wall and shelves full of various whiskeys, bourbons, vodkas, and gins.

"More booze than I've seen in my life," Jimmy said.

"It's not the VFW."

Larry decided to splurge and ordered martinis. "Two olives in each." Worth a try, he thought, even if he was more of a bourbon-on-the-rocks guy when he didn't drink Budweiser. He dug in his pocket and pulled out two dollars.

"That's two fifty, sir." The bartender lowered his chin and looked from Larry to Jimmy.

When the bartender turned his back, Jimmy whispered, "What the fuck? You think he didn't take us as regulars? Not good enough?"

Larry started to reply, but in the reflection between bottles of Jim Beam and Johnnie Walker, he saw a couple at a far table. A darkened area but still light enough to think they weren't hiding. A man in a pink shirt, his black leather jacket hanging on the back of his chair, had his head close to the woman. The blonde with long, loose curls and a low-cut red dress was all smiles and flashing dark mascara eyes.

Larry said to his brother, "Don't be obvious; see that couple in the back, near the wall? I'm thinking Izzy. Clothes, slimy, and all that. The gal. Red dress. Who's your guess?"

Jimmy still had a scowl but gazed at the mirror, then took a slow turn. "Frigging A. If that's our Betsy, looks like she got over his cheating ways. Ain't no two Izzys in this town. Look at those shoes." One long leg stretched out from the table, almost blocking the walkway between tables.

"Sissy shoes. Blue at that."

"Saw those ads on TV. Elvis's new song. Shit, you'd think a man had more sense."

Each took a sip of their martini. "Never liked gin much," Jimmy said and glared at the bartender.

Larry focused on the mirror, but a loud commotion at the front entrance made him turn. As if a storm had blown in, a woman carrying a large bag rushed from the door to the center of the dining area. The doorman trailed behind, "No reservation, please, please…"

About that time, Jimmy geared his attention on the gal with the big paper sack in her hand, Ralph's Camera Shop written on the side in bold black letters. Hard to mistake for a grocery bag. And then it dawned on him who carried the brown paper sack. The striking young Polaroid gal. The girl he'd swooned over for the last few days.

Before Larry or Jimmy could move, she pulled a pistol out and started firing.

The woman in the red dress, who happened to be Betsy Krueger, suddenly plopped over. She fell face-first into the uneaten steak. Izzy's back seemed to open up like it had been filleted. His long leg kicked up, and a blue suede shoe flew off his foot.

Larry and Jimmy decided this was none of their business; they picked up their martini glasses and gulped down the contents. Out the door and into their '62 Fairlane.

"The Polaroid gal doesn't like cheaters."

"No doubt she got that handy Colt 1911 semi-automatic from Hank Krueger," Jimmy said.

"Maybe," responded Larry.

"Guess we won't be getting that extra five hundred dollars from Betsy."

"Krueger won't get his money from Izzy Kaminski either. And he still has to deal with the Panthers not getting what they paid for. Looks like payback all around to me."

Jimmy turned the key in the ignition. The engine sputtered. "Shit."

"Let it settle. Try again in a few minutes."

Sirens squealed in the distance. People ran to their cars.

Jimmy leaned against the steering wheel, "You'd think Izzy would have more sense than to wear blue suede shoes in public."

SUMMER IN THE CITY
John M. Floyd

Tuesday, July 25, 1967

Eddie Gray sat alone on the bench beside the fountain in the park and watched the stranger approaching on the curving sidewalk from the parking lot. It didn't surprise Gray that the man was well-dressed and older and solemn; he'd sounded that way on the telephone two hours ago and had said he was an accountant. What surprised Gray was the wheelchair.

The man rolled the chair to a spot six feet away and stopped. "Mr. Gray?" he said, sweating in the heat. "Coleman Ferris. Thank you for meeting me."

"New clients usually come to my office, Mr. Ferris. In a part of town that's not on fire."

"I don't see any fires here."

"Yet," Gray said.

Ferris nodded sadly. "Quite right." They turned together to look through the trees to the northwest. A dirty smudge hung there in the sky, and even from here Gray could smell smoke.

The trouble had started on Sunday, at the corner of 12th and Clairmount, three miles away. In fact, Eddie Gray was in Tiger Stadium with his ex-brother-in-law, watching the Tigers play the Yankees, when he saw the dark columns of smoke in the distance. Gray wondered what it was, and by the time the game was over, and they were in traffic on Woodward Avenue, he could see for himself. The riots had spread steadily, and now, two days later, dozens were dead, and hundreds of businesses were burned down or looted. The city of Detroit was under siege.

Ferris faced him again and said, "I told you I did time in prison. I asked to meet here because there are those who keep an eye on my office. This is safer, for me."

"Sounds like what you need is a bodyguard. I'm a private investigator."

"No, Mr. Gray, what I need is for you to find my son. I contacted you because he's gone missing."

The story was short and to the point. According to Ferris, twenty-year-old Ronald had taken a job with an Illinois publishing company that hired college students from all over the country to sell dictionaries door-to-door during the summer. Ronnie and another young man—J.T. Watson, from Alabama— were assigned to Flint, seventy miles north of Detroit, and after training in Chicago, they caught a bus to Flint, bought two used bicycles for ten dollars apiece, and found and rented a bedroom in a house on Thayer Street, about a mile from downtown. Using that as a base, they had for the past two months pedaled their bikes all over southwestern Flint, calling on mostly suburban neighborhoods to sell the company's dictionaries.

"Then, this past Sunday," Ferris said, "Ronnie disappeared. His roommate called the publishing company to report it and they called me." He paused and said, "Ronnie had come back here to Detroit for the weekend, to visit, then left my home late Sunday afternoon and never showed up at his room." He paused. "I'm worried, obviously, but even more so now that these riots have spread to Flint. I heard that last night buildings in Flint were being firebombed, cars stoned, store windows smashed, etc."

Gray had heard the same. He thought that over and said, "What kind of trouble has Ronnie had with the law?"

Ferris blinked. "Why do you think he's had trouble?"

"Because you're talking to me instead of to the police."

A silence passed. Finally, Ferris sighed and nodded. "Minor violations, these past two years. Public disturbances, first-offense DUI, that kind of thing. But he's better now. Changed. An old friend of mine at the publishing company suggested I look into getting Ronnie this job, for the summer—to make him grow up a little."

Twenty should *be* grown up, Gray thought. But he didn't point that out. What he pointed out was his daily rate and his promise to phone Ferris with regular updates. After all, he needed the work. When finally they parted ways and Gray drove back to his office from the park, he could hear sirens in the distance. The smoky haze seemed twice as thick as before.

The next afternoon—Wednesday, the twenty-sixth—Gray left Detroit and its troubles and took I-75 north to Flint. He checked in at the Holiday Inn on Bristol Road, on the opposite end of town from the reported rioting. After unloading, he ate an early supper and drove around listening to Jefferson Airplane and Diana Ross until seven o'clock, when he figured Ronnie Ferris's dictionary-selling roommate would have put his bicycle up for the day, and he found the address Ferris had given him for the rooming house, near the corner of Thayer and West 2nd Street.

An elderly lady as short and thin as a child answered Gray's knock at the door. When he told her who he was looking for, she pointed to a flight of stairs, said, "First door on the left," and went back to the noisy TV in the other room. *Gilligan's Island*, from the sound of it. Gray trudged up the steps and saw, through the open door, the biggest guy he'd ever laid eyes on.

J.T. Watson was sitting on the edge of a double bed and reading a paperback Western by the light of a floor lamp. When he saw his visitor, he put the book down, stood up, and said, "You lookin' for me, or Ronnie?"

"Ronnie. But I came to talk to you." Gray introduced himself, held out his hand, and watched it disappear into J.T.'s, which looked big as a catcher's mitt. Gray guessed the kid was at least six-eight and three hundred pounds. Maybe three twenty.

But he proved to be a gentle giant. In a deep but pleasant voice, J.T. repeated what Ferris had said about Ronnie's disappearance and went on to describe his and Ronnie's job and daily routine. Jobwise, it was simple enough: stay for three months, sell dictionaries door-to-door, earn roughly half the price of each book sold, make deliveries in late August of any books ordered, get paid, and go home. He said the company preferred its young salesmen to be from elsewhere—southerners were usually sent north and vice versa—because that discouraged dropouts. Going home was harder if home was far away. As for their workday, they got up at six, had bacon and eggs at Uncle Jack's Diner down the street, pedaled their bikes out to what J.T. called the hinterlands to see Mrs. Jones, sold dictionaries—mostly orders—all day, ate supper together at the same diner around six, arrived "home" before seven, and were in bed by eleven.

"Mrs. Jones?" Gray asked.

J.T. grinned. "She's the universal customer, the housewife who buys our books. Every sales pitch we make is designed for her."

"Do you and Ronnie call on the same areas, all day?"

"No, sir. We usually split up after breakfast. Lately Ronnie goes west on Glenwood Avenue to Corunna Road and its side streets, and I head south over Swartz Creek and past the GM plant, to the neighborhoods down there."

Gray thought that over. "I don't know the town, but from the riding around I did this afternoon, that sounds like a long way."

Another grin. "We cover a lot of miles. I'm so heavy the seat post of my bike bends a little every day, down toward the back wheel, and when I get home, I have to straighten it again."

Grant was surprised the tires didn't collapse. But he could picture this guy bending steel with his bare hands. Then he had a thought and said, "Both of you sleep on that one bed?"

"No choice. Ronnie says it's like sharing a bathtub with a whale."

Gray chuckled. "Better y'all than me." Changing the subject, he said, "So, the last time you saw Ronnie Ferris was Saturday morning, before he left for the weekend."

"Yessir. I really can't figure it. He's missed three days of work, now."

"Okay, one more question. If you were me, where would you start looking for him?"

After a pause J.T. said, "I'd start by asking the other guy that's looking for him."

The room went quiet. "What?"

"Came here last night. Short dude, dark hair, groovy clothes, gold chains around his neck. Said he wanted to talk to my roomie. When I said he wasn't here, he asked where he was, and I told him I didn't know, which was true. He wasn't happy."

Neither am I, Gray thought. *Who the hell was this?* Further questions revealed nothing, and after half an hour he thanked J.T. and left. Outside, he almost didn't notice the red Mustang parked at the curb facing him, several houses up. Someone was sitting in the driver's seat, and in the fading sunlight Gray caught a flash of gold.

He turned in midstride and marched toward the Mustang. He was halfway there when the car pulled out, made a screeching U-turn, and roared away in the other direction.

He watched it turn the corner onto Court Street and stood there awhile, thinking.

What have you not told me, Coleman Ferris?

Gray drove back to the Holiday Inn along roughly the same route Ronnie's roommate must've been taking every day: Hammersberg to 12th and then down Van Slyke past the huge General Motors plant to West Bristol Road. On his car radio, Neil

Diamond was thanking the Lord for the night-time. After another quick meal at the motel restaurant, Gray phoned Ferris from his room with a report. His first words were, "What exactly is your son into, Mr. Ferris?"

"What?"

"I just found out somebody else is after him. What for? Gambling debts? Drug deals?"

For a moment the line was silent. "All this is news to me. Look, Gray, I just want him found, and safe. Maybe he *is* mixed up in something—he's still mostly a kid—but if that's the way it turns out, so be it, and we bring in the police. All right?"

That wasn't all right, but Gray left it at that. The fact was, he was curious now.

The following morning, Thursday, he ran up an astronomical two-hour bill on his room phone talking to an old friend at the Detroit PD. The result was a confirmation of the list of misdemeanors Coleman Ferris claimed Ronnie had committed since his high school graduation in '65, plus a few more. But none of it shed any light on why someone was looking for him.

After lunch Gray drove back to Ronnie's home base and sat there awhile at the curb on Thayer Street. No Mustang in sight this time. Deep in thought, he climbed out of his Pontiac and strolled down the driveway to the back of the house. An old Chevy Impala sat in the one-car garage, and a single bicycle with a basket on the front leaned against a wall inside a screened porch. Probably Ronnie's, since his roommate would currently be out selling books to Mrs. Jones on the other one. Wherever my runaway is, Gray thought, he's on foot or in a car. Which reminded him of something he should've thought about last night, when talking to J.T.

He went back around front and rapped on the door. The same woman answered, and though Gray expected her to say, "Sorry—he's out working," she said, "You again. Do you know what's going on, with those two boys upstairs?" Without waiting for an answer, she crooked her finger in a follow-me gesture and turned away. Gray followed her.

On the way up the narrow steps—which took a long time, since he was behind her—the old woman said, "Since I almost never drive my car anymore, haven't driven it in months, I walked down the street to visit Cora Burnley for an hour this morning—just an hour—and when I got home, I found my back door open, and *this*."

By this time, they'd reached the second floor, and Gray saw what she meant.

The rented room was a mess. Drawers out, suitcases open, clothes everywhere, dictionaries strewn about, lamp overturned, mattress on the floor. And Gray immediately understood. The gold-chained stranger wasn't just looking for Ronnie. He was looking for something Ronnie *had*.

"I need to ask you something, Mrs.—"

"Miss," she said, still fuming. "Miss Dunwoody. What is it?"

"I was told young Mr. Ferris—Ronnie—went to visit his father in Detroit last weekend. Since he didn't have a car...how'd he get there and back?"

"He borrowed one. Or so he told me, before he left."

"Borrowed one from who?"

"His girlfriend," she said.

Gray decided to wait for J.T. Watson at Uncle Jack's Diner. He had three reasons for this: (1) it was already midafternoon, (2) he wanted to catch J.T. before he saw the state of his room and got distracted, and (3) the almost-empty diner gave him a bright, air-conditioned place to sit and listen to music from the jukebox and think. Most of his thoughts involved the fact that he seemed to be learning something new every few hours and still getting nowhere.

As forecasted, the gigantic young dictionary salesman arrived a few minutes after six. He seemed surprised to see Gray but joined him at the table and pulled out a chair. According to the jukebox in the corner, Billy Joe McAllister had just jumped off the Tallahatchie Bridge.

"You buying?" J.T. said, smiling.

"Why not. I'm on an expense account. How was Mrs. Jones?"

"Reluctant. But I won her over, a few times."

The waitress, a weary lady with a beehive hairdo, seemed pleased to see Gray finally order something more than coffee, and when their food arrived three songs later, he asked J.T. the question he'd been waiting for hours to ask. "So, Ronnie has a girlfriend here?"

J.T. nodded, chewing. "Probably should've told you that last night."

"I guess he works fast. You two've only been here a few weeks."

"Eight. But they didn't meet here—they dated in college, he told me. Michigan State. She lives in Mt. Morris, about ten miles north of here."

"Convenient," Gray said. Once again, he had the feeling he was missing something obvious—but couldn't put his finger on it.

"He doesn't see much of her, with our schedule," J.T. said, "but she drives over most weekends and picks him up. She has a little VW bug."

"You know her name?"

"Linda something. Something Polish." He gulped some iced tea that he'd loaded with sugar, thought a moment, and said, "Rosinsky. That's it—Linda Rosinsky."

Gray jotted the name on a napkin and went back to eating. His companion was already done. "Anything else you forgot to say to me, last night?"

"Yeah," J.T. said, and burped. "Want to buy a dictionary?"

Before going to bed that night Gray dutifully called his client again, with two pieces of information. First, he was on the track of a girlfriend of Ronnie's who might know something about his whereabouts, and second, the people who were looking for Ronnie were also looking for something in his possession. Ferris assured him he knew nothing about either. The mysterious son hadn't mentioned a love interest—he'd told his father only that the car was a friend's—and Ferris said he couldn't imagine what special item Ronnie might have that anyone would want. When Gray hung up the phone, he realized he no longer believed much of anything Coleman Ferris said. Something weird was afoot here, and Gray was determined to find the truth. With that noble thought, he hit the sack and slept the sleep of the righteous.

On Friday morning, July 28, he woke up feeling neither righteous nor enthused, but after two cups of coffee he got back on the telephone in his room. It paid off: the operator at Directory Assistance informed him there was only one listing for the name Rosinsky in Mt. Morris, Michigan. It took Gray twenty minutes to drive there, during which he noted that tiny Mt. Morris showed no sign of a mountain nearby, and another five minutes to find the address the operator had given him for one Stuart Rosinsky. The lady who answered the door, the opposite of Ronnie's and J.T.'s grumpy landlady in age, size, and disposition, happily told him their daughter Linda worked at the local library and provided directions.

Linda, when Gray tracked her down at the library's reference desk, was less cheerful—and less trusting—than her mother. She steered him to a private room and agreed to knowing Ronnie Ferris but balked at revealing anything else. It was only when Gray mentioned the fact that Ronnie might be in danger that she relented.

"Someone's looking for him?" she asked, eyes wide behind her cat-eye glasses.

"That's right, and I'd like to know why." Gray paused and added, "I mean him no harm, Miss Rosinsky. I know about his troublesome past, and his father, and I want only to help him."

She studied him for a long moment. "For some reason, I believe you, Mr. Gray—but I'm not so sure about his father."

That makes two of us, Gray thought. "Why not?"

More hesitation. At last, she let out a breath and said, "Ronnie told me something happened Sunday, just before he left Detroit to drive back. He said Mr. Ferris gave him a package to deliver to a street address in Flint sometime during the week."

"What kind of package?" In his mind Gray could see the ransacked apartment at the rooming house.

"Ronnie said it was a wrapped box, and his dad told him not to open it under any circumstances, for fear of damaging the contents."

"But he opened it anyway," Gray said. "Right?"

"Yes." Linda Rosinsky paused, frowning. "He said he knew something was wrong, about the way his dad acted when he gave it to him. After fretting about it for thirty miles on the way here, he pulled off the interstate, unwrapped the box, and looked inside."

Gray said nothing. Waiting.

"It was diamonds, Mr. Gray. Rough diamonds, not the sparkly kind. But Ronnie knew what they were." She looked uneasy, and said, "He used to run around with...well, a bad crowd. But he's changed—and, seeing what was in the package, he was worried about his dad."

She fell silent then, as they mulled this over. Gray knew diamond smuggling had become a big thing—rough stones were often flown in from Africa as part of passengers' bracelets or necklaces to avoid questions at customs and then routed to professional cutting facilities—but it was still a shock.

"What did Ronnie do then?" Gray asked.

"About the diamonds? He wasn't sure *what* to do. On his way here to return my car, he dropped by his room first, and talked it over with his roommate. They decided he should hide the package and wait to figure out the next move. So that's what he did. He and I had passed a stretch of abandoned houses in northern Flint several times before, on our way to his place and back, and after he left his rooming house Sunday night, Ronnie said he decided to stop and hide them there. He sure didn't want them in his room, or here with me, and he was determined not to deliver them to where his father had told him to, at least not yet."

"So, they're still there? At a vacant house on the north side of Flint?"

"Yes, hidden under the front porch steps," she said. "Later that night he drove up here to my place as planned, so I could drive him back to Miss Dunwoody's and keep my car, for work."

"But you didn't drive him back, did you."

She exhaled a lungful of air. "No. When he'd told me about the diamonds, we figured it'd be risky for him to go back to his room, and my dad would freak out if he stayed at our house."

"So where is Ronnie, now?"

"Holed up at my late grandpa's cabin, in the woods west of here, at least until he figures things out, with his father and the diamonds. I'm off at one o'clock and was planning to go check on him." She paused again. "If you can wait till then, you can go with me, if you like."

"I would," Gray said. But suddenly he had a bad feeling. "Do you know the exact address of this house where Ronnie hid the package?"

"Yes. He made me write it down. House number, street name, and exact location—the southeast corner of an intersection a block from North Saginaw."

"Next question: Does Ronnie have a TV or radio at the cabin? To listen to the news?"

"Are you kidding? He doesn't even have indoor plumbing. Why?"

"I think we should make a side trip, before going to see him."

The drive down to the north section of Flint didn't take long, even in Friday afternoon traffic. Neither Gray nor Linda said a word. At one fifteen Gray parked his Pontiac in front of the house where Ronnie Ferris had left his father's box of diamonds.

The problem was the house was gone. Burned to the ground, probably two days ago, when the looting and firebombings started. They'd already passed the ruins of other buildings.

"I was afraid of this," Gray said, as they stared at the smoldering remnants. A blackened section of chimney was the only thing standing. "The riots have all been in this part of town. And apparently most of the arson targets were abandoned and vacant houses."

They left the car and checked underneath the porch steps but found nothing but ashes.

"I didn't think diamonds could burn up," Linda said, her face pale.

"Well, they can. Gold and silver aren't combustible, but diamonds are."

There was nothing more to be said.

They drove back in silence to Linda's house and switched to her car, a white Volkswagen; Gray had decided on their trip back that Ronnie might see his unfamiliar car approaching and run away. With Linda driving and the Monkees blaring from her eight-track, they reached her grandfather's cabin at half past two o'clock and found Ronnie Ferris chopping wood in the front yard. Probably for cooking, Gray thought. The day was too warm for a fire in the fireplace. Linda hopped out and sprinted into Ronnie's outstretched arms while Gray hung back.

Introductions were as tense as Gray had figured they'd be, but after some time Ronnie warmed a bit toward the newcomer, and, if anything, he seemed relieved to share the worry he'd taken with him into hiding. The kid also didn't have the troublemaker appearance Gray had expected. Standing there with his shirt off, he looked a little like that Eastwood guy from *Rawhide* a few years earlier.

Twenty minutes later, sitting on a fallen log beside the cabin after all the updates, Ronnie said, "So, how much of a mess am I in?"

Gray scratched his chin. "Legally, not much. It wouldn't look good that you disappeared, but at this point the three of us and your father and J.T. Watson are the only ones who know about that, and you were duped into transporting the package anyway. Speaking of which, that oversized roommate of yours is almost as sneaky as your father. J.T. didn't tell me you'd stopped there Sunday night and let him in on the secret."

"That's because it was a secret. How about my dad?"

"That's a different story. Smuggling diamonds is a felony— or would be, if we still had the evidence. As it is, I think his trouble'll be with his boss, whoever that is, for losing them." Gray leaned forward and looked Ronnie in the eye. "I think your father did a lot of planning on this. He told me people were watching his movements, and since he doesn't travel easily, I think that's why he wanted you as a delivery boy, for now and probably for later this summer too. In fact, it was one of the things that's been bothering me: I now know the northern dictionary boys are usually assigned to southern cities, and those from the south—like J.T., from Alabama—are sent north. So how did you, a Detroit kid, get assigned to Flint, an hour away from your home?"

Ronnie pondered that, then nodded. "My dad must've arranged it."

"Right. He already told me he knew a guy with the publishing company." Gray paused and added, "I think your choice to go missing scared him in more ways than one. He wanted me to find you because he was afraid others might be chasing you."

"And they were."

"Yes. They must've seen your dad hand you a small package at his place in Detroit and got suspicious."

Surprised, Linda said, "You think they might've followed him Sunday night, to Flint?"

"No. If they had, they'd have later seen him stop and hide the goods at the abandoned house. I think they thought things over and finally decided to locate Ronnie's apartment in Flint, probably from the publishing company's records, once they found out about the summer job. Which they must've done."

All three of them stayed quiet a moment, adrift in their own thoughts about their unknown enemy and its resources. Ronnie, holding Linda's hand, had opened his mouth to speak when Gray frowned and held up a hand to silence him.

The sound of a car motor was approaching.

"Inside," Gray said. "Fast."

They barely made it before a black Lincoln appeared on the curving road from the woods. It parked behind Linda's car and sat there awhile, idling. At last, two men climbed out. One was short with black hair and a string of gold necklaces, the other was almost as big as J.T. Watson. Both held snub-nosed revolvers.

"We know you're here, Gray," Gold Chains called. "You too, Ferris. Come on out."

Inside, crouched beneath a front window, Gray realized his mistake. They must've seen the tag number of the white Volkswagen at Ronnie's father's place in Detroit, and later got Linda's name and address from that. Gray knew his Pontiac hadn't been tailed on his and Linda's trip to the torched home—he'd made sure of that—but Linda's VW must've been followed after they switched cars. The two men had probably parked out of sight when they arrived and spent some time studying the setup, with binoculars.

"All we want is the package your old man gave you, Ferris," the other goon called. "Then we'll leave you be."

Sure you will, Gray thought. To Ronnie and Linda, he whispered, "Go out the back, both of you, before they think to cover it, and get away from here."

"You come too," Linda said.

"No. This must stop, here. Go—I'll find you later."

From the front, a voice called out: "One minute. Then we come in shooting."

Alone now in the cabin, Gray checked his watch, and at fifty-nine seconds he walked through the door. His coat and holster were off, his automatic tucked into his belt behind him.

With raised hands he marched straight toward the men and their car and stopped twenty feet away.

"You counted too long," he said to Gold Chains. "And you forgot that country houses usually have hunting rifles on the wall."

The two men exchanged a glance. The big guy said, "What are you talkin' about?"

"I'm talking about the two kids with me in the cabin. They've had time now to circle around on both sides, and two scoped rifles are aimed at you right now. How do you like that?"

Gray saw the doubt in both their faces, saw their sudden need to look. And waited.

When they did glance away, he pulled his gun and dropped to the ground. The bigger of the two got off a shot, but Gold Chains was too slow. Gray shot both dead center.

Minutes later Ronnie and Linda showed up, and the three of them stared down at the bodies in the gravel. In a firm voice Gray said, "Okay, kids—no more delays. When we get to a phone, I'm turning this over to the police, and all three of us'll need to make statements. I wish your father luck, Ronnie, but it's time to cut bait. You understand me?"

"I understand," he said.

They drove back with long-legged Ronnie in the passenger seat of the VW and Gray folded into the back. The bodies of the two men in the Lincoln had been dragged into the cabin and the guns left on the floor beside them. When Gray and the others arrived at the Flint police station, he phoned Coleman Ferris and told him he'd found Ronnie, but said no more. He didn't want Ferris running—wheeling his chair?—away before the Detroit cops pulled him in. The bodies were recovered, Ronnie gave the police the delivery address given him by his father, and around seven thirty he and Gray and Linda were released, but were asked, as in the movies, not to leave town. Gray had no intention of leaving. He had one more person to visit, in Flint.

After retrieving his car from Linda's driveway and dodging the frantic questions her parents were asking all of them, Gray drove south again, to the rooming house on Thayer Street. This time he knocked softly, and when Miss Dunwoody answered the door, he asked her to step outside with him, onto the porch. As politely as he could, he then asked if he might use her keys to check the car she kept in the garage out back. Surprisingly, she fetched them and waited on the porch until he came back, at which point he returned her keys, thanked her, and walked in and up the stairs. He found J.T. reading the same paperback on the bed in the now-straightened room. The friendly giant was leaning back against a propped-up pillow.

"More questions?" he said.

Gray pulled up a chair and sat. "Statements, mostly."

J.T. closed the book and laid it on his chest. "I'm listening."

"You followed Ronnie that night, didn't you, after he told you about the package."

"How would I do that?"

"With Miss Dunwoody's Impala," Gray said. "She told me yesterday she hasn't used it in months, but when I looked at it a few minutes ago, its driver's seat was cranked all the way back. She's five foot one, at the most. And by now you'd know where she keeps her keys."

J.T. nodded slowly. "Continue."

"Then you watched from a distance as Ronnie hid the diamonds, and when he left, you took them yourself, drove back, and returned the landlady's car to her garage. What you wouldn't know is that Ronnie told Linda Rosinsky about the abandoned house, and you also wouldn't know it was later firebombed during the riots. Not that it mattered."

For a moment neither of them spoke. The floor lamp, its broken bulb replaced, cast stark shadows on the wall. From the open window, Gray could hear crickets in the bushy lot across the street. A warm wind ruffled the curtains.

"What gave it away," he said, "was that you withheld too much information. Ronnie's stop here Sunday night, the package, his girlfriend…why would you not tell me those things, unless you had something to hide?"

J.T. was quiet for a long time, then let out a sigh. "You know, of course, that I could snap your neck like a toothpick. I'm quick, for my size."

"I'm sure you are," Gray said. "But I don't think you'll do that. I don't think you're even sure what to do with all those diamonds."

J.T. seemed to consider that. "You're right. I'm not."

"Well, I am. You need to turn them in to the police. Or give 'em to me, so I can."

Again, they fell silent.

"Tell me where they are, J.T. Those guys who searched this room weren't amateurs. How could they have missed them?"

"Guys? More than just the one with the gold necklaces?"

"Maybe it *was* just him, for this. But I know he had a partner."

"Where are they now?"

"Let's just say they won't be bothering anybody else."

J.T. smiled a little, at that. "You're a pretty tough guy, aren't you, Mr. Gray."

"I'm a pussycat," Gray said. "Where'd you hide the diamonds?"

"In the seat post of my bicycle. It's just a hollow tube, and when the seat's screwed on, it's plugged tight."

Gray nodded. "Good place."

"I thought so too." J.T. swung his feet off the bed, and the frame groaned dangerously. "Come on, I'll get 'em for you."

They walked together to the top of the stairs, where he turned and said, "There are fifteen stones, in all. Think anybody'd mind if I kept one?"

"I would," Gray said.

"Even though they'd be ashes now if I hadn't taken them?"

"Even though."

Ten minutes later the diamonds were in Gray's sport coat

pocket. He could feel them bumping against his holstered gun as he clomped down the porch steps. Behind him in the darkness, J.T. said, "Are you going to turn me in?"

Gray looked up at him. "I can't. Mrs. Jones'll be expecting you tomorrow."

J.T.'s chuckle sounded like an old boat motor. "How about Ronnie?" he asked. "Will he be okay?"

"I have a feeling he'll be fine, and the girl too. But I think you'll be riding alone, from now on."

"Sleeping alone too," he said. "Thank God."

"By the way, he said to tell you to keep his bike."

"Good. Mine bends too easy."

They shook hands and Eddie Gray climbed into his car, pausing to check his watch by the dome light. Almost nine p.m. Not late, but a long day. He'd located the person he'd been hired to find, he'd been shot at, he'd killed two henchmen, he'd recovered a cache of smuggled gems, and he'd managed to finish a case that had earned him no money at all.

He switched on the radio as he drove toward his motel and caught the last of the hourly news before the music resumed. The violence and burning in Detroit had fizzled out, the newscaster said, along with the riots in surrounding cities. Good news, for a change. As luck would have it, though, the first song after the break was The Doors, with "Light My Fire." Somehow, that struck Gray as funny.

He continued south, along the path J.T. Watson would probably travel tomorrow morning on his bike, in search of book buyers.

Gray wished him luck.

PIECE OF TRASH
Lynn Maples

February 11, 1968
Memphis, Tennessee

The waitress emptied her apron of crumpled currency.

"Will this be enough?"

Stewart Theebus folded the top half of his newspaper and eyed a wad of bills that replaced the check and tip he had left for the waitress. From what he could quickly calculate, she had just emptied her life savings onto the table.

"Breakfast is a buck sixty and I only left you a fifty-cent tip, Theona. Either your math is a little off or something has happened." Theebus discarded the newspaper and motioned for her to join him.

"It's J.R. He's in trouble. He's been arrested. My boy didn't do what he's accused of doin'." She smoothed her apron and took a seat across from him. She didn't look at him. Instead, she began to unfold the crumpled bills.

Theona Bellows had been serving him breakfast for nearly five years, and over time they had glimpses into each other's life. The private investigator learned that she'd been waiting tables at Harlem House on Beale Street for the past ten years. It was one of the few diners in Memphis that allowed interracial dining and primarily catered to Black customers. And to be honest, Theebus and his choosy palate didn't care. As long as the grits and fatback were served hot each morning, he was there. Theona's smile and friendly personality were just a bonus. It was a great way to start the day.

But this morning was different. Theona wasn't smiling. Her lips quivered as she breathed deeply. Slowly in. Release. Repeat.

"I don't know who else to ask for help. I can't ask the cops. They won't listen. Now there's talk of a strike by the sanitation and sewer workers since those two young men were crushed inside that garbage truck a week back and the city refuses to do anything. The mayor and police are too busy trying to keep us in our place. To make sure we don't make trouble. But they don't have no problem handin' down trouble. And that's what they gone and done. I need your help. Please."

She unfolded the last bill, tucked it with the others, and offered the money to him. "It's all I have. Whatever it takes to hire you...I can get...if this isn't enough."

"Theona, I really couldn't take—"

"Don't go doin' no charity on me. I don't need it. I need my boy. Are you going to help me or not?" She shook the cash at him again, dropped it on the table, and began to sob.

That was it. He fumbled for his cloth napkin, offering it to her, and picked up the cash Theona insisted he take. He didn't bother to count it.

"If I'm to help you, I need to know what happened. Let's start with why J.R. is in jail." Theebus reached into his blazer's interior pocket to remove a small notepad and pen. It was his first step in any investigation.

Theona choked back one final deep breath before vomiting details of her son's arrest. Memphis police arrived at her home the night before looking for J.R. after a woman reported her Chickasaw Gardens home had been burglarized. According to neighbors, a young Black man fitting J.R.'s description was seen at the home around that time, and evidence left on the scene indicated it was J.R.

"What evidence?" Theebus jotted down notes as quickly as Theona relayed the story.

"They found a sanitation worker's hat in the backyard," she said. "It was J.R.'s. I wrote his initials in black marker on the inside brim, so no one would be stealing it since the city don't pay for worker uniforms. That was all they needed to arrest him. They didn't listen to a word he had to say. Said he was a lying Negro. And they took him."

Each word made Theebus's stomach churn in disgust. The plantation mentality perpetuated by the white community meant Blacks were skilled at taking it from white folks. Stories of police strong-arming the Black community was all too common across the South. Especially in Memphis.

He pocketed his pen and notepad. "I'm sorry this happened, Theona. I can't make any promises, but I'll do what I can. I still have some friends in the department. They may listen. I also need to talk to J.R., if that's all right?"

"C-c-certainly."

Theebus stood to put on his winter coat and reached for his hat. Theona's slim hand touched his wrist. Their eyes met.

"Thank you." She attempted a weak smile.

A high-pitch ping-ping came from the kitchen's window followed by "Order up!"

"You may want to get that," Theebus said, slipping his hat on. "No one likes cold grits."

A slow southern wind made the fifteen-minute walk to Central Police Station on Adams Street tolerable despite the near-freezing temp. Theebus pulled his coat collar around his neck, passed by the Peabody Hotel, and nodded to the Black bellman holding the door for guests. Usually, he was greeted with a smile and a tip of a hat. Not this time. The bellman barely made eye contact and didn't bother with a smile.

He passed another regular on his route. Same response. The

chill from the winter breeze was nothing compared to the reception Theebus was getting from the Black citizens along his path.

He paused at Court Square to watch a small group of sanitation workers talking among themselves and eyeing a police car parked nearby. Five years ago, the police wouldn't have been sitting and observing from a distance. Instead, they would be forcefully disbanding the gathering, as Blacks were still not allowed to be in public parks and other publicly owned recreational facilities. Desegregation was gradual in Memphis.

A red Chevy Chevelle slowed past the police car, edging its way toward the group of men. The revving of the engine followed by the sound of broken glass and racial slurs told Theebus all he needed to know.

"Porch monkey want a banana?" yelled one of the young white men as he threw several rotten banana peels at the men and waved his middle finger outside the car's passenger window. The car swerved toward the sidewalk, hitting the curb and landing with a hard thump back into the street, barely missing Theebus.

He caught a glimpse of the driver and passenger. A blond guy with a sneer sat behind the wheel. His pudgy friend laughed and banged the dashboard with his palms. The car sped down North Second Street before disappearing around the corner on Court Avenue.

Theebus turned to see if the police were in pursuit. They weren't. Instead, the two officers elbowed each other, laughing at the frightened group. One cocked his head, nodded, and smirked when Theebus shot them a look.

"Assholes." He sighed and approached the group of men who instinctively began to disperse.

A tall Black man in his mid-forties glared at him and leaned over to whisper something to several other men. Each turned to look at Theebus.

He recognized the man as one he had arrested for simply saying no when told to leave a city park after several white citizens complained. The disobedience resulted in a night in jail and a scar where Theebus's boot smashed the man's face into the curb's edge.

He was not that type of person. He turned in his badge after serving a decade at the Memphis Police Department and tried to make amends as a private investigator.

The group of men quieted as Theebus passed by, giving him a distrustful side glance. Despite all his effort in the African American community, he was still recognized as a flatfoot by most. Once a cop, always a cop.

"Theebs!" A deep voice echoed down the stairwell, causing pauses and glances from those bustling in the concourse of the Central Police Station. Theebus looked up to see his former partner descending the broad stone staircase. Standing six foot three, Detective Calvin Anders was not to be missed by his size or his volume.

"Theebs, what brings you in?" He shook Theebus's hand and motioned him toward one of the green marble columns that framed the Chief of Detectives' office to speak discreetly.

"Let me guess. Another one of those colored cases you seem to wade into since you left the department."

"Yeah. It's something that came up this morning over breakfast."

Anders raised an eyebrow. "You still hangin' out at that colored diner?"

Theebus nodded. "Best grits in town."

"That may be, but you know how things are. Folks around here have been on edge since desegregation started years ago. People are slow to change. Hell, we've had colored officers for the last twenty years," Anders said. "But still, when one of our own goes rubbing shoulders with the coloreds, well, that may cause you some issues."

Theebus was unfazed. He knew his former partner meant no

harm, but the message was clear. The police department hadn't changed.

"It's nothing I haven't faced before. I need some information and to see my client's son. Think that can be arranged?" Theebus asked. "He was booked in sometime last night. Name is J.R. Bellows."

"Bellows. Bellows." Anders took out a cigarette, offered one to Theebus, and lit his, taking a quick puff. "That name sounds familiar."

They entered the outer office. It was lined with six desks each facing the other and running along large windows. Nameplates identified who sat where. A detective that Theebus didn't recognize sat across the room typing a report, not bothering to acknowledge their entrance.

Theebus looked at his old desk across from Anders's. The nameplate for Detective P. Thatcher had replaced his, and family photos and a clay trivet with a small handprint indention had been added. He sat in the chair next to Anders's desk usually reserved for suspects and victims.

"What'd he do?" Anders asked. He put out his cigarette and opened a metal cabinet labeled with the letter B. He thumbed through files.

"Burglary, but his mother...my client...says he didn't do it. That he's been singled out because he's Black."

Anders rolled his eyes. "Same song. Second verse. Look Theebs, I'm sure if the officers that arrested him didn't have evidence he committed the crime, they wouldn't just arrest him for no reason. Come on, you know better than that."

"At one time, I thought I did," Theebus said under his breath. "According to his mother, they do have evidence, but it's circumstantial. They found his hat at the residence where the burglary took place."

"Sounds pretty tight to me." Anders took out a few folders, flipped through the contents, and continued his search.

"True, except he's a sanitation worker and it's not uncommon for those guys to lose things while on the job. I'm thinking that it's just misfortune. I know his mother and I doubt he's the type of young man who would be getting into trouble intentionally."

"Really." Anders shut the file cabinet and dropped a manila folder on the desk. Several black-and-white photographs slipped from it—photos of a sit-in at a local restaurant and several mug shots of young Black and white men and women.

"Those photos say differently."

Theebus shuffled through the photos, pausing to look at the mug shot of J.R. dated April 12, 1965. In another picture, J.R. was seated at The Kress Five and Dime Department Store lunch counter with a half dozen Black and white young men and women who had staged a sit-in. Nearly a year after the Civil Rights Act desegregated public places, sit-ins were still a common occurrence in Memphis.

"Looks like your client has a record." Anders flipped pages of a stapled report. "He was arrested for loitering, causing a public disturbance, and inciting a riot. Says here he even has ties to some local civil rights group calling themselves The Invaders. They're supposedly peaceful but have been known to mix with the Black Panthers. Bet Momma didn't tell you that about her sweet boy."

Anders put the report on the desk with one page showing a list of names and COINTELPRO stamped across it in red letters. "Oh, and it's not uncommon, but he's been on the FBI observation list ever since. The feds here in Memphis passed it along to us when he was hired by the city to pick up trash since that's the only job most guys with records can get. We're supposed to keep an eye on workers so that incidents like this don't happen. And with rumors that the coloreds aren't too happy after those two men died last week and all those so-called Union meetings this past week, well...let's just say things are tense around here. So, it's no wonder the kid was brought in."

"A young man participating in a sit-in or misplacing his hat doesn't make him a thief," Theebus said. "But it does make him a target."

Anders's jaw tightened. "Watch it, Theebus. You don't want to go down that rabbit hole without evidence."

"That's where being a private investigator and a cop differ, Anders. A cop needs evidence to solve a crime. I just need a motive. You've been a great help and I appreciate it. I think it's time I go talk to J.R. See if I can find a motive."

"Your mom sent me." Theebus sat across from the tall, lanky young man. "She told me why you're here, but I need you to tell me why you're here. And be honest."

J.R. settled back in his chair, rubbed his face with his palms, and paused to take a deep breath. He peered through his fingers, looking past Theebus at the one-way mirror directly behind the private investigator. He pocketed his hands and questioned Theebus.

"You some kinda lawyer?"

"PI." Theebus held his business card between two fingers, offering it to the young man.

J.R. took the card and nodded. "The ex-pig that my momma talks about. You think I'm supposed to trust you just because my momma does? Man, you one of them. And you're white. No white man has ever helped me. So, what about it? How you gonna help me get outta here?"

Theebus ignored J.R.'s aggressive distrust. The previous run-ins with the police soured any future interaction. He decided to be blunt and direct with J.R.

"I know you have a record. I also know law enforcement has been keeping tabs on you. Doesn't seem to be right, but then again, a lot of things don't seem right nowadays. That's why I told your mother I'd see what I could do to help you. I can't make any promise, but I can do my best to get you out of here and clear your name. That is if you are innocent as your mother claims."

The young man shifted in his chair. "I am."

Theebus reached for his notepad, flipped a few pages, and began to recite details from the police report. Once done, he took a pen from his pocket to take notes. "Sanitation route records have the truck you were working on in the neighborhood around ten yesterday morning. According to the report, the resident said she discovered her back door open when she arrived home midmorning. That would put you in the vicinity of the crime when it took place."

"Yeah, sounds about right, but like I told the police, I don't know nothin' about some missin' silver." J.R. leaned in, glanced past Theebus's shoulder again at the mirror. "Trash is nasty. We have to get it from the backyards or wherever they don't want no one to see it and haul it to the truck out in front of the house. Most of the time folks don't even bother to bag it up or put a lid on it. And when that happens, we have to clean it up, so those white biddies don't go complaining we done made a mess. Ya see, man, I was in such a hurry to get the job done that I forgot my hat when I was picking up that mess. By the time I realized I'd left it somewhere, it was too late to be goin' back and look. Guess I shoulda done that, huh?"

Theebus pocketed the notepad.

"Mistakes happen." He tapped on the mirror, signaling to the officer waiting on the other side that the conversation was over.

Both stood as the door opened. Theebus paused, motioned for the officer to stop for a moment, and turned to ask one final question before J.R. was led from the room.

"J.R., I know you've associated with this group called The Invaders. Would you or they have any reason to make someone mad? Mad enough to set you up?"

The young man's jaw tightened. He looked at Theebus. Then at the officer who wrapped a hand around his arm.

"Garbage men are invisible. People don't see us. They smell us. Ignore us. But we see them and all their dirty little tidbits."

Theebus nodded. He watched the officer tug on J.R.'s arm, then escort him back to the cell area, noting the number of times J.R. glanced over his shoulder and at the police officer. He'd found the motive.

Theebus followed the stone walkway to the Chickasaw Gardens' home of Altha Marie Goode and rang the doorbell twice. If it had been a hundred years prior, the estate could have easily passed as a plantation, complete with a Black woman answering the door and asking, in a thick Southern drawl, if she could help him. He introduced himself, flashed identification, and was escorted into the front parlor.

The sound of thick heels against wood stairs and flooring was all the introduction Theebus needed. Altha Marie Goode strode into the parlor, purse secured in her elbow's crease as she clipped on an earring.

"You'll have to make this quick, Detective..." Altha hesitated, clearly not catching his name when her maid had shared it.

"Theebus. Stewart Theebus."

"Yes. As I was saying, you'll have to make this quick. I have a luncheon with some of the Cotton Carnival committee at Lowenstein's downtown and I don't want to be late. What is this about? I'm a little confused about your visit as I gave a statement to the other officers." She put her hand on her hip and frowned. "Is that Negro denying he did anything?"

"I'm not here representing the police, ma'am." Theebus gave her a business card. She eyed it closely. Her jaw tightened as she read the words Private Investigator. "I'm here representing J.R. Bellows. I was asked to look at what the police did not."

"And what exactly is that?"

"I'm not sure," he said, removing a small notepad and pen from his coat pocket. He recounted her statement from the police report. "Now are you typically alone during the day, Miss Goode?"

"Missus Goode. And, yes, I am. My husband is Wilson Goode. He's often away, either in court, his office, or—like today—in

Arkansas overseeing a real estate development with his business partner. Why do you ask?"

He flipped a few pages of the notepad. "Your maid. Was she here yesterday?"

"Yes. Why?"

"I don't see a statement from her. Is there a reason for that?"

Altha tilted her head with a slight nod and raised an eyebrow.

"The police didn't bother talking to her because they know those people protect each other. You can't believe a word they say."

Theebus gripped his pen, imagining it was Altha's slim neck. "You don't trust your housekeeper?"

Altha let out a sigh and tilted her head with a slight rise to peer around the PI as if that made her voice carry further. "Rose, come in here, please."

The slim Black woman who had greeted Theebus earlier appeared in the arched doorway, holding a mink cape and hat. Altha crossed the room to stand next to the maid, adjusted her purse to take out a pair of white gloves, and waved her hand toward Theebus.

"Rose, this detective would like to ask you a few questions about that Negro who broke into the house yesterday. He seems to think you may know something."

Rose stiffened. Worry crossed her face. Her eyes darted from her employer to Theebus.

Altha paid no attention to the reaction her statement had made. Instead, she slipped her gloves on, weaving her fingers between each other, and removed the mink cape and hat from Rose's arms. The curt beep of a car horn signaled that Altha's lunch companions had arrived. She opened the front door, waved, and returned her attention to Theebus.

"If you have any further questions for me, Detective Theebus, then I suggest you contact my attorney...who happens to be my husband." Altha smiled curtly. "Now if you'll excuse me."

"Would you like cream and sugar?" Rose Pollard asked, trying to hold the coffeepot steady as she poured. She set the pot next to a small red transistor radio on the kitchen table and clicked it off, giving him her full attention.

"Black is fine," he said taking a sip of the hot liquid. He found the delicate, floral-patterned Royal Albert teacup intimidating. He was used to flimsy disposable cups that came with the dime coffee he bought on the street corner, not the gold-rimmed dainty cup that cost nearly as much as a month's worth of breakfasts at the Harlem House. He set it down carefully on the matching saucer. He nodded toward the French door leading outside to the detached garage.

"I'm assuming that's the door used for entry?"

Rose nodded.

"No broken glass? No forced entry?"

Rose shook her head.

"And you or Mrs. Goode didn't leave the door open by any chance?"

"No, sir. Miss Altha don't drive. She usually has a taxi or one of her friends to pick her up. The back door is used mostly by myself and..." She paused, took a sip of her coffee, and grasped the cup firmly between her hands.

Theebus noticed the hesitation. And her thin silver wedding ring.

"Do you have children, Rose?"

She smiled. "I have a daughter, Loretta Jean. She's twelve."

"Then you know what J.R.'s mother is going through," Theebus said. "She's worried sick about her son sitting in jail, accused of doing something both say he didn't do. And if you know something, I'm sure she'd be mighty grateful. I know the police didn't ask you anything because they assume that Blacks are going to protect Blacks. But I don't think like that. I think people know right from wrong, and I give folks the benefit of the doubt."

"She must be awfully worried. I wish I could do more to help, but likes I told Miss Altha, I didn't see or hear anything. I was upstairs. All I know is Miss Altha came home, started screaming about the mess outside. There was trash strewn everywhere. Looked like some mad man been diggin' through it. The back door was open. That's when we noticed the serving set gone missing from the dining room." Rose pointed to the small spoon next to his cup and saucer. "That's the only piece left because it was in the sink."

Theebus picked up the thin spoon, looked at both sides, and noted the letter G monogrammed on the fiddle-shaped handle tip.

"It was a wedding gift," Rose said. "Miss Altha was upset about the silver set missin'. It was one of the last things her momma gave her before passing on, bless her heart."

Theebus glanced through the French door. The revving of a red Chevy Chevelle pulling into the driveway and stopping in front of the detached garage caught his attention. Two laughing young men exited the vehicle. He recognized the pudgy passenger snuffing out a cigarette, following the driver to the house.

Rose shifted from her seat, reached for the two coffee cups, and put them in the sink as the young men entered the kitchen. She smoothed her apron and gave a weak smile to the new arrivals.

"This is Mrs. Goode's nephew, Chuck, and his friend, Moochie," Rose told Theebus. She took a step back as Moochie darted in front of her and into the fridge looking for food. He grabbed a jar of milk, took a drink, and offered it to the tall blond driver.

"Who do we have here?" Chuck took a swig, twirled around Rose's empty chair, sat down, and stared at Theebus. He sniffed. "Smells like bacon."

Moochie chuckled. "Bacon. Oink, oink!"

Theebus introduced himself, offered his hand, and withdrew it as Chuck didn't bother to do the same.

Instead, Chuck took another drink of milk and wiped his mouth with the back of his hand. "So, you're a dick."

The detective nodded. "I'm looking into the burglary on behalf of the accused. You boys know anything about what happened yesterday? I don't recall seeing either of you mentioned in the police report."

Chuck licked his bottom lip, squinted his eyes, and pointed his pinky finger at Theebus. "You a Negro lover?"

Theebus could see Rose shift uncomfortably, lowering her head. He knew exactly how to deal with young, privileged bullies. He'd seen Chuck's kind many times before. Usually smiling as the judge patted them on the head and dismissed charges as being teenage antics.

"Are you a troublemaker? Seems like I recognize you and your buddy from earlier today along Court Square trying to run over some sanitation workers. And then here you are. At the scene of a crime involving a sanitation worker. Coincidence?"

Small, spit-laden pieces of partly eaten chicken spurted from Moochie's mouth as he dropped his food stash on the floor and pointed at Theebus. "You accusin' us of somethin'? 'Cause if you are, my dad's a city council member, and I'm pretty sure he knows how to deal with assholes like you."

Chuck raised his hand, signaling Moochie to shut up. He stood and opened the kitchen's back door. "I think it's time you left."

Outside, as Theebus passed underneath the kitchen window, he could hear Rose taking a verbal beating from Chuck. He hoped his unseen misdeed wouldn't get her into any more trouble as his hand slid into his pocket over a thin, hard object. He removed the monogrammed spoon and studied it closely. Things like this usually end up in a pawnshop. And if his hunch was correct, he'd find the missing serving set at one of the pawnshops along Beale Street.

He paused to write down the license plate and a description of Chuck's red Chevelle. He'd bet a bowl of grits that anyone who saw the car would remember it. Especially on Beale Street.

Sam Dennis rubbed the monogrammed silver spoon between his

fingers and examined it closely. He glanced at Theebus's business card and then at the PI.

"Nope. Can't say that I have anything like that here." Sam handed the spoon to Theebus. He seemed eager to distance himself from the PI as he continued, "But you're welcome to look around. Pete can help you while I take care of something in the back."

Sam picked up the business card, shook Theebus's hand, and quickly disappeared down a narrow aisle between overstocked shelving leading to a small office.

Theebus saw Sam reach for the telephone as the office door swung shut.

"Is there anything else I can help you with, sir?" Pete asked as he stepped in front of the PI.

Theebus shook his head, then paused as he turned to leave. He smiled at the teenager. He was around the same age as the two troublemakers.

"There is, Pete. You wouldn't happen to know a couple of guys named Chuck and Moochie? Drive a red Chevy Chevelle?" Theebus twirled the spoon between his fingers.

From Pete's subtle intake of breath, Theebus could tell he recognized the names.

The teen looked over his shoulder. The office door was closed, and a gray silhouette paced behind the clouded glass window. He tilted his head for Theebus to follow him to the end of the counter, closer to the pawn store's entrance.

"This could get me into loads of trouble." Pete pointed at the spoon. "But from the looks of it, you already know. I heard what you told Mr. Dennis about the theft and J.R. Bellows. His mom is nice. She always cuts the chocolate pie slice extra wide for me when I get lunch at the Harlem House."

Theebus nodded and wiggled the spoon. "What do you know about this?"

Pete glanced toward the office. "The matching set is back in Mr. Dennis's office. He's been trying to sell it ever since Chuck and Moochie brought it in yesterday. But he ain't had any luck since it's not a complete set. I guess when he saw that spoon, he knew the jig was up. And I bet you money he's back there calling Chuck right now."

"I'd count on it," Theebus said as he pocketed the spoon.

"I know those two no-goods. Always stealing stuff for fun and bringing it into the shop for a few bucks. Mr. Dennis never says anything because their stuff fetches a pretty penny," Pete said. "Guess that's why he has no problem with what Chuck and Moochie do with the money."

"Oh? And what's that?"

Pete looked out the store's entrance and pointed to a police car down the street sitting on the corner of Beale and South 4th.

"They been paying 'em off, from what I understand," Pete said.

"And it looks like they've graduated from larceny and bribery to character assassination and obstruction of justice." Theebus shook his head. "Great business partners your boss has."

The sound of the office door opening, followed by hurried footsteps, ended their conversation. Theebus thanked the teen and quickly exited the pawnshop, stopping for a moment to examine the police car sitting at the corner. Then he looked at his watch. Three o'clock.

Anders should be wrapping up reports at the police station and Theona Bellows would be finishing her second shift of the day. He had enough time to make a call to Anders from the pay phone at Harlem House and brief Theona on his suspicions.

"An innocent Black man is sitting in jail because he happened to witness something he shouldn't have while doing his job. And the police are covering up the misdeeds by allowing Chuck and Moochie to set him up and looking the other way."

Theebus tapped the table harshly with his finger. Theona sat calmly next to him.

"That's an interesting theory, Theebs." Detective Calvin Anders crushed his third cigarette of the conversation. "And strong allegations. You're accusing the police of accepting bribes from the sons of two prominent Memphis families to keep their mouths shut about a few adolescent high jinks. And then the said stolen item just happens to be in a pawn shop, not a half block away from where the accuser's mother works. Sounds coincidental to me. There're a lot of reputations at stake here. The department. Those kids. Their families. Yours."

"J.R.'s." Theona broke her silence, tears streaming down her cheeks. "Detective Anders, I know my boy. He wouldn't do this. He's been in trouble before, but it's because he's been fighting for what's right. For what're his God-given rights. Not just as a Black man. But a man. Surely you can understand that."

Anders leaned back against the blue vinyl booth, let out a sigh, and met his former partner eye to eye. "What's the plan?"

Theebus took out the monogrammed spoon and a wad of bills, grinned, and began to count.

"One phone call and then it's time to go shopping."

The soft jingle of the pawn shop's bell announced the arrival of Rose Pollard. She strode down an aisle, casually looking at items behind the glass counters, and paused to pretend a small silver platter had caught her attention.

Sam Dennis stopped what he was doing and eyed her closely. He took a few seconds to determine if she was buying or selling. *Buying*, he thought. Definitely buying from the way Rose lingered over the display of silver serving platters, gravy urns, and utensils.

"Looking for something in particular?" Sam asked.

Rose smiled. "Well, anything and everything, truth be known. I just got married, and we're setting up a house over on Barton Street. And I need just about everything. But I want something nice. Something fancy. Like..." Her eyes widened. She pointed at a small, rectangular wooden box partly hidden from sight. "Like that!"

Sam grinned.

"Good eye." He set the silver flatware set on the counter.

Rose ran a finger across a spoon, admiring it and pausing her fingertip on the monogrammed G. "It's lovely. How much?" She unsnapped her purse and reached in to remove a lump of bills.

"Well," Sam stuttered slightly at the sight of the cash and leaned on the counter, rubbing his chin. "It's a fine set. How about say...fifty even?"

"Hmm..." Rose counted out the money. She paused, sat the money on the counter, and picked up the first set of spoons from the case. "This is a forty-piece set, correct?"

"Well...um..." he hesitated. "You got me. It's an incomplete set, but I'm sure you can buy a spoon to replace the missing one."

"Oh, I don't think that will be necessary." Rose smiled and pulled out a small teaspoon matching the ones in the case.

Sam straightened himself. He looked confused, his eyebrows narrowing as he stuttered.

"H-h-how do you..." He stopped in midsentence as Theebus entered the store. He slammed the case shut and reached for the missing spoon. Rose jerked it back and stood beside Theebus.

"What are you trying to pull here?" Sam demanded as his hand slid beneath the counter. "You better git outta here before I call someone who will make you wish you'd never stepped foot in here."

"Someone like Chuck or Moochie." Theebus stood his ground. He'd hoped mentioning the accomplices would get the pawnbroker to talk long enough for a confession.

Over Sam's shoulder, Theebus saw Pete, the helpful teenager, let Anders slip in the back door. The timing was perfect as the pawnbroker slowly removed a gun from under the counter and pointed it at the couple. Anders nodded to Theebus as he raised his pistol behind the pawnbroker. Theebus stepped in front of Rose.

"I think you better git before someone gets hurt," Sam said, twitching the pistol, motioning them to leave.

"You've got a lucrative little scam going on here." Theebus stood his ground as Anders stepped closer to Sam. "Paying for merchandise some rich kids bring in after a night of adolescent mischief. Brings in big bucks. And if they get caught, they take the fall. But not this time. You're going down. Larceny can get you five, ten years."

"Nooooo!" The bullet whizzed past Theebus's ear, barely missing Rose Pollard as he shoved her to the ground. He stumbled toward Sam, attempting to grab the man's arm. Sam tumbled forward, collapsing unconscious from a quick blow to head from the grip of Anders's gun.

Theebus let out a sigh. One down. Two to go.

Theebus, Theona, and Rose watched as Chuck and Moochie stood sulking behind the police intake desk, listening to their charges and to a heated discussion between Anders and two smartly dressed men in suits. Their plan to expose the young men's misdemeanors and character assassination had worked. When the police arrived at Sam's pawnshop, he freely gave a confession of his arrangement with Chuck and Moochie and how he came into possession of the stolen monogrammed silverware.

The lawyer and city councilman exchanged glances at the trio of crime solvers—pausing longer than necessary at Rose—and pointed the wayward young men toward the police station's main hallway and outside to a waiting car, leaving Anders to explain the conclusion.

"That was Wilson Goode and City Councilman Schwartzman, if you couldn't guess," he said. "I'm sorry to say that there appears to be no honor among thieves. Our little plan to set a thief to catch a thief has backfired. It appears that Wilson Goode is friends with a circuit judge who dismissed the charges against the two boys on account of no priors. Sam Dennis is being charged with multiple counts of larceny, which he admitted to for a reduced sentence."

"And the police payoff?" Theebus asked.

Anders didn't answer.

Theebus shook his head. It wasn't a surprise.

"Does that mean J.R. is free to go?" Theona asked.

"Yes, ma'am. We're finishing up paperwork."

Theona closed her eyes, put one hand on her chest, and waved another above her head. "Thank you, Jesus. Thank you, Lord."

She hugged Theebus, then held him at arm's length, shaking her head gleefully.

"Thank you, too," Theona said. "Worth every penny."

"That reminds me." He dug into his jacket pocket and removed the cash she had given him earlier. He offered it to her. "Consider it my civic duty."

"But…"

"I insist. After all, I think there are a few times I shorted you a tip or two over the years, and this would make up for it." He grinned.

Theona pocketed the money and wiped a tear from her eye. "And you, Rose, we all owe you big time. It was very brave what you did back there. Thank you for getting involved. If you're needin' a job after all of this, I'm sure we got a spot open at Harlem House for a new waitress."

"Thank you, but that won't be necessary," Rose said. "I turned in my resignation after Detective Theebus called and told me what he suspected. I'd endured enough abuse from those two for a while now. Your son didn't deserve what happened. Besides, I need to spend what time I have left with my husband and daughter. I found out earlier this week I have breast cancer."

"Oh, my poor girl." Theona held Rose tightly, cupping her head and rubbing her back. "If you need anything…anything…you let me know. And you bring that daughter of yours in tomorrow morning for breakfast on me."

"Mom." J.R. stood in the doorway. "Is it true? I can go?"

Theona wiped a tear. "Yes, son. Detective Theebus done it. You are free."

He sighed, hugged his mother, and shook Theebus's hand.

"I never thought I'd be thanking a white man for anything."

Theebus nodded. "Times are changing."

"Time?" J.R. looked at the office clock. It was nearing seven o'clock. His energy changed, and he pecked his mom on the cheek. "I know this is sudden and all, but I gotta go. There's a Union meeting for the sanitation and public works employees. We're gonna strike tomorrow."

March 1968

Theebus slipped the sandwich board over his head and stepped out of Harlem House with Theona Bellows and an identically dressed J.R. They walked silently down Beale Street, passing onlookers and a growing number of police cars all making their way to a crowd of sanitation workers organizing along Main Street. Each wore a sandwich board or held handwritten signs with thick black letters proclaiming "I Am a Man" and various Union demands.

J.R. elbowed the detective lightly. "You don't have to do this. This isn't your fight."

Theebus looked around. In the growing crowd, he recognized many of the men finalizing details of the march and could see the determination on their faces. The line stretched for several blocks. Men. Women. Black. White.

Along the sidewalks, the baton-wielding Memphis police were dispersing to stand three to four feet from each other, forming a barrier, as if to dare the Black men to cross it. To rock the boat...or a police car, like the one that started the first riot weeks ago. Right before the tanks rolled down Main Street, tear gas fumes filled the air, and Dr. Martin Luther King locked arms with the strikers.

In a growing crowd behind that barrier stood Chuck and Moochie, hurling vulgarities and each gripping a hard object in their right hand. Theebus looked at Theona and took her hand in his.

"You're wrong, J.R." Theebus took a step forward and began to walk with the crowd. "Nobody should be treated like a piece of trash."

LADY IN THE POLKA-DOT DRESS

Michael Chandos

"This is Francis St. John reporting from a temporary press center close to Good Samaritan Hospital. Early yesterday morning, Senator Robert F. Kennedy, the winner of the 1968 California Presidential Primary, was rushed into surgery here after being shot in the head by an assassin.

"A few moments ago, at 1:59 a.m., Frank Mankiewicz, Senator Kennedy's spokesman, informed the press crew that doctors pronounced Senator Kennedy dead at 1:44.

"A busboy identified by police as Sirhan is in custody. Sirhan appears to have operated alone, but, like the JFK assassination, conspiracies abound. The LAPD and the FBI will have a tough time separating the truth from all this crazy fiction."

He paused.

"I was with the senator's group when the shooting occurred. People struggled to seize Sirhan's weapon, but he continued to fire wildly. Five people were wounded, including my good friend William Weisel from ABC who was standing just in front of me and perhaps stopped a stray bullet headed in my direction.

"LAPD is scheduled to update the press corps on Sirhan later this morning. You can be sure I will be there.

"This is Francis St. John, KCLA News."

* * *

Apprentice Private Investigator Diaz slogged into the Boyd Detective Agency bullpen. The narrow room had four desks facing each other in pairs down the middle with telephones and typewriters at each desk. The early morning sun poured in through the southern windows and filled the room with a warm, friendly glow, so the fluorescent lights overhead were not turned on. Bookshelves laden with city directories, reference books, and maps filled the far end of the room. Neatly stored on the bookshelves were the tools of the surveillance trade: cameras, binoculars, tape recorders, caffeine pills, urine collection bottles, and aspirin. A chalkboard faced the front wall.

Diaz carried a brown Marine Corps knapsack over his shoulder. His long black hair was gathered at the back like a matador's and his clothes were loose and comfy. His Cuban-heeled platform shoes hammered the linoleum. He walked to his desk and sat down heavily.

"What's happenin', Mr. Perfect! Up all night?" said one of the other two men in the room.

"Clipper, I've told you before, my first name is Perfectico," said Diaz.

"And I've told you before everyone here gets a nickname," said Sarge. "Like Sarge for me and Clipper for Reynaldo. As the supervisor for the surveillance investigators, I get to make the choice. Mr. Perfect almost suggests itself, Perfectico."

"Don't become unglued, *ese*. If we didn't like you, we'd call you something rude like *Quinto*," said Clipper with his usual toothy smile.

"Maybe something else will come up for you later on, after you've booked your five thousand hours and passed the state of California test, and you become a real, licensed private eye," said Sarge.

"Okay, boss. I'm too tired to argue," said Diaz.

"Did you get the money shot on that wandering husband?"

"Yeah, *jefe*, good telephotos of him and his hippie girlfriend. She's a looker if you like them skinny. Rose-colored shades, hip-huggers, tall heels, and her possibly natural blond hair, all curly and down to her waist."

"I assigned you to watch him, not her."

"Like I said, she was tall, tan, leggy, *and* braless. A looker."

"A looker?" said Clipper. "Oh, I thought you said hooker. And remember, Mr. Perfect, every sexy young woman in the beach cities is blond and tan."

"Get the film into Felix and ask him to run a contact sheet before enlarging anything," said Sarge. "You can't go home until he develops the negs and prints the sheet. Meanwhile, type me a summary. Did you take good notes and do an exposure log? And no one noticed you?"

"Sarge, I'm driving a grungy, bullet-nosed '51 Studebaker that used to belong to my grandmother. The rusty brown paint makes it almost invisible at night. The only guys that ever notice me are the hot rodders who want to buy it. The report is almost done already, Sarge."

Diaz got up and dug the Leica M3 Rangefinder camera and a notebook from his knapsack. He walked down the hall to the darkroom. "Hey, Felix, you got any bennies?"

Diaz dropped his paperwork on Sarge's desk. "Here's my shift report, the contact sheet, and the exposure log, Sarge. The surveillance report includes the wheres and whens, including the address of the cheap apartment that his wife doesn't know about where he balls his lady. I had a nice conversation with the manager at the front desk, too. She told me a few juicy things. I've marked the shots I think are the best."

Diaz put his flamenco shoes up on the corner of his desk and leaned back in his creaky, junior-guy-in-the-office chair. The cuffs on his bell-bottoms hung down six inches. He started to fade, and he jerked himself awake and sat up again.

Sarge stood and held up a file folder. "We have a new case this morning that requires a moving surveillance, in a car and on foot. We know a lot about the subject and where he likes to go, so we don't have to follow him too closely. We're mostly interested in *where* he stops and *who* he talks to. Need facts and photos."

"I'll take it," said Diaz. "I need the hours."

"How long have you been up?"

"Oh, maybe twenty hours. I got lotsa gas still, Sarge. I'm young. I can do it."

"Clipper, see Rich, he's the responsible agent. You, Mr. P, need to finish up here and head on home. I'll call your granny if I need you, otherwise I'll see you at eight a.m. tomorrow."

"*Sí, jefe.* I'll do my expense report next."

Mr. Perfect separated his personal belongings from the agency's surveillance gear and put the equipment on the shelves. "Hey, some reporter named St. John on the car radio was jabbering about an emergency dragnet. Did I miss something during those two shifts on surveillance?"

"You know there was an election?" said Clipper.

"Yeah. The primary. I voted for Kennedy. Did he win?"

"Yes, he did, and then somebody shot him in the head at the Ambassador Hotel. He died at the hospital early this morning," said Clipper.

"Holy shit! That's beyond bummer! Did they get the shooter?"

"They arrested one guy at the scene, but the news is full of the usual garbage," said Sarge. He held up his left hand to count off the rumors. "An LA TV station described a woman in a polka-dot dress running from the scene yelling 'We got him!' There are rumors about assassins from the Mafia, Cuban mercenary killers from Miami, second shooters, and hit men disguised as security guards, and, of course, we simply must include rogue elements of the CIA. They've got big imaginations in the LA press."

"If it bleeds, it leads," said Clipper.

"Do we have a piece of that?" said Diaz.

"Son, we chase beaters and cheaters. We are not the police. But we still must be careful when we investigate. You never know what kind of creepy bug is under that rock you just turned over." Sarge returned to his desk.

"You never were a cop," said Clipper. He stood eye to eye with Diaz, left hand on Diaz's shoulder, right hand emphasizing the point. "Listen, Perfectico. I stopped a guy for speeding once that turned out to be running from a violent holdup. I thought he was handing me his license. It was a sawed-off shotgun. I saw it coming soon enough that I only caught a couple pellets. Remind me to show you the scars sometime. Pay attention out there, rookie, and remember Sarge's warning. You'll live longer."

"Wow, Dallas in LA," said Diaz. He picked up a small notebook bound in heavy cardboard and black leather. He waved it in Clipper's face. "We'll see what Mr. Perfect's Little Black Book can hustle up tonight." He wedged the notebook into his left inside coat pocket and patted it.

"Outa here in five, Sarge."

Tia's Restaurant looked like any American local eatery if you replaced the burgers, fries, and shakes with tacos, refried beans, and, well, shakes. It was smaller than the usual diner with only four crimson leatherette-covered swiveling seats at the counter plus a row of four- to six-person tables. Each table was covered with a green, white, and red checkered plastic tablecloth with a cluster of equally plastic flowers in the center. Bottles of local and Mexican hot sauces finished the layout. No Louisiana Tabasco here. Flavors went from Tourist to Omigod. Her place was popular. Gang bangers and police both ate here. If Tia ever had any trouble, she had plenty of available protection.

Tia served combo plates and nearly anything Mexican you could imagine, and a lot of it was on Diaz's large oval dinner plate. He was at the counter.

"You are hungry tonight, *guapo*. Keep eating like that and

you won't be my little Perfectico anymore," she said.

"I just worked two long shifts on a stationary surveillance. When I'm waiting in the pursuit car for the target to do something, I don't eat or drink much because I can't leave for the bathroom. The subject might escape and do bad things while I'm gone. Clients don't like that. Ay, I get so hungry, but the hunger helps me stay awake."

"Listen to you. Just like a private eye on TV. But…white chinos, a flowered shirt, a white sports coat, and a panama hat. Do you think you are in Miami?"

"It's a warm June in South LA, Tia, and I have the night off. I'm going dancing. I have the personal phone numbers of beautiful women in my coat pocket. They are just waiting for me to call."

"Oh, you young men, always chasing."

"Men chased after you too, I bet, *mi reina*."

"*Sí*, but I'm afraid the best ones weren't fast enough. I ended up with a robber doing time in County jail and a wavering son."

She refilled his glass with sweet iced tea, glanced at him twice, then put the pitcher down and folded her hands.

"Perfectico, can you do me a favor? If you can help solve my problem, maybe you don't pay for your next dinner."

"No bother. I'm always happy to help," said Diaz. He put his fork down and turned to her. "You look a little nervous."

"You know your cousin Pirro recently got a job in hotel security."

"Yes. Good for him. He's smart. Pirro should progress well."

"Lately he's been working the night shift at the Ambassador Hotel, but he hasn't come home the last two nights, and his boss called a little while ago to ask where he was today. If Pirro isn't here and he isn't at work, I don't know where he is." Her eyes teared up a little. "I don't want him to follow his father's example. Can you find him?"

"Not to worry, *mi alma*." Diaz got up from his chair and put his arm around her. "I am almost a fully licensed private investigator. I locate missing people for a living, and I'm pretty good at it. Please, have a seat in my office."

She sat at a table opposite Diaz, wringing her hands and looking away.

"I need to know a few things. First, I need the name and number of his boss."

"I'll write it down for you."

Diaz opened his notebook to a clean page and offered her his pen. "Thank you. This helps. Is he still associating with our local gang?"

"He still hangs out with them. They make fun of his security uniform and tease him about carrying a gun. He has to leave the pistol at work, you know. Will they talk to you?"

"No problem. We're all still friends," said Diaz. "Where is he living?"

"In a rented room on Crenshaw toward Inglewood. Off the alley behind a noisy Tejano bar. Oh, it was horrible in there, but it was cheap and close to the bus. I helped him clean it up and the landlord repaired the door lock. It was okay then."

"And he's still driving the black Mercury?"

"I think so," she said.

Tia teared up again. "Pirro is a big boy, but the world is such a tough place, Perfectico. You learned that in the Marines. But my Pirro, he is just not ready. Too trusting maybe. I worry so much about him."

"I'll find him, and I will ease your worries. And I'll give him a punch for scaring you." Diaz sat back in his chair. "Now, let me have coffee and one of your legendary sopapillas."

Pirro and Diaz grew up in an odd, three-block neighborhood. The north end stubbed into a freeway with no underpass, and the south dead-ended against the back of the high school athletic field. A youth gang was a natural development in that geography, but it was a small one with multiple generations of members. Diaz had belonged when he was in high school. All the neighborhood boys and most of the girls did too. Everyone hung out in the center block, usually on the porch of a burned-down home.

"Why are you dressed like a pimp, homie? Is this what the successful Dick Tracy wears in LA?" said an older boy sitting on a ratty couch. The other three boys laughed and whistled.

"I am off duty and ready to fly, Antoine," said Diaz.

"I'll alert all the underage girls. Still drivin' your spaceship?"

"It was free. And it works. Maybe, with all this money I'm making, I'll get one of those new Mustangs. Maybe a Thunderbird."

"That will go better with those clothes anyway. You secretly working?" said Antoine. He handed Diaz a beer.

"If it was a secret, would I tell you? Tia asked me to find Pirro. He's not been coming home from work."

"Oh, that boy is f'ed up."

"Drugs?"

"Might as well be. He's apeshit over some foxy lady he met in a bar. She's got him all wrapped up," said Antoine. "Drove by with her a couple times. She wouldn't even get out of the car. Looked pissed to be here. I think he took that security job just to impress her."

"Cuban," said one of the other boys. He looked around at his friends. "Well, she sounds Cuban, anyway."

"She wears these big, round shades, looks like a cartoon character," said another. "And mean eyes, when you can see them. Black line makeup around black eyes. *In*tense. Hair wrapped up with a wicked hair pin that looks like a dagger. Deep red lipstick, too. Maybe she's a killer vampire."

"And polka dots, can you believe it?" said Antoine, shaking his head. "Always something with stupid polka dots. Big ones, little ones. Always something. Scarf, blouse, skirt. Crazy about 'em. But he hasn't been comin' around the old neighborhood much since he met her."

Antoine leaned into Diaz.

"She's way above his class. She should be cruisin' the beach hotels lookin' for rich businessmen on holiday," said Antoine, "not screwing a young Mexican dropout from Central LA. I don't know what she can possibly see in Pirro."

"Pussy crazy," said one of the boys.

"Is she a hooker?" said Diaz. "A fancy call girl soaking Pirro for money?"

"He doesn't have that much money," said Antoine. "I don't know what she does for a livin'. Always talkin' to Pirro like a football coach. Remember that shit in high school? Talkin' loud, straight into your face. Pointin' a finger at his eyes. Red nail polish."

"His mother says he's living in a scuzzy shack out back behind a Tejano bar on Crenshaw. True?" said Diaz.

A boy held up a wagging finger. "Oh no, that wasn't good enough for her. I think they're in the old Cabrillo Hotel, in one of those rent-by-the-week little apartments. Probably changed his phone number too."

"He struts around in that stupid security guard uniform. A TV hero with an empty holster and an empty head," said Antoine. "It's crazy. Drugs would be easier to understand."

"I guess I'm off to the Cabrillo. Thanks for the cold beer. I'll drop some more by later," said Diaz.

"If I were you, I'd skip him and head to the Tejano for the chicks," said Antoine. "And don't get arrested in those clothes."

The old Cabrillo Hotel was typical of forties LA. It was a three-story stucco building shaped like a narrow U with the remnants of a garden plaza in between. Faded images of palm trees and beach scenes decorated the faded rose walls even though it was seven miles inland from the Southland beaches. One lonely tall palm tree in need of trimming still grew in the center of the overgrown plaza.

Before he parked, Diaz looked for Pirro's Mercury in the hotel parking lot. The cars and trucks were a mix of Depression-era junkers, commercial vehicles, and snazzy modern sedans. It was easy to pick out the locals renting an "apartment" for a week's binge or a shack up. He found the Mercury in the far corner where the lot lighting didn't work. The darkness was for people who didn't want to be seen. Diaz grinned. Pirro was probably fooling with his major league lady in their room. Surprise, cousin!

Diaz parked on the street and went into the hotel office. No one was around. The Dodgers were playing on a television set with a rolling screen that hung from the ceiling in the corner. The plants in the lobby were real, but also in need of attention. Diaz waited at the desk and watched the game. After a minute, he hit the chrome service bell.

"Yeah? What?" emanated from somewhere down the hall.

"Are you the manager?" called Diaz.

Amid scooting and shuffling noises, a sixtyish white man in a rumpled white shirt and thin black pants approached the desk. He looked Diaz over. "We don't allow no hookers in here. Take your girls down the street." He turned to go back to his office.

"Hey, I'm not a pimp. I'm a PI. See? My company ID card."

The manager took the card, leaned into the desk lamp to read it, and handed it back to Diaz. "What bad TV show did you escape from?"

"Look, I'm working a missing persons case for a very nice old lady. Can I ask a couple of questions?"

"Be quick. I'm working on my books in the office, and I need to get them up to date."

"I'm looking for a twenty-five-year-old Mexican man, about six feet tall, not fat, works as a hotel security guard downtown somewhere. Might be living with a tall, well-dressed woman. They've been here a month, maybe a little less."

"Yeah," said the manager. "But she isn't here all the time. She one of your girls?"

"I'm not a pimp. I'm a private eye," said Diaz slowly.

"So you claim."

"They're here, right? Have you seen them today?"

"No. Yesterday I think I saw them drive in, but not today," said the manager.

"What room are they in?"

"I can't tell you that, normally."

Diaz pulled a ten-dollar bill from his wallet and laid it on the counter.

The manager studied the bill. "I guess you aren't LA's most successful private eye, huh?" The sawbuck disappeared.

"Do you have a house phone? Can I call his room?"

"Yeah, I suppose. Dial eight then two oh nine," said the manager. "Phone's over there on the little table. Are we done now?"

The manager didn't wait for an answer. He shuffled back to his office.

Diaz went to the phone. Like the plants and the TV, it needed attention too. Diaz pulled a handkerchief from his breast pocket and carefully held the handset away from his ear. He dialed the eight and then Pirro's room number. After six rings, Diaz dropped the handset into the cradle, went out the office front door, and looked for the stairs. These prewar places never had elevators.

He walked up to the second floor. The first room he saw was room 233. Pirro's was around the other side of the U. He proceeded down the dimly lit hall.

It was almost eight p.m. on a Thursday, so most people were home. Music, food smells, and voices came and went as Diaz walked past the apartment doors. He turned the corner and there she was. The girlfriend.

She was wearing the circular shades, at night, and a silk head scarf, white with small red polka dots. Her plain off-white skirt and white cotton blouse were made for travel, and she was carrying a soft-sided, brown leather suitcase.

She didn't seem to notice Diaz as they passed. He stopped and turned around.

"Ma'am? Are you with Pirro?" said Diaz.

"Pirro who? I don't know him," she said over her shoulder. Yes, Cuban. She continued around the corner without stopping.

Diaz caught up with her.

"Answer my question," he said to her back.

She stopped, turned slightly, and took off her shades. She stared holes into Diaz. Hard eyes, not blinking, radiating heat. "I have an appointment. Excuse me." She turned to continue down the hall. Diaz reached out and caught her sleeve. The dagger hairpin flashed in the hall lights.

She shook off his grasp with a strong twist. "Are you a cop?" Her red lips were set into a thin straight line. She put the leather bag down.

"No, I'm a private investigator. I've been asked to find Pirro. I know you have been with him for several weeks. I've talked to people who described you and your polka dots. I don't know why Pirro is living with you, but I intend to find out who you are and what you are doing with Pirro. Now, tell me. Is he still in his room?" Diaz gestured down the hall.

"You want to find Pirro? Sure. Let me show you." She picked up her suitcase, seized his upper coat sleeve, and turned him to hustle down the hallway. Diaz couldn't shake her grasp. At 209, she looked up and down the hall, opened the door, and shoved him into the room. He stumbled over Pirro's body and almost fell to the floor.

Diaz's mouth hung open, but no sound came out. He reached over to Pirro. The body was cool to the touch and Pirro's skin was a pale tan. Pirro was lying facedown, arms and legs spread open, head turned to the right. A wide pool of blood clotted on both sides of his chest. His eyes were open. He appeared surprised.

Diaz jumped to his feet. "Did you kill him? What did he do to you to deserve this?"

"The stupid bastard screwed it up, didn't get close enough to Kennedy and never even pulled his gun. And then that damn Arab came out of nowhere and did the job," she said. "Pirro was a loose end. And now so are you, *pendejo*."

Enlightenment came to Diaz. "You tried to kill Kennedy." His face flushed and his eyes stopped blinking. His Marine training surged back. He raised his fists and set his War Face.

The Cuban lady hit Diaz in the mouth with a left cross worthy of Sugar Ray, and he staggered against the wall. She pulled the hair stick from behind her head and held it like the long silver spike it truly was. Her brown hair tumbled around her face, but it didn't hide the fury in those black eyes.

Diaz was bleeding from his nose and cut mouth. When she raised her arms, he tried to grab them both. He got the left arm but missed the right and she plunged the spike through his left hand. Diaz screamed and pulled his hand free. She came closer for another strike.

She grabbed his face with her left hand. The long nails dug in, almost in his eyes, and he retreated. He tripped over Pirro and went down backward to the floor. She immediately straddled him, reared the arm with the spike and plunged it into his chest, aiming for his heart. Diaz's scream went soprano. Blood flowed and soaked his flowered shirt and white sports coat. She reared back again and struck him again. Diaz lost consciousness. His eyes and soundless mouth were shocked open.

Diaz struggled back into consciousness. His shirt and coat were soaked with blood. He pressed his pierced left hand to the twin bleeders on his chest. He spat blood from his split lip and loosened teeth, and his ruined nose bubbled red foam.

Diaz rolled over on his right side. He scooted and half-crawled to the phone next to the couch. He dialed zero and the manager answered.

"Ambulance. Police. Room two oh nine. Emergency. Murder." Diaz shot the words out.

"What? Who is this?" said the manager.

"The PI. Room two oh nine. Police. Murder. Hurry. Ambulance. Hurry."

"Damn it. You pimps and your girls are always getting killed in my hotel. I clean up after your parties and fix the broken furniture. And do you ever give me some of the action? Never."

"No pimp. Hurry. Two oh nine."

Diaz faded to black again.

"Oh, all right. This will cost you a twenty this time."

"About time you woke up," said Sarge.

"You look like a third-rate wrestler after a night of professional losing," said Clipper. "Did you get jumped?"

"Murder. A woman did it," croaked Diaz.

"There's a homicide cop in the hall who wants to talk to you about that. Can you talk around those stitches and bandages?" said Sarge.

"The lady was in polka dots, Sarge, like on the radio."

Sarge paused. "I see. I'll get the detective ASAP. You wait here." Sarge gave him a slight smile.

Clipper leaned against the bed. "Didn't you listen to my story about the shotgun? When you're out on a job and you decide to stare into a deep, dark hole, you better think first about what might be in there.

"You were lucky this time. Mr. Perfect's Little Black Book saved your life. The notebook absorbed most of the blows. Her knife still pierced your chest for an inch or so in two places. The blood flow must have convinced her you were mortally wounded.

"You're not looking too perfect right now. Maybe the pain will help you remember this incident. Be cool, Perfectico. We'll talk more, eh?"

A man in a suit walked up to Diaz's bed. "I'm Detective Sundberg. Tell me about this lady in the polka dots. Start from the beginning and go slow. I'm a terrible note taker."

SET THE CONTROLS FOR THE HEART OF THE SUN

Jeff Esterholm

There were two killings of note that year. One took place on a motel balcony in Memphis and the second in the kitchen of a Los Angeles hotel. Paul Cimarron lived in the Upper Midwest, in a port city on Lake Superior. The city of Superior in 1968 was insulated by physical distance and weather from the socio-political tumult that resulted from the assassinations. Although Paul Cimarron had photographs of Martin Luther King, Jr., and Robert F. Kennedy reverently Scotch-taped to the cracked plaster wall beside his kitchenette table, a larger collage made up of glossies from *Look*, *Life*, and *Time* memorializing John Fitzgerald Kennedy, assassinated when Cimarron was a teenager, dwarfed those of the other two figures. The riots in the streets of larger cities? At nearly twenty-three, Paul Cimarron—*the* pot entrepreneur to his friends—found more to be anxious about waiting for a package arriving from the Netherlands. Amsterdam. He was concerned about rip-offs, though he was the one intent on pulling off the grift.

He'd driven to the post office daily for the past week and a half in his '64 Dodge Dart, a midnight blue not-bad junker he bought secondhand off his uncle Dick. He went there again.

"Hiya. A package come in for me? Paul Cimarron?" He had

a post office box, but this package from his Amsterdam contact was going to be, as he told his friends, massive. Luckily, Cimarron thought, he had the Dart. He was sure he wouldn't have been able to carry the package back to his apartment without the car. He was feeling wired—if someone touched him on the arm, he would explode. That feeling.

He failed to catch the postal clerk eyeing him. The clerk recognized the young man and his name, before grunting, "Yes, I believe there is a little something here."

Cimarron nodded, said, "Cool." He checked the wanted posters on the bulletin board while the postal clerk, an Elmer Fuddly grandpa who he knew delivered mail years ago to his parents' three-bedroom ranch out in the park, waddled off to the back of the large room and the steel shelving filled with packages of all shapes and sizes. He looked at the FBI's most wanted. Black and white, somewhat grainy. Not a longhair among them. Cimarron muttered, "Criminals," and shook his head over his parents' generation.

"Here it is." The postal clerk set the package on the counter. "I'll need your signature right here."

Disappointed—the package was so much smaller than he had expected—he would have to tear into it back at his apartment. Paul Cimarron signed his name with a bit of autographical flourish, was handed the carbon, and walked out of the post office's main entrance onto Tower Avenue, the box from Amsterdam under his right arm. The Dodge Dart was three spaces down on the southbound side of the street. Cimarron put the package on the passenger seat and pulled away.

Watching him from an unmarked Ford Galaxie parked across the street was Denny Nord, a member of the city police department's fledgling Narcotics Division.

On a cross street to the north, an electric blue Cadillac with Minnesota plates sat idling. A certain Mr. Osborne, in town from Minneapolis, was watching Cimarron.

Nord eyeballed the Dart from his rearview mirror, followed

it until it took the left-hand turn going east. *He's going to his apartment on North 21st. Give him time to break the package open, split it up. Catch him as he's leaving to deliver to his crew.* Nord opted for a quick lunch at Sully's Café on the eastside.

Osborne's Cadillac rolled out from North 14th Street onto Tower Avenue, passing the narc in the Ford Galaxie going in the opposite direction.

Back at his basement apartment, Cimarron set a Beatles' album—*Revolver*, his favorite—on the turntable of his Montgomery Ward portable stereo. He lit a cone of sandalwood incense in the mushroom-shaped burner, a gift from his girlfriend going to the U down in Madison, and passed through the red-beaded curtain into the kitchenette. He set the package on the table after sweeping aside his dirty breakfast and lunch dishes. Swinging to the tabletop a tackle box that was not a tackle box, Cimarron opened it and moved aside a scale, a roll of plastic bags, and other tools to get to a Stanley retractable razorblade. Using the blade, he slit the packing tape that held down the package's flaps, singing along with George Harrison on "Taxman," his voice an imitation of a nasally Liverpudlian, and entirely missed the knock at the door, the door's soft opening whine, the footsteps.

Cimarron jumped when the hand rested on his shoulder.

Denny Nord had wanted to kill Paul Cimarron, beat him beyond recognition, the penny-ante pusher who'd been a pain in his ass for the last year. Better yet, let him live, but never want to talk. And *then* the detective from the Narcotics Division would walk out with the package from Amsterdam. There was something to be said about keeping things on the q.t.

Nord arrived at about two, two thirty that afternoon after lunch at Sully's. The kid's basement apartment. The door opened an inch. Nord toed it wide. It was a mess. Blood and personal property damage. *Revolver*, side one, *thup-thupped, thup-thupped,* the tonearm ticked repeatedly after the final track. He lifted the tonearm from the album with a handkerchief, clicked off the turntable, put the LP back in its sleeve, and adjusted the cheapo stereo system so his colleagues from the department wouldn't screw it up more when they came bulling through.

Blood and damage. Damn, he thought, looking around. No sign of Cimarron. No sign of the package from Amsterdam.

Nord's plan had blown up.

Osborne and his driver waited in the electric blue Cadillac until dark to visit Paul Cimarron's apartment. Cimarron had the one visitor—Osborne guessed a cop or a PI—and he left with nothing visible. Now, there had been no more coming, no more going. No lights shown through the open windows. No voices. No FM radio or rock and roll albums spinning. Osborne knew Cimarron liked that, while he preferred what he considered the more so-phisticated sounds of Mantovani. The window screens were torn, but that was from age, lack of the caretaker's due diligence.

Osborne knocked. He turned the doorknob and whispered, "Turn on the light."

His driver looked at him. "Not a flash—"

"Hit the switch." Osborne's whisper was a bark.

The light was not bright. Better, less suspicious, he thought.

The space was an artful disaster, Osborne could see that right away, as if a professional wrestling card, the living room edition, had played out. Yet, strange to see, the homemade shelving sys-tem of planks and cinder block held the Montgomery Ward portable stereo perfectly, though the black-and-white portable television tumbled down, the tube cracked. Furniture tipped over. Choreographed. The beaded curtain over the doorway to the kitchen was a wreck, red beads scattered over the floor.

There was blood, but very little of it, as if someone had snot-ted his bloody nose in his hands and then wiped those hands off on the apartment's surfaces. Strategically.

It was wrong. It was all wrong.

Steven Mayhew sat in his office above Worldwide News and Views, the downtown corner shop source for newspapers and magazines of every stripe, from *Tiger Beat* and *16 Magazine* to *Buff Swinger* and *Playboy*. Candy bars people hadn't yearned for since the Great Depression were laid out in the shop's display case, along with cigars, cigarettes, and pipe tobacco. The latest entry was a fast-selling product: Zig-Zag slow burning cigarette papers. Mayhew wondered about the cigarette papers occasionally, but now he was more inclined to pull at his hair. He was letting his crewcut grow out, the crewcut he'd had since 1952, a young enlistee serving in Germany during the Korean War. Jane, the woman with the doctorate in English who taught at the university in town, and Mayhew had been dating for about six months and initially she liked his whiskery skull. Now, she told him to go for that longhair look. Mayhew was giving it a shot.

It looked like crap.

Tanner agreed. "I'd cut it if I were you." Tanner was his secretary, and, no surprise, she kept the place running so the rent check could be handed over every month to Skorich, the owner of Worldwide News and Views as well as the rest of the buildings on the block. "That's if I were you, but I'm just the secretary."

He set aside the mirror he'd been tilting this way, that way; his older brother had the mirror in the Navy during the war in the Pacific, meant to signal search planes if you were floating in the middle of the ocean on a rubber raft. "I don't know, Tanner. I look like a porcupine with limp quills."

"You can wet it and brush it down for now, Steven. You've got a couple of borderline weepy parents. Well, one is anyway. They would like to meet with you."

He waved off Tanner's coiffure suggestions. "Send them in. Just tell them I'm a work in progress."

"Oh, I'll do that, all right."

Like Steven Mayhew, Patricia and Randall Enstad were in their thirties. She was originally from Solon Springs, a rural community about a half hour's drive out of town, and he was a lifelong Superior resident, born at home, just like his nine sisters and brothers, and raised in the city's hardscrabble North End. The Enstads now lived what anybody in the city would assume was the good life in Billings Park, on the westside.

Mayhew welcomed the Enstads, offered them coffee which they declined, and the three of them sat quietly until he said, "What can I help you with today?"

Randall was stone, not wanting to be where he was at that time of day. Midafternoon. He wanted to get back on the road; he was a salesman. He wasn't prone to say a word. Patricia glanced at her husband, then back at Mayhew. She was frustrated. She took a deep breath, released it with aggravation.

"I'm not a marriage counselor, if that's what you were looking for," Mayhew said, taking them both in.

Patricia Enstad rolled her eyes. She apparently didn't appreciate Mayhew's sense of humor. With her tightly compact bouffant the color of freshly minted pennies and her elfin look, she reminded him of the leprechaun who shilled cereal when he watched Saturday morning cartoons and ate his Wheaties. "We are aware that you aren't a marriage counselor, Mr. Mayhew." Her blue eyes pinned him as if she were a lepidopterist and he was a run-of-the-mill, dusty moth. She would have killed him, or the bug zapper would. "Has anyone ever discussed your manner with you? You don't know what people are coming in for, and you joke?"

Randall Enstad maintained his Mount Rushmore solo performance, but, at that last line of Patricia's, his tight lips slid into an angry, grinding gash.

"Miss Tanner, my secretary, she has. Many times." It was true. He didn't know what he would do without Tanner. He wished more of her instruction would take. "I apologize, Mrs.

Enstad and Mr. Enstad. My job, I'm a private investigator. You're interested in my services for—"

Patricia Enstad put her purse on Mayhew's desk, sliding his signal mirror aside—inwardly, he rolled his eyes—and snapped the purse open. "Our son, Paul, has disappeared. Here's a snapshot from last Christmas. It's the most recent photograph that we have."

Mayhew picked up the photo. A black-and-white snapshot. Christmas, 1967. A young man grinning goodbye, about to leave by someone's back door, his hair wavy and shoulder length, the color light brown to red, Mayhew guessed—he would have to ask—wearing wire-rimmed glasses, a heavy military field jacket with a black-and-white-striped winter scarf wrapped around his neck. He flashed the peace sign at the photographer.

Patricia Enstad appeared anxious about this *most recent* photo, not wanting to lose it. "His hair, it's dark blond, and he's about five-nine, one fifty-five, one sixty." She smiled. "For a hippie, he's pretty fit. Those magazine articles, you know. You never know what you're in for." Her voice cracked. Her husband, Randall, hadn't said a word.

"How old is Paul?" Mayhew asked. He kept a finger on the edge of the photo, not wanting Patricia to snap it up. "If you don't mind, I'd like to have copies made up of this. You'll get the original back."

She nodded. "It was his birthday last week. He turned twenty-three"—she quaked, snapping her purse shut—"and missed his birthday dinner at Cronstrom's."

After glaring briefly at Randall, she turned back to Mayhew and continued. "He was gone, out of town, right after Christmas. He flew to Hawaii, spent the winter there, sent a postcard saying he was living on the beach. Where do these kids get the money to do this sort of thing? Flying to Hawaii." She laughed falsely, rolled her eyes.

Randall turned to Patricia and said, "You know where Paul gets his money."

"Not from me. Not after you kicked him out."

Mayhew encouraged Randall to say more. "Where does he get his money, Mr. Enstad?"

"Drug money," Randall said with disgust.

"That's why he kicked him out of the house."

Mayhew held up his hands, attempting to direct the verbal traffic darting in front of him. "Let's get the ground rules laid out before we go any further, folks." He told them he would take the case, what his rates were if they were interested, daily, weekly. And, it had never occurred in the past, but the monthly figure too. Were they still interested in hiring him?

"Yes!" Patricia said.

Randall offered an unenthusiastic, "Sure. You probably can't be any less helpful than the police." He glanced at Mayhew's hair. "Maybe."

Mayhew ignored that and asked, "Who have you worked with in the department? Did you file a missing person report?"

Randall shook his head. "No, we haven't. Paul's been arrested before. Marijuana. There was a hearing scheduled. That never happened. He was gone by then."

"He ran?"

"He wouldn't run," Patricia said. "He believes it should be legalized. I told him, 'We're pretty advanced in 1968, kiddo, but legalizing marijuana?' And Paul didn't call it marijuana. He used something exotic like 'bhang.' Bhang, right?" she asked her husband.

He nodded.

"So. You've spoken to someone in Narcotics?"

"Nord, Denny Nord."

Mayhew winced inwardly at the mention of Nord. He didn't doubt that Nord would do the same hearing his name. "Detective Nord didn't have you fill out a missing person report, refer you to anyone else?"

Patricia shook her head. "It sounded to me like he was more likely to put out an all-points bulletin on Paul."

"He should," her husband said. Then he softly growled, "What that boy has done to our family name."

"At least he *changed* his last name," Patricia said, patting Randall's knee, but she knew it didn't make the upheaval in their life any better for her husband.

"Changed it to what?" Mayhew asked.

Patricia said, "Cimarron. He goes by Paul Cimarron now. He liked cowboy movies when he was growing up. Fighting off the hired guns, rescuing the schoolmarm. Riding off into the sunset."

As luck or something worse would have it, Denny Nord was the older brother of Mayhew's English professor girlfriend, Jane Nord. The two men did not get along. Denny had been trying for years to set up Jane with single guys on the force. Uniforms. Plainclothesmen. She already knew about "single guys on the force." They were not single. Multiple snubs and taking up later with Mayhew, a private investigator licensed in Wisconsin *and* Minnesota, perturbed Denny not a little.

"What do you think? I really should talk to your brother. Would he give me the time of day?" He knew he would have to, and it was his way of letting Jane know that he would have to. Mayhew and Jane were having dinner at Cronstrom's Supper Club, where the Enstads had planned on celebrating Paul's birthday.

Jane laughed. "He'd probably say, 'I'm at lunch, so take a hike, dick.' That's what he would probably tell you. I'm right about 'dick,' right? You're a private dick?"

Mayhew scrunched his eyes, feigning pain. He didn't favor the old lingo, too many old jokes attached to the words. He chewed his upper lip before taking another bite of his breaded walleye. He chewed the fish, raised a finger for another old-fashioned. "Yeah, yeah. Funny girl, Jane. But seriously, you know and I know I have to talk to him."

"Great. At least there aren't any family gatherings coming

up. I won't have to hear him whine. Or ask me for the umpteenth time why I won't go out with Detective Snively instead of you. And my responding, also for the umpteenth time, that Steven Mayhew is a decent guy, with no wife and without twelve kids on the side. I have that part right, right?"

Mayhew smiled, nodded. He liked this woman a lot.

Leslie Weathers. That was the name of Paul Cimarron's girlfriend. Mayhew had phoned Patricia Enstad about that, girls in her son's life, so he got word about the steady who, as far as Patricia knew, was going to summer school in Madison. Mayhew brought up something else.

"I want to ask about something you said. Your husband kicked Paul out?"

"When Paul was seventeen. He was uncontrollable, Paul was. He went to parties, got drunk, who knows what else. We didn't know what to do. The fight didn't help."

Mayhew let that last sentence hang there after traveling through the telephone line, and seeing that she wasn't going to add anything, he said, "The fight."

"It was like Joe Frazier and Buster Mathis going at it in my kitchen here. Randall outclassed Paul. I was screaming, but not like I was anyone's fan."

The Weathers family lived in south end, across the street from the IGA, two blocks south of Twin Ports Dairy. Mayhew slowly passed their home on Tower Avenue and then doubled back, up the alley. There was an orange VW bug parked alongside the garage and a trash can that sat in a wooden frame. Mayhew pulled into the vacant space next to the bug. It was daubed with black paint, looked like a giant ladybug.

From the screen door on the back porch, Mayhew could hear music, a rhythmic drone, and voices, maybe two voices, he couldn't be sure. He rapped at the door's wooden frame, perhaps too lightly at first, then tried again, harder. The music abruptly stopped, the tonearm lifted, and there was silence.

"Yes?" a young woman asked, coming from inside the house, walking barefoot, soles tick-tacking across the kitchen linoleum. She stood on the other side of the screen, glancing at the latch, ensuring that the hook was in the eye. Good girl. She was tall and Twiggy-thin, strawberry blond hair long, past her shoulders. He could smell pot and incense intermingling.

"Leslie Weathers?"

Her look was vapid, her smile quixotic. Mayhew thought she might start laughing. "Yes."

He held his business card up to the screen so she could read it, but she didn't appear to be interested. "My name is Steve Mayhew. I work for Randall and Patricia Enstad. I'm looking for their son. Paul."

Leslie Weathers's smile flatlined. She blinked, an action that seemed to take forever.

"Paul's mom thought you might be in Madison, taking summer school classes. But, obviously, you're here."

At mention that she was, in fact, home, Leslie Weathers slammed shut the heavy inside door. The screen door slapped in its frame. Mayhew frowned. It hadn't been locked after all. He started back, off the porch, crossing the backyard to his car when the Weathers's door swung open. Leslie stepped out onto the porch. "My folks aren't home." A case of nerves in her voice. "They're out at the cottage on Lake Nebagamon. Summer session was done. I came home."

Mayhew stood in the backyard on a narrow concrete walk alongside a picnic table and an empty clothesline. A dog barked farther down the block and semis rumbled down Tower Avenue. "Can I ask when you got back from Madison?"

Leslie told him and he nodded. She could have seen Paul before he disappeared.

"Have you seen Paul?"

It took her too long to say no, Mayhew thought, even though stoned.

"Ask you one more thing? That music you were listening to when I knocked. What was that?"

"Pink Floyd, English band. 'Set the Controls for the Heart of the Sun.'"

Mayhew smiled. "Yeah. I thought so." Then he turned and walked to his car.

Leslie Weathers's face clouded over, quizzical. After Mayhew drove away, she picked up the card he'd left on the picnic table and pocketed it.

The midnight-blue Dodge Dart, Uncle Dick Enstad's former ride, Paul Cimarron's only one, was found submerged in the Saint Louis River after a fisherman's line became entangled with the rear bumper and the license plate. The county water rescue team saw that the driver's side and passenger side windows were open. Fair enough on a summer night. But no body. Investigators speculated: Did Paul Cimarron get out and make it to shore, or was he swept away? The water rescue team, happy for a July dive rather than one in February, when vehicles dropped through thin ice, found no trace of a young man's corpse hung up on anything below the river's surface. In their opinion, the river had swept him away, into Lake Superior's cold maw, cold no matter the season.

The police station was on the ground floor of City Hall, a building constructed at the tail end of the nineteenth century, the Gilded Age, sitting at the corner of Broadway and Hammond. Denny Nord was typing, his index fingers doing a practiced pas de deux across the keys that continued for a fraction of a second after he looked up and saw Mayhew on the other side of his desk. He sat back in his wooden chair. Nord was old school, and the thought crossed his mind that the PI was going to ask for his sister's hand. No such luck.

"Hiya, Denny." Mayhew took the chair that Nord nudged his chin at. "You familiar with Randall and Patricia Enstad?"

"Jeez, you don't waste words on pleasantries, do you? 'Hello, Detective Nord.' 'Why hello, Mr. Mayhew.' The Enstads?" Nord shrugged. "Not too." But their kid, yes, Paul Cimarron was on his mind. A lot. He had been typing up a report related to the drug case, the Dodge Dart at the bottom of the Saint Louis River.

"You busted Paul, their son, for selling nickel and dime bags? Something bigger?"

Nord slapped his desk, spread his arms. *Those* Enstads, *that* Paul Cimarron. Yet he shook his head.

"Enstads. Cimarron. Don't shit me," Mayhew said.

Nord checked his watch, looked back up at Mayhew. "Tell you what. Let's go for a burger and a beer. Your treat."

At the Ore Dock Tavern on 5th Street, the two sat at a table away from the bar and its regulars, ate hamburgers charred on the bar grill, and drank Grain Belt taps. Elvis on the comeback trail played on the jukebox until a Rolling Stones single was punched in. "Jumpin' Jack Flash." Nord shook his head at the change. Mayhew moved forward, offering that the Enstads were his clients. Nord was surprisingly forthcoming about the specific case, the charges against Cimarron, when his court date was, how the kid had missed it and disappeared, just like that, until he didn't.

"You've located him?" Mayhew asked.

Nord took a deep breath. "Not *him*. It'll be in the papers tomorrow. No. Not him, but his car." Not the package from Amsterdam, goddammit. The package. He didn't bring that up. Or whatever the hell happened in Cimarron's apartment. "Sheriff's department is operating under the assumption that"—wide-eyed, he fluttered his fingers off to the side, the river's flow—"he's at the bottom of Lake Superior now."

Mayhew guessed that the detective from the Narcotics Division didn't look at it the same way as the county did. He let that ride. There was something under Nord's skin about the Cimarron case, maybe as simple as the one that got away, maybe something more than his fingers mimicking the Saint Louis River, maybe resulting in the angry throb of the vein along the side of his forehead. "You think he got out of the car?"

Denny Nord would not say.

The detective dropped Mayhew off at his car in the police department parking lot. As Mayhew climbed from the unmarked Galaxie, Nord asked, "You'll tell me if you locate him, right?"

"I'll do as much as you'd do for me, Denny."

Nord said, "Nothing less for my future brother-in-law."

Mayhew, walking over to his car, thought, sure, but you'd probably shoot him. Nord wasn't right. No way, no how.

The first thing that Mayhew noticed when he returned to Leslie Weathers's house was that the Volkswagen was gone from its parking spot near the garage. The second thing he noticed was that Leslie had not left in the car. She sat at the redwood picnic table in the shade of her parents' house, chain-smoking cigarettes, not reefer. He got that word from Jane. A can of Schlitz, beaded with condensation, was beside her on the table.

"Can I join you, Leslie?" he asked, walking across the backyard.

"Free country," she mumbled. "That's what I hear."

He looked at his lonely car, sitting by itself on the gravel parking spot, then at the young woman with the red-rimmed eyes. She wasn't high, not like she'd appeared to be on his last stop. "You've heard about Paul's car?"

She nodded.

"You know what he was involved in?"

"Of course," she snapped. "Or I wouldn't have helped him." Leslie spoke as if she had nothing else to lose. "Damn, man. We were going to split, just the two of us." She took a long slug from the can of beer, caught how he was looking at her, and said, "Don't worry, I'm twenty-one."

Mayhew shook his head. "He was dealing dope. You were helping him?"

"Not with that. But with the car. And trashing his apartment. That narc from downtown had been hassling Paul, you know? Busted him, but then, get this, wanted in."

"Detective Nord?"

"No shit, Sherlock. Talk about corruption. The Man wins that crown hands down. The narc was horning in on Paul's trip, you know? Telling him, 'I know someone in Amsterdam. Dude can send you top-quality shit.' Hear me out, man. Dig this. The narc was even putting Paul up against it with his supplier from the Twin Cities. Mr. O, Paul called him." Her foot kicked a beachball across the yard, bouncing it off the garage. "And that dude, he is one dangerous—"

"Paul wasn't in the car when it went into the river, was he?"

She laughed. "Nope. Listen. It was like with his apartment. He had it all planned out, that Paul. Listen, listen. Dig this. We sank that car with the windows open, the trunk popped, just so we'd be sure it would go down and not bob around like it was waiting for a bite. It served its purpose. But, damn, Paul"—her eyes teared up, her nose ran, she used the bend in her wrist to wipe it—"he nearly went down with the ship, man. He built this crazy Rube Goldberg thingamabob, a wooden pole with like a footpad at the end of it, his own creation. He angled that sucker into the car, gave it the gas. Man! The pole cracked and held, and he jerked toward the river with the car. I grabbed his skinny ass and he let go of the pole. He told me I saved his life. And I did. And the car, it plowed into the river a way, then, bloop, bubble, bubble, it sank."

"That's some story," Mayhew said.

Leslie Weathers crossed her heart. "It's the truth, man."

"Some think Paul's at the bottom of Lake Superior."

The tears returned. "Oh, man, that cat makes me so blue. I

dig him so, showed him your card. He must've freaked. I woke up early this morning and he was gone. He booked it, man. Took Ruby."

Mayhew gave Leslie a questioning look.

"My car, man. Ruby the Ladybug. Dig. His taking her? That hurts more than his splitting."

She wasn't sure where he'd been before coming back to town. She had no idea where he'd be going. "He did talk about us going to Hawaii. He talked about it a lot. Live on the beach." She tested the Schlitz can. Empty. "So that's the story, Mr. Private Eye. What're you going to do with it?"

Later, Mayhew met with Paul Cimarron's parents. They were his employers, not the police department's narcotics detective. They had heard from the police, not Denny Nord, about the Dart in the river, their son's apparent drowning. They were happy to hear, and more importantly believe otherwise based on what Mayhew had to tell them. Even Randall Enstad smiled.

Denny Nord did not fare well. Leslie Weathers gave her detailed account to investigators with the police department. Nord's union supported him as it was bound to do, but, in the end, he lost his job, not disappointing Mayhew one iota.

Paul Cimarron?

No one in the Upper Midwest admitted to ever hearing from him again. It was like he rode Ruby the Ladybug off into the sunset, straight into the heart of that sinking sun.

PLUTONIUM BLONDE
Graham Powell

I was awakened by someone pounding on my door at, well, I guess it was morning from the sunlight streaming in the window. I dragged on my bell-bottoms and hurried to see who the hell it was. It sounded like the fucking cops. As I pressed my eye to the peephole, I scowled. It wasn't the fucking cops; just *one* fucking cop—Inspector Eberhardt.

I opened the door as far as the chain would allow. "What do you want, Eb?"

He laughed, then coughed, then spat. "I want to come in, dipshit, what do you think I want? I got a case for you."

I opened the door. "It better be goddamn important to get me up so early."

"It's ten o'clock!"

"Like I said."

He passed me a manila folder, and I rubbed the sleep out of my eyes and started leafing through it. "Which is it—missing kid, missing lover, or missing bag of cash?"

"It's a woman. Sylvia Vossey. Parents Sam and Greta. They've driven all the way from Sacramento, so be nice."

I flipped through the file quickly. Sylvia was twenty, a sophomore at Stanford. English major. There was a photograph— platinum blond hair, bright blue eyes, and a smile that looked genuine.

Eberhardt glanced at his watch. "They'll be here soon. You'd better brush the crumbs out of your beard and get dressed. When are you gonna shave that thing off, anyway?"

"I haven't shaved since they shot Bobby Kennedy. Anyway, chicks dig the beard. It tickles their thighs."

He laughed while I grabbed a clean shirt from my closet. "Ever think about coming back to the force?"

"Do pigs fly?" I said, tying my hair back into a ponytail.

"Nope."

"Call me when they do."

Eberhardt shook his head. "I never understood that, Horse. Why'd you quit? You brought in as many drug busts as the rest of the team combined. You had a future."

"The truth? I got to like the hippies I was spying on better than I liked the cops. Hippies just want to get high, play their records, and screw. You guys want to bust heads. After a while it made me sick."

"So, you went over to the other side. That makes you a shithouse rat."

"Yeah, well, I'd rather be a rat than a stainless-steel son of a bitch like you. Do you still want your finder's fee? Twenty-five percent, right?"

Eberhardt's smile lost its humor. "Yeah," he said. "I do."

I kept my place neat, so I just had to tie my hair back, move last night's dishes to the sink, and put away the bong. Good thing too because they were early.

Eberhardt answered their knock. The Vosseys were just beyond middle age and dressed for church—Sam in a charcoal gray suit and fedora, Greta in a black dress with white lace collar. They were nearly as wide as they were tall, square in every way.

When they saw me, they recoiled in unison.

"This is Harrison, the man I was telling you about," said Eberhardt. "Don't be alarmed by his appearance. He's worked undercover for many years, infiltrating various drug gangs and radical groups."

"That's right," I said. "Maintaining this disguise helps me stay in character, like method acting."

Eberhardt nodded. "I can vouch for him, he's reliable. Harry, meet Sam and Greta Vossey."

"Sir, ma'am," I said. "Please do come in."

My little couch was crowded with the two of them, so Eberhardt stood while I sat on the recliner and took out my steno pad. "The inspector says your daughter Sylvia is missing. What can you tell me about it?"

Sam sat there holding his hat on his lap as Greta did all the talking. "Sylvia and I usually spoke once or twice a week while she was at school, and *always* on Sunday," she said. "But she didn't call last week, so on Sunday I called her dorm and her roommate answered." Her lips trembled. "Amy said she was gone! Sylvia told her she had to 'get her head together,' then she packed a bag and left!"

"Amy's the roommate? Did she have any idea where Sylvia was headed?"

Greta shook her head. "It's been over a week now. I've been calling every day, but she hasn't come back yet." Her eyes brimmed. "If something has happened, I'll *never* forgive myself."

"I wouldn't worry, Mrs. Vossey. Since she left of her own volition, I'd say she's probably just taking a little vacation. Now her roommate Amy—what's her last name?"

"It's Lambert. I've got her number and address right here."

I copied that down. "Does she have any other friends there? Someone she might stay with for a while? Or was there any-one...special?"

"Oh, yes, there was someone, a very nice young man named Bill Jennings. He was a year or two older. I think he was working on an advanced degree. Electrical engineering, something like that. Yes, go see Bill—he should know where she is."

"Did she maybe leave a forwarding address at the office?"

"The office!" Greta snorted. "They were worse than use-less—wouldn't tell us anything at all! And the police were hardly better." She remembered Eberhardt's looming presence and quickly added, "Except for the inspector, of course."

I kept at it for a while longer but there was nothing more to get. When we'd finished, I closed my notebook. "I believe Inspector Eberhardt has discussed my fee?"

Greta nodded. "Yes, one hundred dollars a day with five days in advance."

Sam Vossey reached for his wallet and took out five new hundred-dollar bills. As he handed them to me, he spoke for the first time. "I don't care where Sylvia's been, or what she's been up to. I don't understand the things that happen today. Violence, chaos—"

"Yeah, the country's gone to hell since Dylan went electric."

His eyes were damp. "Please just bring my little girl back to me."

"I swear I'll do my best," I said.

After they'd gone, I turned to Eberhardt and said, "So the price is a hundred a day now? Your cut not big enough already?"

"You're worth it, aren't you? And they can afford it."

"I set my own prices, Eb. Do this again and I'll find another shill." I got out my pouch and stuffed my pipe full of some nice Mexican weed.

Eberhardt sneered. "How can you poison yourself with that shit?"

"It expands my mind, helps me cogitate. Now beat it, I've got work to do."

He left in a huff but as long as he was gone, I was happy. It was time to get moving. I grabbed my messenger bag from the closet and stuck in an extra pad, a few manila envelopes, and yesterday's newspaper. Then I climbed in the Rambler and headed down to Palo Alto.

I always liked going down Palm Drive onto the Stanford campus. The rows of palm trees, the mission buildings with their whitewashed walls and tiled roofs—it's a place time left behind.

The traffic cop giving me the stink-eye kind of broke the spell.

The dorms were located on "the Row," and they weren't the rambling, institutional buildings you find so many places these days. They were big, to be sure, but they were houses, not storage facilities for the students.

The room that Sylvia Vossey shared with Amy Lambert was on the corner of the second floor. The girl who answered my knock was blond, average build, an inch either side of five feet, dressed casually in a light shirt and jeans. She looked up at me, my long hair and beard, and her mouth fell open.

"Amy Lambert? My name is Harrison—you can call me Horse—and I'm trying to locate Sylvia Vossey. May I come in?"

"Sylvia?" she said, opening the door wide. "Is something wrong?"

Inside it was spartan—two beds, two desks with chairs, a chest of drawers. Amy sat on her bed while I took one of the desk chairs. There were tie-dyed sheets serving as curtains, and a poster for the Bonzo Dog Doo-Dah Band. I had a feeling we were on the same page.

"Sylvia's parents haven't heard from her in a while," I said. "They're getting worried and asked me if I could make sure she's okay. Have you seen her lately?"

She couldn't keep from staring at my hair. "Uh, no, I haven't seen her for a few days. I guess it's like two weeks now. Something happened with Bill, I think they had a fight, and I think Sylvia went to crash with some friends for a while."

"That's Bill Jennings, right?"

She nodded.

"Do you know what they fought about?"

"No, Sylvia kept that stuff to herself. I know he's been busy with some big project lately. I heard them arguing about it."

"Oh yeah? He didn't have enough time for her?"

"I don't think that was it, he'd do anything for her. He was just worried about something, you know—preoccupied."

I chuckled as I wrote that down. "You're an English major."

"Minor," she said. "My major is pedagogy."

"Sounds kinky."

She smiled. "So, are you a real hippie?"

"What gave it away?"

"Well, you sure don't look like any cop I've ever seen."

I shrugged. "I'm just helping the Vosseys. Sylvia's still their little girl, and they're worried sick about her. Ever since Monterey Pop there've been a lot of weirdos around. Not all of them are as nice as me." I looked over my notes. "You say she might've gone to crash with some friends. Anybody in particular?"

Amy thought that over. "There was some new guy, an older guy. Older than you—in his forties, maybe. She was in some funky music store up on Telegraph Avenue…"

"I know it," I said. "I live right around the corner from there."

"Yeah, so they got to talking. I think his name was Dick." She frowned. "He might have worked there, I can't remember. He had a bunch of obscure records, stuff like Django Reinhardt and the Bonzos. Books, too, he gave her a few of those."

"All you have is 'Dick,' no last name?"

"I'm sorry, that's all I know."

"What about Bill? You know where I might find him?"

"I can give you his address," said Amy. "He's usually out at DC Power, though."

"DC Power?"

"It's like this annex for the engineering school, up in the hills a few miles south of here. They can tell you how to get there at the office."

I looked over what I'd written. "That gives me a place to start, at least. I'll talk to Bill and track down this man Dick, and we'll see where that goes." But I made no move to leave.

"So…" she said. "Do you, like, smoke pot?"

I pulled my pipe out of my pocket. "Who doesn't?"

The two of us smoked up all the weed I had and got to feeling mellow. I couldn't help but notice the curious way she was looking at me.

She asked, "Why do they call you Horse?"

I ran a hand through my hair. "Don't you think it's because of my glorious mane?"

She gave me a salacious smile that belied her tender years. "I sure hope not."

I shut the door.

A while later she laughed and said, "Oh my God, that tickles!"

The DC Power building was about five miles away, up in the rolling hills to the southwest of Stanford. I needed a pretext to go asking around, so I took a big envelope from my bag, stuffed the *Chronicle*'s sports pages inside, sealed it, and scrawled "Hand deliver to Bill Jennings" across the front. Then I put on my sober face and went inside.

On the wall across from the doors was an office directory full of useful information. I scanned it quickly before walking to the reception desk. It was occupied by a woman in late middle age. The nametag on her blazer read "Winter." She looked at me with distaste. "Can I help you?"

Winter by name, Winter by nature.

"I sure hope so," I said. "I'm supposed to deliver this package to Dr. Shoerdsma, but this is my first time here. Can you tell me how to get to his office? He said it's important."

Still frowning, she said, "Go to the end of the hallway until you reach the computer room and turn left. Shoerdsma is in the second office."

As I hurried off down the hall, I could feel her gaze like a cold wind on my back.

Every door had its nameplate, sometimes two, and I glanced at them as I went by. No Jennings.

Up ahead the hallway formed a T with a cross corridor. The broad wall ahead of me had only a single door. A sign over it read "Computer Room."

I turned to the left as instructed and found that Ms. Winter had left me a surprise.

Just around the corner there was one of those chairs with a desk attached, like kids sit at in school. It made the full-grown man sitting there in a three-piece suit look ridiculous. He was maybe in his mid-twenties, his hair military length and full of Brylcreem. He looked like a cop, and not just any cop—a Hoover.

He looked up sharply. "Yes?"

"Thank god you're here," I said. "Have you seen Bill Jennings around? Dr. Shoerdsma needs him to look over these papers and get back to him right away."

"What's in them?" he said, holding out his hand.

"I was told to deliver these to Mr. Jennings."

"I'm afraid he's not here right now, but you can leave them with me."

"No can do, I was told to put them in Jennings's hands myself and return them as soon as he was finished."

Hoover Jr. said, "Well, he isn't here. You can leave them with me if you want. I'll give them to Dr. Kroger." He pulled a pen and notebook out of his pocket. "What's your name, anyway?"

"I'm with Grimm and Moody, couriers in Sausalito," I said.

"Which one are you?"

"Depends on the day, am I right?" I glanced at my watch. "I've got a couple more deliveries to make before I knock off— how late are you going to be here?"

"There's someone on this desk around the clock." He frowned. "Who did you say you were with?"

"Grimm and Moody. In Sausalito. Say, if you leave before I get back, could you tell your relief to keep an eye out for Jennings?"

"Yeah," he said. "I'll do that."

I booked it as fast as I could without raising suspicion.

So, Hoover Jr. didn't have to check to see if Jennings was around. He knew. That was interesting. I thought about it all the way back to Berkeley.

The Art Music Company was still open when I got there. Yogi was leaning on the counter, reading the new issue of *Rolling*

Stone. "What's up, my man?" he said, his gold tooth flashing. "How you been?"

"Busy, man. Hey, got a question—"

"Me first, man." He bent his head close. "You holding?"

"Sorry, man, I smoked the last of my stash earlier."

He took it philosophically.

"Do you remember a guy named Dick who used to hang around here a lot?" I said. "An older guy. I think he may have worked here at one time."

Yogi thought about it. "Yeah, man, I think I know the dude you're talking about. Used to listen to a lot of cool old classical stuff. I mean, you can't dance to it, but all those guys like Bach and Handel were groovy, especially when you're, uh, in the right mood." He winked.

"Like I said, man, I'm not holding. Do you know where this guy lives?"

"That's not really my scene but I know some people who've been to his place. It's up in Marin County somewhere, San Rafael or Santa Venetia. I heard his old lady took a hike. He's got a big ol' empty place, so he lets people crash for free."

"Do you remember anything else?"

"Just the books he used to bring around. Talk about some freaky shit!"

"Yeah, I heard about the books."

"He must've been flying high when he wrote that stuff, it sent me right around—"

I grabbed his arm. "Wait, *Dick* wrote those? He *wrote* them?"

"That's what I just said, man."

"Where's your phone?"

I was in luck—Amy was still awake.

"Hey," she said, sounding pleased. "I've been thinking about you all day—"

"Sorry, Amy, this is for work and it's important. Are any of the books that Dick gave to Sylvia still lying around?"

"Let me see…yeah, I've got one right here. It's called *Confessions of a Crap Artist*."

"What's the author's name?"

Dick's address was in the phonebook.

The next morning, I drove out to Santa Venetia, a little burg tucked into the hills of Marin County, up across the Golden Gate from San Francisco. It's tough for a hippie to hang around in the suburbs without attracting attention, so I drove around, passing by the house every half an hour or so. Just before nine I spotted someone stirring. I pulled to the curb and cut the engine. A moment later I was pressing the doorbell. Footsteps coming closer, then the door opened.

It had to be her. She was taller than I expected, maybe five foot seven, but her blond hair, almost white in the sun, was unmistakable, and her blue eyes were friendly.

"Can I help you?" she said.

"My friend Yogi told me I might be able to crash here. Is this the right place? I have a little money…"

"Don't worry about that, come on in. I'm just making breakfast. Are you hungry?"

"Wow, that would be great." I stuck out my hand. "My name is Harrison. People call me Horse."

"I'm Sylvia," she said, smiling.

I looked her over while she scrambled some eggs. Whatever she'd been up to in the past couple of weeks didn't seem to have taken much of a toll. In white Capri pants, a periwinkle blue shirt, and sandals, she looked like she'd just stepped off a yacht.

After a few minutes Sylvia brought my plate and sat opposite me, sipping her coffee and reading the *Chronicle*, the two of us like a mismatched Ozzie and Harriet.

There was an odd sort of rattle coming from somewhere in the house. It seemed familiar but I couldn't quite place it. "Say, what's that noise?"

Sylvia laughed. "You'll get used to it after a while."

"But what—"

Just then it stopped. A few minutes later a middle-aged man with dark hair and an unruly beard came in and flopped down onto one of the chairs. His eyes were bloodshot. Without a word, Sylvia went into the kitchen.

"Good morning," I said. "You must be Dick. My name's Horse."

"Nice to meet you," he said absently. "Or have we already…?"

"No, I just got here."

Now Sylvia was back with a big mug of coffee. Dick slurped down half of it, then fished a pill bottle out of his shirt pocket. He shook out a couple of pills and swallowed them.

"What are you on?" I said. "If you don't mind my asking."

"On? I'm on deadline, that's what I'm on. This is due at the publisher by the end of the week, and I've got a hundred and twenty pages to go." He rubbed his face. "If I'm lucky I can have them done by Friday."

"Just be careful with those bennies. I've seen a few friends get too far down that path." There was an awkward pause that I felt compelled to fill. "What kind of stuff do you write?"

"Science fiction. Spaceships, robots, that kind of thing."

"Like Robby the robot?"

"Not quite. More like…if I were a robot, how could you tell?"

He stared at me until I was squirming. Then he shrugged. "I've got robots in the story I'm working on now. They're smart, as smart as us. If they get any smarter, they might decide they don't need us anymore."

"Hell," I said. "If they get smart enough, they might be able to *save* us."

Dick set down his mug. "Huh. Maybe." Then he stuck out a hand and we shook. "Nice to meet you, Horse, and thanks."

"For what?" I said, but he was already gone. A minute later the rattle started up again.

"He's at it twelve hours a day," said Sylvia. "Sometimes more. I guess he's found his thing. So, what's *your* thing, Horse?"

I wondered how much I should tell her. She wasn't here under duress, wasn't stoned out of her mind, didn't seem to be on the run or in any kind of danger. "I'm afraid I haven't been honest with you. I'm a private investigator. I've been looking for you for a couple of days now. Your parents hired me to make sure you're okay."

She frowned. "My parents?"

It took me a while to get everything set up, so I didn't call Eberhardt until lunchtime.

"What do you want?" he barked in my ear.

"I found your girl, Eb. If I bring her to the station, she'll get spooked. I'd rather find a neutral site. How about City Lights?"

"The bookstore? Why do always want to meet there?"

"Because the staff are all flaming liberals and won't let you pull any shit."

"Don't you trust me?"

"Yeah, I do. But I don't take things on faith. Three o'clock sound good to you?"

He grumbled a little more but finally agreed.

We pulled to the curb right on time. I turned to the girl beside me and said, "You ready for this?"

"Ready as I'll ever be," she said.

I spotted Eberhardt's bulk as soon as we entered, waiting with the Vosseys in an open area used for readings. When they saw us approaching, Mrs. Vossey rushed over and wrapped her arms around the girl beside me. "Oh, thank God, thank God almighty!" she said. "I was so worried about you! Please don't ever do that again!"

"I won't, Mom," she said. "I didn't mean to scare you. I just needed some time to get my head together."

Her father gave me a firm handshake, his eyes watery. "Thank you, Mr. Harrison. I have to say I had my doubts about you, but you've brought my girl home safely. That I can never repay."

Even Eberhardt got into the act, grinning as he slapped me on the back. He leaned close and said, "Another satisfied customer, eh?"

"In a way," I replied. "Okay, Jen, show them your Equity card."

"Her what?" said Eberhardt.

"Actor's Equity," I said. "That's not Sylvia Vossey."

"Then who the hell is she?" said Eberhardt.

"Everyone, meet Jen Freiberg, an actor and a friend of mine."

She curtsied elegantly.

"Jen?" said Vossey. "It's Sam—we played together in *Three Sisters* at that little theater in the Castro a couple years ago, remember?"

"Holy shit, Sam, is that you?"

"*Everybody shut the fuck up!*" shouted Eberhardt. He jabbed a stubby finger at Jen. "You finished? Then beat it."

"All right, Jack," she said, flashing a peace sign. "See you in the funny papers, Horse."

Eberhardt turned to the other two. "You got some explaining to do. For starters, who the hell are you?"

"We're actors," said the man. "My name's Sam."

"I'm Abigail," said the woman. "We have the same agent."

"That's right," said Sam. "Some guy came by his office last week, wanting to hire an older couple. He paid well, too, a couple hundred bucks each. Said it was some experimental breaking-the-fourth-wall thing. I figured he was just a pretentious ass."

"Did he say anything else? Give any other instructions?"

They mulled it over. "Oh, yes," said Abigail. "Come to think of it, he did. He told me to ask after Sylvia's boyfriend, Bill."

"Bill?" I said. "Bill Jennings?"

She nodded. "He made a point of it."

"Can either of you think of anything else?" said Eberhardt.

They shook their heads.

"Okay, you two," said Eberhardt. "You go wait by the car while we decide what we're gonna do with you. You'd damned well better be there when I come out!"

When they'd gone, he said, "How did you know those weren't the Vosseys?"

"I found Sylvia, told her that her parents hired me. Turns out they're on vacation in Miami."

"Then why the drama club bullshit? Why didn't you just tell me what was up?"

"I wasn't sure if you were involved. Was this Lieutenant Stone's idea?"

"Oh, fuck you," said Eberhardt. "How can you ask me that?"

"Because I don't know what's going on or who might be involved. I confronted the fake Vosseys like that because I wanted them off guard, vulnerable. I wanted the real story. I guess I got it."

"Did you?"

"Yeah," I said. "I don't know who's behind this, but it's not Sylvia Vossey they're after. It's Bill Jennings."

I went by my place for a shower and a change of clothes, then headed back up to Santa Venetia. Traffic northbound across the bridge was wretched that time of day and it was dark when I got back to Dick's house.

The rest of the house was up. I guess they woke at nightfall like vampires. There were mods and rockers, knee-high boots and headbands. They'd moved the furniture up against the walls to form a makeshift dance floor and were bobbing and weaving to *Beggars Banquet* on the hi-fi. Sylvia stood in the doorway to the dining room, arms crossed, looking like a bored kindergarten teacher watching kids run around at recess.

"Hey there," I said. "How's it going?"

"The usual, I suppose," she said. "There's some food on the table if you're hungry."

There was a buffet laid out, with little sandwiches, cocktail wieners, that kind of thing. It had been well picked over already and there were dishes abandoned everywhere. While I was eating, Sylvia came in and said, "I guess I'd better take Dick a plate."

"Is he still working?"

"He says he's in the home stretch, should be done tomorrow or maybe the next day."

While she was gone, I took the dirty dishes into the kitchen and started washing. She didn't say anything when she returned, just picked up a towel and went to work drying. Within fifteen minutes the place looked respectable again.

"Thanks," she said. "You didn't have to do that."

"I couldn't leave it all to you, and besides, I like to keep things tidy."

She smiled. "Sounds like you're turning into 'the man.'"

"Bite your tongue, kid. Or, if you prefer, I'll do it for you."

"I don't think so, Horse. You're a nice guy, but I don't think so."

Sylvia turned to go, and I made to follow. She planted a firm hand on my chest and said, "No, Horse, I mean it. I'll see you in the morning. Good night."

It was past midnight when I fell asleep on a sofa, alone.

About six hours later I was awakened by the smell of freshly brewed coffee. I stumbled into the kitchen, rubbing sleep out of my eyes.

It was Dick. He was sitting at the breakfast table looking cheerful. "Good morning!" he said. "How are you today?"

"Ugh," I said. "Your guests wouldn't shut up and go to bed."

"Really? Kids these days!"

I glared at him through bloodshot eyes. "You're awfully chipper."

"Damn right," he said. "I finished the book. Knocked out

the last chapter yesterday afternoon. By lunchtime it will be off to my agent and then the publisher. So, for a couple of days at least, I'm at liberty."

"You should celebrate," I said, without much enthusiasm.

He laughed. "I slept in, that's about all I can afford these days. I must've been out for fourteen hours."

I thought about all the pills he'd been popping and said, "Really? Fourteen hours?"

He shrugged. "I took something to help me relax. When I'm on deadline I'm like a different person. I need something to help me be myself again."

Fourteen hours…

After a while, Sylvia poked her head in and said, "I'm going to the store, do you need anything special?"

I looked at Dick and he shrugged. I said, "No."

Once she left, I excused myself, saying I had to go to the toilet. Instead, I made my way to Sylvia's room. I pressed my ear to the door and heard nothing. Quietly I turned the knob and pushed it open a crack. Inside it was dark. I opened the door and flipped on the light switch.

There was a sudden movement to my left, but before I could turn, the lights went out again.

Gradually I returned to consciousness. The sky above me was bright, but something was blocking the sun. I shut my eyes tight and opened them again, and saw it was a face, haloed by the light above. "Are you an angel?" I said, awestruck.

The angel looked away and said, "Good, he's awake."

"Sylvia?"

She helped me sit up. "What happened?" I said. "I came in and…"

I realized we weren't alone in the room. Over in the corner stood a man of about Sylvia's age. He was built like a linebacker, tall and square, dark hair, and plenty of stubble. The expression he wore was of a kid caught doing something he shouldn't.

"Is this Bill?" I said.

Sylvia nodded. "Bill Jennings, this is Horse Harrison."

Slowly I got to my feet and smiled. "You're a hard man to find, Bill."

"I'm not going back," he said. "You can't make me."

I felt around my jaw. There was a painful knot that hadn't been there before. "You're right, I can't make you and I'm not sure I want to try—but how about we talk?"

We gathered in the kitchen, the three of us and Dick, who was puttering around the stove.

"Here's what I know," I said. "Someone is using me to find you. They know enough about your private life to assume that if I found Sylvia, I'd find you too. Could this have anything to do with your work at the artificial intelligence lab?"

"How did you know that?" said Bill.

"They're the only ones who seemed interested in you. Was there a guard on the computer room the last time you were there?" Bill shook his head. "Well, there's one now."

"Oh, God," he said. "What am I going to do?"

"Tell me what you were working on."

"There were two parts to the program," said Bill. "My part analyzed patterns, made connections—figured out what's going on." He took a sip of water. "It started with several sets of data, each connected to some of the other sets, like a spider's web or a fishing net. We'd input some new information and ask if it matched the pattern. If the program got it right, some of the connections would get stronger. If it didn't, some other connections would get weaker. We'd run a few hundred sets of input a day, and the program gradually grew more accurate. We called this 'training the program.'"

"What kind of information were you putting in?" I asked.

Bill licked his lips. "I wasn't supposed to know," he said. "I was only working on the program, not the data. But it hadn't been very well scrubbed—labels hadn't been redacted, tags hadn't been removed."

"So?"

"It was military data. Train schedules leading up to the Soviet invasion of Hungary in '56. Missile deployments before Francis Gary Powers's U2 was shot down. Radio chatter in the days before the North Koreans captured the Pueblo. If we'd had the program back then, we could have anticipated any or all of those and prevented them."

I got up and started pacing. "Okay, so that's your part of the program, to figure out what's happening. What's the other part?"

"To figure out what to do about it. I heard there was a big project at the War College, playing out all these different scenarios, documenting what commanders might do, the thinking behind it, and what the best response would be. The reaction team then turned that into computer code. But," he shook his head, "something's wrong somewhere."

"Like what?"

"At the start we were getting the usual range of responses to our programmed simulations—like trade sanctions after the invasion of Tibet, or when we let the Berlin Wall go up in exchange for the Soviets withdrawing their tanks. But over time, more and more scenarios began to converge on one action in a way that suggests they're being manipulated."

"And that action is?"

"A US first-strike nuclear attack."

We all fell silent.

"Jesus," I said at last. "Why would anyone do that?"

"Because they hate the Russians. Because they think they can win. Because they're crazy. It's coming, and it's coming soon."

"Why do you say that?"

"You know this thing in Czechoslovakia? The 'Prague Spring'?" said Bill. "I've seen the data. It's not going to end well."

* * *

"All right," I said. "So, what do we do about it?"

"We could go to the newspapers," said Sylvia. "The *Bay Guardian* would print it for sure."

I shook my head. "How many people read that, even in San Francisco?"

"What about *Rolling Stone?*"

Bill said, "These people don't care about bad publicity. They'd just deny everything and then relocate to Caltech or MIT."

"You're right," I said. "We need find a way to spike their guns."

"You know what makes a machine dangerous?" said Dick.

We looked up in surprise. I'd forgotten he was there.

"A machine is dangerous because it has no conscience. It follows orders. You step on the gas, the car goes. You pull the trigger, the gun fires."

"Yeah," I said. "But how does that help—"

"They'll even kill each other if you tell them to," he said.

Bill got a funny look in his eye and started rubbing his chin.

"Would that work?" I said.

After a few minutes, he said, "Me and the other guys used to run a program—more like a game—called Core Wars. The idea was to grab as much of the computer as you could and delete the other players' code. I might be able to adapt it..."

"How long will it take?"

"At least all day. Then maybe another hour or so to upload it over the phone lines."

"Can this be traced back to you? Can you cover your tracks?"

He rubbed his jaw some more. "I can put in a counter, so that it won't activate until it's been run, I don't know, fifteen times."

I glanced at my watch. "You'd better start right away."

"There's something else," said Bill. "From here I can only access the public resources. The mainframe we need is on a private net-work in a secured area."

"So?"

He swallowed. "I'm going to have to go there."

"Oh," I said. "Yeah, that might be a problem."

Just looking at Bill, you could see his nerves were wrecked. Without moral support he'd fold like a tea towel. Sending him alone would be worse than useless.

"We'll go together," I said.

Relief flood over his face. "Thanks, Horse. I won't forget it."

"Hold on," said Sylvia. "You can't go out there looking like that."

I gave myself a once-over. "Something wrong with the way I look?"

The others all glanced at each other, silently asking *who's going to tell him?*

I smiled. "I have this situation under control. I'm going to run along now—Bill, you'd better get to work."

On the way home I stopped off at a friend's and bought a couple of ounces of combustibles.

The plan was to get to DC Power late in the day when there wasn't much activity. At precisely three o'clock that afternoon, I rang the bell at Dick's house. Sylvia opened the door. "May I help you?"

"Good morning, ma'am. Have you accepted Jesus Christ as your personal lord and savior?"

She rolled her eyes. "I'm sorry, I don't have time—"

"Sylvia, it's me," I said.

She goggled. "*Horse?* Where's your beard? And your hair? And where did you get that *suit?*"

"I'm going undercover again," I said, "but this time I'm infil-trating the squares."

We tried the same gag on Bill, but he thought I was from the

FBI and nearly jumped through a window. After Sylvia calmed him down, she leaned close to me and said, "I don't think he slept any."

He looked rough. I just hoped he could hold it together for a while longer.

We didn't speak during the drive, but when we arrived at DC Power, I parked the car and turned to Bill. "Let me do the talking—you just focus on what you need to do. I'll handle the rest. You ready?"

He took a deep breath and nodded. "Ready."

Ms. Winter was behind her desk. To Bill, she grudgingly said, "Morning," but all she had for me was a glare.

When we reached the end of the hall we found Hoover Jr. on duty. It took me a minute to realize it wasn't the same guy.

"May I help you?" he said.

"Yes. My name is Harrison, I'm a San Francisco detective. This man with me is Bill Jennings. Inspector Eberhardt asked me to find him."

Hoover got out a logbook and pen. "Your name?"

"It's Harrison."

"First name?"

I grimaced inwardly. "Horace."

From the corner of my eye, I saw Bill stare at me in surprise.

Hoover had us both sign the book and said, "Wait here, I'll get Dr. Kroger."

When he'd gone, Bill cocked an eyebrow and said, "Horace?"

"You tell anyone, I'll shoot you dead. My mother was a Latin teacher."

Then we had to shut up as Hoover was returning with a man of middling height and age with baggy eyes, baggy jowls, and unruly tufts of white hair. "Bill!" he said. "So glad you're back. How've you been?"

Bill looked like a dog that had shit on the carpet. "Much better now, sir. I guess I just needed a break."

"Did you make the changes that we had discussed?"

"Yes, sir. The program will…respond more aggressively now."

Kroger nodded. "Good, good. Is your punch card deck ready? Then why don't you go ahead and start loading it?"

Bill got his deck from the keypunch machine and Hoover let him into the data center.

"Did he give you any trouble?" said Kroger.

"No. I was able to get onto him through his girlfriend. They were flopping at a friend's house up north of the city. Last night I took him out, got him drunk, and managed to talk him into returning to work."

Kroeger nodded solemnly. "What do you think of his character? Am I going to need to…do something about him?"

"I don't think so. He's basically an overgrown boy scout, idealistic and loyal as they come. But that also makes him squeamish. It would eat away at him. IBM or Xerox might be a better fit."

"Yeah." Kroeger sighed. "He's a good kid. A good old limp-dicked son of a bitch. Maybe I can get him appointed as a visiting professor at some backwater, keep him out of circulation. It's better than the alternative, eh?"

I didn't want to think about the alternative, so I just nodded.

Ten minutes later, Bill was back. "I'm all done, sir. You can try it anytime."

"Thanks, Bill," said Kroeger. "I think this will complete your project, right?"

"Yes, sir, I'll be returning to regular classes next semester, unless you need some more fixes."

"I don't think that will be necessary, but if we need you, I'll let you know."

No one challenged us as we walked to the car. Bill practically fell into his seat.

"Get me that pouch from the glove box," I said.

Bill gave it to me, and I started packing my pipe.

"Is that…?" he said.

"It sure as hell is. If you're going to be a threat to national security, you may as well go all the way."

We made our way back up to Santa Venetia, the car smoking like it was on fire.

It was after dark when we arrived back at Dick's house, and we were both feeling a lot more relaxed. There was a party going on like the night before, but they'd swapped the Stones for the Beatles' *Rubber Soul*. Maybe it was just me, but the vibe seemed a lot more relaxed—peace, love, and rock 'n' roll.

As soon as we stepped in the door, Sylvia ran up and embraced Bill. He gave her a passionate kiss, and I smiled. Like the Lone Ranger, my job was done, but as I turned away, someone grabbed my hand.

It was Amy. "Well, hello, stranger," she said. "Sylvia told me you'd gotten yourself cleaned up."

"How do you like it?"

"Not bad," she said, smiling wickedly. "But I will miss the beard."

WHERE DREAMS AWAIT
Nils Gilbertson

May 1969
Berkeley, California

He thought of Korea as he trudged up the steep sidewalk. Dragging heavy legs up the hill, a familiar mantra marched across his consciousness. Snow-dusted memories blocked out the sun in the sky and the hot pavement and the beads of sweat forming on his brow. Instead, they sent shivers through him. He stopped to catch his breath and check the number on the mailbox against the scribbles on the cocktail napkin in his pocket. Perfect match. He tilted his head and examined the place. It was a sprawling hillside home with wood shingle paneling and broad windows that he was sure provided a stunning panorama of the bay. Before climbing the stairs that led to the front door, he pulled a pack of Chesterfields from his jacket pocket, slipped a cigarette to the good side of his mouth, and inhaled deeply. Turning and scanning the street that snaked through the hills, he couldn't quite catch a glimpse of the view beyond the reach of the neighborhood trees. Those types of views weren't for fellas like him.

The housekeeper led him up an ornate oak staircase to the third floor and sat him on a leather couch in front of a stone fireplace at the base of a large partition. To the right, a sliding glass door opened to a balcony and the million-dollar view.

"Mr. Randolph will be with you shortly."

He leaned back on the inviting couch and fought the heaviness of his eyelids. As he scanned the room, he noticed a sharply dressed boy drawing with crayons at the table beyond the partition. The boy met his gaze and stared, unable to return his attention to his picture.

"Hi there," the man said.

"Hello," said the boy. He paused, appearing to contemplate his years of firmly taught manners. "What happened to your…"

"My face?"

The boy nodded.

The man rose from the couch and approached the table. "I hurt it fighting in a war far away from here."

"The one they show on the TV?" the boy asked.

"No, it was years before Vietnam. But far away, just the same."

"My papa says it's important that we fight for what's right even if it's far away."

The man grinned. "Your papa and many others. But no need for a boy your age to worry about that."

He nodded and took a breath as though already aware of the ubiquity of evil. "Does it hurt?"

"My face? Not anymore." The usually numb flesh tingled. In the window's reflection, he caught a glimpse of the mangled corner of his lip and the mottled, drooping skin that masked his cheek. After all these years, he still saw a stranger.

There were footsteps on the stairs, and he recognized the man from the picture in UC Berkeley's Sproul Hall. The vice chancellor was tall and lean, with silver hair and eyes like razors. He stared for a moment before sticking out a bony hand and saying, "You're Edward Ash, private investigator, correct? I'm Vice Chancellor Philip Randolph."

"It's a pleasure, Vice Chancellor Randolph."

"It's all mine," he said. "Can I get you a drink?" He approached the bar cart by the window.

"Rye, if you have it," said Ash.

"How do you take it?"

"Usually through a straw, but I'll manage."

The vice chancellor grunted with feigned amusement and fixed the drink. As he handed it to him, he examined the investigator's scarred features. "I hear that you suffered your injury in the Korean War."

"That's right."

"Thank you for your service. It's because of men like you that we got the job done there in a few short years. If young men these days were half as tough as we used to be, the conflict in Vietnam would be long over with." The vice chancellor glanced at the boy. "Go downstairs and play, Bobby."

The boy nodded and stole one last look at Ash's face before scampering down the stairs.

The vice chancellor took a seat across from the couch, struck a match, and lit his pipe. "I'm a busy man so I won't waste any time. I understand that you exercise discretion when tracking down missing persons. That so?"

"I keep things as quiet as I can."

"Good. I've heard as much from my acquaintances, whose opinions I hold in high regard. They recommended you for a sensitive matter relating to my daughter, Isabelle." He slid a photograph across the coffee table. In it was a young woman with long brown hair, rouge-dusted cheeks, and a smile like a beautiful mask. "She's a senior here at Cal. During her first two years, she was a straight-A student and member of Delta Gamma sorority. At some point, she was charmed by some hippie types and took on the free spirit act." He chomped on the stem of his pipe. "At first, I didn't think much of it—only a phase. But soon things got out of hand. Drugs, parties, reckless participation in far-left protests. I haven't heard from her in weeks. She hasn't been in class and none of her friends have seen her. It's not the first time she's gone missing, but it's the longest. And, given the radical nature of the protests and increasing tensions on campus, I fear she's in danger."

Ash downed some whiskey and wiped the dribble from his cheek. "The boy's her brother?"

"I don't see how that's relevant."

Ash shrugged. "I'm curious by nature."

"Half brother. Isabelle's mother died in an accident years ago."

"Sorry to hear it. You mentioned that there are dangerous activities you fear that Isabelle is engaged in. What are they?"

The vice chancellor stiffened. "Mr. Ash, I provided a detailed dossier summarizing the information I've gathered—"

"Humor me."

He cleared his throat. "Drugs, communist-adjacent affiliations, sexually deviant behavior. This whole nonsense with the new park has Governor Reagan upset, and I don't blame him. I'm afraid that things are coming to a head, and it won't be pretty."

"And you want me to find her before things get ugly?"

"Exactly, and do so in a manner that doesn't bring attention to my role as vice chancellor. I'm on the front lines of maintaining order at this institution, and the personal nature of things necessitates that you handle this with the utmost care. But I fear for her safety if things continue to escalate." He said it as though embarrassed by his concern. "I did my best to fight the creation of that hippie sanctuary—*People's* Park. Talk about letting the inmates run the asylum. It's what we get for giving in to the free-speech demands over the years. Tell me, Mr. Ash, what happens when our guiding principle is to allow people to do and say whatever they want? Where does it end? Should the communists speak? The fascists? The deviants and rogues of society?"

Ash shrugged. "The way I understand it, it's about letting all ideas see the light of day, so the best ones win out."

The vice chancellor chuckled. "And has the twentieth century validated that theory? You're too old for such naiveté."

Focus leaked from Ash's brain like there was something broken in it. He did his best to pay attention to the conversation and suppress jagged memories of limbless men, their exposed intestines rotting in blood and shit-stained snow. But his mind lost track of all sense of time and place, leaving him stuck in a purgatory between the past and the present. At some point, the present wrestled back his consciousness, refocusing, assuring its host that the eyes on him were not an enemy, but a small boy hiding on a staircase, listening.

"But I digress," said the vice chancellor. "My primary concern is to ensure the safety of my daughter. You've read the list of contacts I recommend speaking to?"

"You bet," Ash said. As he sipped his drink, he pinched the corner of his scarred jowls shut.

"Wonderful. I expect regular updates." Ash watched the man chew on his next question. "Out of curiosity, Mr. Ash, does your disfigurement interfere with your job?"

"How so?"

"Make it difficult to blend in with a crowd?"

"To the contrary," Ash said. "It's a hell of a lot easier to blend in when people do their damnedest not to look at you."

They shook hands and Ash finished his drink. On his way out, he found Bobby drawing on the deck that anchored the front door. The boy ripped a sheet from his coloring pad and handed it to the investigator.

"I drew it for you," he said.

Ash glanced down at the sloppy portrait of a man with half of his face engulfed in flames. He kneeled beside the boy. "Thank you, Bobby."

"Will you find my sister?"

"I'll do my best."

The front door opened, and the housekeeper summoned the boy in. He went without a look.

Navy-blue beams crossed the Delta Gamma sorority house's white façade and surrounded the large Greek letters—ΔΓ. Ash took the brick walkway through the manicured bushes to the front door. Two attractive young women on the porch greeted him with looks of restrained fear.

"Hi there. My name's Ash, I'm here to talk to…" He glanced down at a crumpled note. "Lucy Dalton." Before either could respond, a tall thin girl with bobbed blond hair opened the front door.

"Mr. Ash?" she asked.

"Yes."

"I'm Lucy Dalton. Mr. Randolph said that you'd be coming by. There's a spot out back where we can talk."

She led him through the house to a picnic table in a well-kept garden. Ash offered Lucy a cigarette, but she declined. "We're not supposed to smoke at the house."

The investigator lit his anyway and asked, "So, any idea where your friend Isabelle is?"

She creased her brow. "If I knew, don't you think I would have told Mr. Randolph?"

He shrugged. "I like to ask the easy questions first."

She shook her head. "I have no idea. Isabelle and I used to be close, ever since we were little girls. We grew up together and rushed the house as freshmen. A couple of years back, she started acting weird and hanging out with the alternative crowd. Doing drugs, hooking up with all sorts of—people." She lowered her eyes.

"Any other change in her behavior?"

The girl nibbled on her lip as she thought. "We were room-mates living in the house. One night Isabelle stumbled in late when I was sleeping. She crawled up to my top bunk and shook me awake. She was sweating and smelled like—I don't even know what. She was out of her mind, insisting that her mother was outside, dying on the front porch. She begged that I call an ambulance to save her." Ash noticed Lucy eyeing the pack of cigarettes on the table as she spoke. He offered it to her. She glanced back through the glass doors, took a cigarette, and leaned forward to let him light it. "It made no sense because her mother died when she was younger."

"How'd she die?"

"Hiking accident in Yosemite. It was her and Mr. Randolph. She lost her footing and fell; it was horrible. Isabelle acted out for a while, but by high school, she was doing great."

"Except..." Ash prompted.

"Except," said Lucy, "occasionally, during sleepovers, she would have these night terrors, wailing, begging for her mother."

"Like the time here with you?"

Lucy shook her head. "No, that time was different. She was awake, on something. Her eyes were so dark, like she was possessed."

Ash let the girl gather herself. As he did, he tilted his head back and blew smoke toward the clear blue sky, contemplating the heavens beyond. How anyone ever got way the hell up there, he could only wonder. He whispered familiar words under his breath.

"When Isabelle started hanging out with these alternative types," he asked, "was there anyone she started spending time with? A man, or woman, who she was seeing romantically?"

Lucy blushed at the suggestion. "There was a professor named Alvin Singler. He teaches political theory."

Ash jotted down the name. "What does he look like?"

"Young, for a professor at least. One of the new-age types. Shaggy hair, mustache, doesn't bathe as much as he should."

"So, the same as everybody else in this town?"

Lucy gave him a timid smile. He returned it for a moment before turning away. "What do you know about their relationship?"

She shrugged. "Not much. He has a reputation about relations with students, and I saw her with him around campus a few times before she stopped coming around altogether."

He nodded. "That's very helpful, Ms. Dalton—"

"Lucy."

"Thank you, Lucy."

Ash stubbed out his cigarette and started to leave. She stopped him and said, "There's one more thing, about the time she came into my room that night." He watched as the girl fiddled with her bracelet. "Isabelle had a knife, she tried to use it on herself—her wrists. Luckily, it was a butter knife, and she couldn't do more than scrape up her arms. She told me it was the only way to save her mother from her father."

Ash thanked Lucy again and left. In front of the house, a group of protesters with picket signs stating "Get the Hell Out of Vietnam" and "Peace in People's Park" marched by. Ash followed them.

At People's Park, young men and women passed sod rolls, planted small gardens, and huddled in meditation circles. Others dumped fresh vegetables into a pot of gray, mushy soup that reminded Ash of the gruel they rationed out to the shivering, famished soldiers in Korea. Below a tree, a mustached man in a clown outfit announced himself as the Jolly Savior and recited vulgar parodies of Bible verses as a long-haired woman strummed a guitar at his side.

Ash walked past the clown to a clearing where a more lucid man was standing on a tree stump with a loudspeaker. He was young and had a thick beard and curly hair. Ash approached, close enough to hear, and lit a cigarette to mask the pungent odors. "People's Park," the man said, "represents a new type of society. One that doesn't run on the blood and sweat of working men and women, one that doesn't place profit over humanity. It is a refuge for those of us who see land as something we must share for the good of all." The small crowd of students hummed in agreement. "If we continue to live in harmony, in contrast to the bourgeois ways of our mothers and fathers, our small stake of liberated land will inspire others to follow suit. This refuge represents not what we are, but what we may become."

As Ash continued through the park, he observed other members of the demonstration. Some fit the news's portrayal of hippies with wild beards, drug-fueled erraticism, and tattered clothes. Others, though, were typical college students, young people with spirited gazes who were seeking something that would give them purpose. He thought of the words of his troop commander decades ago: *The only thing scarier than a soldier with a gun is a soldier with an ideology.* He thought of stacks of frozen bodies, makeshift sandbags, their rot delayed only by the cold.

Ash took Telegraph to campus and found Professor Alvin Singler's office, located in Wheeler Hall. When he arrived, the door opened and a young woman in a flowered blouse and jeans scurried out. The investigator knocked on the open door and said, "Professor Singler? I'm Ed Ash, private investigator. Can I have a word?"

The professor leaned back in his chair and kicked his bare feet up on his messy desk. He had a bushy handlebar mustache and bushier eyebrows. Dark, greasy hair hung to his shoulders, and he wore a tattered vest over a loud, pit-stained shirt. Unlike most, who averted their eyes from his face, the professor studied Ash with apparent interest. "Please, come in. What should we have a word about, Mr. Ash?"

Ash closed the door behind him, moved some wayward papers and a copy of Mao's Little Red Book from the seat across from the professor, and sat down. "I'm looking for Isabelle Randolph. She in any of your classes?"

"Oh, my dear Belle," he said, as though reminiscing on a long-lost love. "No, but I had her in my lecture a few semesters ago."

"What lecture was that?"

"Twentieth Century Revolutionary Theory."

"That's where you teach the kids five-dollar words to justify the drugs and orgies?"

His eyebrows extended with delight. "That's the charge I address at faculty meetings."

"When did you—"

"Excuse me, Mr. Ash," he said, removing his feet from the desk and leaning forward. "Would you answer a question of mine first?"

"Go ahead."

"What happened to your face?"

Ash paused before speaking. "It happened in Korea. I took some shrapnel in Incheon, when we moved to take back Seoul. Ended up getting airlifted out and the docs stitched me up best they could."

"They didn't do a bad job."

"They didn't do a good job either."

The professor sighed. "Another casualty of the American war machine. It's a shame since the North Koreans were fighting for nothing more than the right to self-governance. And the politicians sent poor boys like you over as mere cogs in the machine. It's even more troubling that the illusory success in Korea justified the rampant military adventurism and neo-colonialism we're seeing now in Vietnam."

"I didn't come here to talk global politics, Professor. You mentioned that you taught Isabelle Randolph a few semesters ago. Did you have a romantic relationship with her?"

"I had a spiritual relationship with her."

"Did it have a physical component?"

"How do you mean?"

"Did you fuck her?"

The professor's grin was a nervous one now. "There are some students I take a special interest in due to their passion for revolutionary politics. I try to open their minds and help them channel that passion into developing a philosophy of what a better world—one not defined by mindless consumerism and profit-seeking—would look like."

"I'll take that as a yes. When's the last time you saw Isabelle?"

"Oh, weeks, months ago." He paused. "Let me guess, her daddy's trying to track her down before the revolution comes?

Save some face? I don't see Isabelle anymore; she outgrew me. But I learned a thing or two from her when we were close."

"Was she your student when you were having sex with her?"

"Sex to us," he pondered, "is not a matter of conquest. To us, an adult woman is free to seek physical pleasure without the stern admonishment of a phallocentric society. Do you understand?"

"About every fifth word. I get the idea that you go to great lengths to incorporate yourself into the counterculture scene here. Given what you know about Isabelle, where would you expect I could find her?"

"You plan to drag her home to her fascist father?"

"That father can make your life very difficult if I don't give you passing marks."

Ash watched as his words transformed the glazed look in the professor's eyes to fiery passion. "I'm not afraid of Philip Randolph's intimidation tactics. I know a thing or two about him, things that he's done."

Ash thought back to Lucy's description of Isabelle's mother's death. "Like what?"

"It wouldn't be worth much if I go around spouting off about it, would it?" Professor Singler said. "To put it in capitalist terms, the scarcity of the knowledge is what makes it valuable."

"How about this, Professor. I don't give a damn about Vice Chancellor Randolph, but everything I've heard about his daughter suggests that she's a troubled girl running from things she doesn't understand. Everyone feels the tension in this town. I see cops eying protesters like prey; I hear the governor on the radio talking about sending in the troops. If you care about that girl, you'll tell me where I can find her to keep her out of harm's way—understand?"

Professor Singler nodded and chewed on his upper lip. "She was never one for the ideology," he said. "To her, the movement was always an emotive outlet. At bottom, she was scared."

"Her and the rest of us. Where is she?"

"Last I heard she was living in a communal home on the

North Side. It's a hub for the student movement. They have a function tonight to celebrate the takeover of the park."

"A party?"

He grinned. "Like something you've never seen."

On the way to the address that evening Ash stopped at a corner bar called The Tipsy Beaver. It was an old-school spot that was out of place during the hippy revolution. Liquor bottles lined the counter behind the bar in front of a cracked mirror, and dim bar lights cast shadows over the Cal paraphernalia on the walls.

Ash ordered rye, neat. The bartender looked at him sideways when he asked for a straw but nodded as he noticed the investigator's sagging lip. Ash slurped the drink and thought over the conversation with Professor Singler. He considered that the party was a setup, misdirection to throw him off the trail, or worse. He also couldn't shake the thought of the vice chancellor's wife, her accident. Was Randolph so concerned about his daughter's whereabouts only because she knew the truth about what he might have done? Ash examined the picture of Isabelle and reasoned that the sins of her father weren't worth the trouble. Not yet. As he drank, he mumbled a comforting mantra and let the words cleanse his mind.

The sky's turning dark, the hour is late. It's time to drift off, to where dreams await.

The address led Ash to a dilapidated mansion hidden from street view by overgrown bushes. He followed a few students past the gate and through a small garden to a brick staircase. Hanging from the front columns were sheets with antiwar slogans painted on them. At the top of the stairs, a few men and women shared a joint while discussing what a disaster the Nixon presidency would be.

"Hey," said one of the men. He brushed back a floppy mop

of hair as though he cared deeply about appearing not to care. "Can I help you out, man?"

"C'mon, Jerry," said the woman beside him. "All are welcome." She wore a brightly colored poncho and Ash wasn't sure whether there was anything underneath it. She took a long inhale from the joint and coughed skunky smoke into Ash's face. Stepping toward him, she brushed the back of her hand against his scarred face. "You're beautiful," she whispered. "You want a toke?"

"No, thanks. I could go for a drink though."

She grinned, scrunching freckled cheeks. "Follow me."

The shadowed hallway led to an open central room where Jefferson Airplane blared, and projections of colorful kaleidoscopes twisted on the walls. Men and women, lost in the music, minds foreign to bodies, danced and swayed.

"This way," the woman said. She took his hand and led him to a kitchen where there was a large punch bowl that sweaty, half-dressed young people were dipping cups into. She filled two and handed one to Ash. She took a long drink. Ash sniffed it.

"I'm Eden, what's your name?"

"Ash."

She rolled her head around her neck and said, "Don't you trust me, Ash?"

"What is it?"

She leaned in and whispered, "It's freedom from this world." Swollen pupils blackened her eyes.

"Do you know this girl?" Ash asked, raising Isabelle's picture.

The young woman laughed as she raised her arms above her head and swayed. A glance confirmed that there was nothing underneath the poncho; her small, firm breasts peeked out from the side of the garment. She twirled and then nestled close to him. "Have a drink," she said, "and I'll find her for you."

Ash took a small sip. Sweet and earthy. She pushed the cup back and he downed it on instinct.

"You're in for a trip."

Music bled from undulating walls as he journeyed through the house. The main room pulsed with passion and sweat trickled down the smooth scars that traversed his face. Sounds and flashing lights transported him to the icy hills—gunfire piercing the darkness with sharp flashes of light—cracks and whips—an explosion that knocked his head backward. His heart rattled his rib cage, and he dropped his rifle and felt the sticky wetness streaming down his cheeks. Smears of blood stained his ice-cold flesh and screams of drug-fueled jubilation were, at once, hollers from the commanding officer radioing for an airlift. Time disappeared altogether and past and present and future were one.

Ash stumbled outside and the gunfire ceased, and he guzzled air to feed starved lungs. The music was a distant memory, but he felt it reverberate through the caverns of his past. His mind grasped for the words that had kept him safe since he was a boy, but they wouldn't come. Instead, stacks of frozen corpses twitched to the rhythm of synthesizers. He keeled over and vomited into the dirt and watched his sickness nurture the earth.

He sat on the ground and peered through large windows inside at the lights and uninhibited dancers. In the corner of the courtyard, there was a serious conversation about the Vietnam War, and he couldn't make sense of how the two existed in the same plane of being.

There were two women before him but then only one. She smiled at him. He pulled the picture from his pocket and watched her crawl from its corners and become one with the beautiful, dazed woman in front of him. Her figure echoed in the night.

"You—you're—" He inhaled and summoned any remaining coherence in the corner of his mind. "Isabelle Randolph."

She helped him to a bench. "I hear that the man with the broken face is looking for me."

Before he could respond, she pulled him toward her and kissed the scars from his ear to the corner of his lip.

"Isabelle, I'm here to—I ought to keep you safe—"

"Shh," she whispered. "My father, I know. But no one's safe in this world. *Safety* is a construction by people like my father to keep us trapped—keep us from exploring who we are." Her eyes darted in their sockets as though chasing wayward strings of light. "Ask my mother."

"What happened to your mother?"

She held his cheeks in her hands and stared at him in the quivering darkness. "Don't trust men like my father."

Ash tried to keep focus, but imaginary pins prodded his cold, damp hands. "But why—"

"Shh." She kissed him again. "Meet me tomorrow at People's Park." She drifted from the courtyard and disappeared through a sliding door into the aquarium of sin. Guitar chords rang through the night and pierced Ash's eardrums as though the sound emanated from plucked strings of nerves. He did his best to gather himself and follow her, but the ground traded places with the night sky, and the stars throbbed in the heavens below. He reached out to touch one, but it sent a wave of electricity through him. Light and sound and color swirled, and the universe collapsed into its own darkness.

Ash woke to Bobby Randolph sitting on the carpeted floor, staring at him. He peeled open his dry mouth and reached with a trembling hand to the glass of water on the table. It was the same room where he'd met with the vice chancellor the day before.

After downing the water, he said, "How the hell'd I get here?"

"You were talking in your sleep," the boy said.

"It's a habit."

"Something about the sky being dark, and dreams."

"The sky's turning dark, the hour is late. It's time to drift off, to where dreams await," recited the investigator.

"What does it mean?"

Ash kneaded his throbbing head. "You ask a lot of questions."

The boy sat still, as though he'd heard the suggestion before.

"It's a rhyme my mother used to tell me when I was a boy. I had trouble sleeping and she'd sit by me and whisper it until I'd fall asleep. I say it when I'm in a tough spot and my mind gets away from me. It keeps me focused. Did it so much in the war that it got stuck in there."

The boy opened his mouth to respond but, before he could, Vice Chancellor Randolph was at the top of the stairs. "Leave him be, Bobby." The boy took a deep gulp and started down the stairs.

Ash tried to find the right question, but his mind felt like porridge, and he was vaguely disturbed by his return to the material world. The vice chancellor read this and said, "Berkeley PD found you wandering the street on the North Side at two in the morning. Said you didn't make a lick of sense and were jimmying the lock of a coffee shop, insisting it was a portal to the past."

Bits and pieces started coming back to him and Ash questioned which fragments were real. "I tracked a lead on Isabelle to a party at a communal home. Took a drink to blend in but it must've been spiked with LSD. How'd I get here?"

"You were smart enough to name-drop Officer Burrell; I guess he's your buddy. They called him and you did your best to explain things. He phoned my people and I had them bring you here." He paused. "I'm afraid you won't have much time to rest. The radicals are ramping up their efforts to obstruct construction in People's Park. Early this morning, at my recommendation, Governor Reagan sent in the National Guard to push them out, fence off the perimeter, and use whatever force is necessary to maintain order." Lines hung heavy on his tired face, but his eyes were relentless. "There will be violence, Mr. Ash. I need you down there."

"I was with her last night," Ash whispered, speaking thoughts as they returned to his desiccated brain.

"Excuse me?"

"Isabelle—I found her. I tried to follow her, but the drugs

knocked me on my ass. She said—" He looked up and met the vice chancellor's eyes. "She said to meet her at the park."

As he spoke, the housekeeper appeared at the top of the stairs. "Mr. Randolph," she said, "I have Lucy Dalton on the phone. She says it's about Isabelle."

"Let me talk to her," Ash said.

The vice chancellor, his stone face grappling with his decision, nodded.

"Lucy?" Ash said on the downstairs phone. "This is Ash."

"Mr. Ash," she said. "I saw Isabelle."

"Where are you?"

"In Sproul Hall. She's near Sather Gate at the front of the mob marching on People's Park." She took a breath. "The police have tear gas and riot gear..."

"Lucy, you go straight home, you hear me?"

"Of course."

"What's Isabelle wearing?"

"An orange-and-green patterned dress and a headband."

He hung up and, as he turned to leave, saw Bobby standing close behind him. In a hushed voice, the boy said, "The sky's turning dark, the hour is late. It's time to drift off, to where dreams await."

We want the park! We want the park!

Thousands of protesters marched down Telegraph Avenue, chanting, hurling bottles at the officers guarding the perimeter of People's Park. Ash hustled to an alley where he had a view of the approaching mob. Toward the other end of the street, he saw police officers and guardsmen in gas masks loading riot guns with canisters of tear gas. When a brick landed near the front line of the officers, they fired the canisters. As he turned to shield himself, Ash caught a glimpse of Isabelle, fire in her eyes, marching near the front of the advancing masses. The explosion of tear gas canisters filled the streets with a thick haze and chaos engulfed the boulevard.

Ash pulled the shirt from his back and wrapped it around his head, leaving enough to see where he was going. He kept his eyes on Isabelle, who marched on in the face of the melee. Protesters threw bottles and rocks and the officers returned with tear gas and shotgun fire. Someone opened a hydrant on the corner and a powerful surge of water took out officers and protesters alike. Eyes singed, Ash ran toward the girl. Traversing through water and gas and officers beating and dragging limp bodies on hot pavement, he found himself fighting another war—one that had been stalking him since he'd returned home from the last.

As he grabbed her arm and choked—*get down!*—Isabelle's look told Ash that she knew who he was and why he was there. He bent her low and directed her further down Telegraph, past the park. Sidestepping torched vehicles, he turned back and saw a group of officers in riot gear with nightsticks and shotguns pursuing the belligerent crowd. Time slowed as one officer raised his shotgun. Ash stepped behind Isabelle, shielding her, propelling her forward. The staccato of gunfire ripped through the madness and Ash felt the familiar sting of 00 buckshot. Before the world disappeared, her hand slipped from his. He wondered if it had been there at all.

Ash awoke in a room at Alta Bates Medical Center to find his buddy and former platoon mate, Officer Wayne Burrell, smoking a cigarette and reading a dirty magazine.

"What the hell?"

"What?" said Officer Burrell. "The magazines they got here are shit."

"What—am I—"

"Don't worry, Ash; it's 1969. You're not in 1950 Korea anymore." He paused. "Your face is still fucked up though. And between the pellets in your ass and your trip the other night, I hope the vice chancellor is paying you handsomely."

It started to come back to him. "Where's Isabelle? Is she all right?"

"I've been working my ass off trying to track her down, but there's no record in any hospital. No reports of her injury or arrest."

Ash eased up in bed. "You come here to tell me that?"

He leaned in close. "My officers tell me that, when you were drugged-out the other night, you asked questions about the vice chancellor's wife—about her death. Could be nonsense you were spouting on account of the Electric Kool-Aid, but—"

"You know something?"

He grinned. "I got a buddy in Mariposa County who worked on the investigation. Always seemed real bothered by how the powers that be kept things quiet, no hard questions asked."

"You have their report?"

"Probably buried in an old cabinet down at the station. I'll take a look. Come by next week when your ass heals up and this park fiasco dies down. Reagan's got this place on lockdown."

"Thanks, Wayne."

"Don't mention it." He looked down at the busty model on the front of the magazine and tossed it onto the hospital bed. "Enjoy the rest of your stay."

A couple of weeks later, Ash walked through downtown Berkeley toward the police station to pick up the file on Isabelle's mother. People's Park was still fenced off and guarded. Protesters, many of whom had participated in the violence that stained those very streets, marched peacefully, hand in hand, past the barricades.

Ash watched from a distance and wondered if the lines of demarcation facilitated peace or propagated violence. It wasn't so simple. Whether it was a war or a revolution or a missing girl, nothing was ever truly simple. In all that he'd seen, he felt an urge to conclude that abstract notions of *right* and *good* and *true* didn't exist at all. But he sensed that this, too, was misguided. The elusive nature of goodness did not render it nonexistent.

He lit a cigarette, slid it to the good side of his mouth, and watched as young women placed flowers in the barbed wire fencing. One girl looked familiar, as though from a not-too-distant dream. He whispered a mantra under his breath as she disappeared back into the crowd.

WE ARE THE STONEWALL GIRLS
Joseph S. Walker

When I was a kid, my uncle Max, a private detective with his own firm in Manhattan, was the toughest, smartest, bravest man on the planet. Once or twice a month he would visit to sit on the back porch, drinking beer and telling me about crooks he'd caught and crimes he'd solved. He let me wear his snap-brim fedora and look at, but not touch, the .45 he carried in a shoulder rig.

My mother stayed in the kitchen while we talked. The fact she didn't fully approve of Max only made him more fascinating. She never tried to stop her late husband's brother from visiting, though. "It's hard for a boy, having just a mother," she told one of her friends on the phone late one night. I'd taken to eavesdropping when she thought I was asleep, practice for my own career as a gumshoe. "Neil needs to be around men sometimes."

After high school, following Max's advice, I went into the Army. To my mother's overwhelming relief, I was not sent to Vietnam. I served three years, mostly in Germany and mostly as an MP, in the meantime earning an accounting degree. Max said a good PI needed to be able to follow the money. As soon as I got out, I joined Max's firm. For the next four years I lived my childhood dream, playing Robin to his Batman. The day I turned twenty-five, we went downtown, and he watched me receive my own PI license.

Not long afterwards, Uncle Max unexpectedly dropped by my apartment one night and discovered that I liked to be around men in other ways. Heading out the door, unable to look at me or the naked stranger in my bed, he told me I was fired.

On a Friday in June, a little over a year later, I walked into Sandy's, a bar in Greenwich Village. It was the hottest day 1969 had yet produced, the streets and sidewalks blistering stovetops under a white sun. At least I didn't have to follow Uncle Max's strict dress code anymore. Jeans and a T-shirt were misery enough; a coat and tie would have been torture.

Sandy's was a long, dim room with fans stirring the humid air. A few people hunched at the bar. One man sat alone at a table in the back. He stood as I approached, holding out his hand. "Mr. Fell? I'm Frank Grierson. I took the liberty of ordering you a beer."

Grierson looked to be in his mid-fifties. He had a thinning head of salt-and-pepper hair, a hint of a paunch, and the most open face I had ever seen, a face that promised honesty and asked the same. I shook his hand and sat. "Thanks, Mr. Grierson. Call me Neil."

"Neil," he said, sitting himself. "And I'm Frank, please." He had his own beer, and he took a long drink. "This heat is unbearable."

"Brutal." The fact he hadn't immediately commented on how young I was earned Frank a couple of points. "How can I help you?"

He took a deep breath. "I only hope you can. I've been to the police, and some of the larger agencies. None of them wanted anything to do with me after I explained the situation. Some of them were frankly abusive. They made the most obscene assumptions.

When I couldn't think of anything else to do, I went to the Mattachine Society. A young man there gave me your card."

The Mattachine Society advocated for the rights of homosexual men. In recent years, its New York chapter had gotten more visible and strident, organizing demonstrations and media events. A friend working there had a stack of my "Discreet Investigations" cards to hand out if the chance arose. Uncle Max hadn't just fired me. He'd spread the word to other firms, making me too radioactive to hire. To keep working as a PI, which was the only thing I wanted to do, I looked for clients among the gay men and lesbians who were also unwelcome in their offices. The problem was that many of them were poor, and the ones who weren't associated private eyes with blackmail and public exposure. I was getting one or two cases a month, barely making ends meet with odd jobs and security shifts.

Frank was my first potential client in weeks. Looking at him, I guessed what was coming. His lover had vanished off the face of the earth. I would find the guy living on Long Island with a wife, two and a half kids, and an Irish setter.

"Whatever you have to say will be between the two of us," I said.

Frank rolled the glass between his palms. "What do you know about the boys who hang out in Christopher Park?"

So much for my powers of prognostication. "You mean the hustlers?"

"You could call them that," Frank said. "They'd more likely call themselves queens."

I held up a hand. "I'm not here to judge, Mr. Grierson, but if you're involved with one of those boys, I can't help you. It would cost me my license, and we could both end up in jail."

A flash of irritation crossed Frank's face. "That's just what the police and the other detectives thought," he said. "Nobody will hear the truth. They all want this to be something dirty."

"I'll hear you out. That's all I can promise."

He closed his eyes a moment, getting ready to tell a story he'd already tried to tell many times. "I live just around the corner from the park, in a brownstone on Washington. I could move, but I like the Village."

"What do you do?"

"Nothing. Twenty years ago, I invented a gadget that allowed General Electric to make light bulbs a little bit cheaper. I get a fraction of a penny every time they sell a bulb." He took a drink. "They sell a lot of bulbs. My days are mine. I read, write letters, go to museums. I suppose it's a useless way to live, but it suits me."

"All right. Go on."

"Every day I walk my dog, Pokey, and we go through the park. The boys are almost always there. I should say, Neil, that I am not gay. I have no moral objection to homosexuality, but no part of me is attracted to these boys. I'm just interested in them, as individuals. Almost nobody is. People are either afraid of them, or they use them. And of course, they put up such a front. All of them, not just the ones who wear women's clothes or shoes or makeup, which most of them do, at least sometimes. They act fierce and fearless and what they think of as sexy, which is mostly a kind of bitchy attitude they take from old movies. Everything they do is a performance. They make it impossible to really know them."

"But you do."

Frank smiled. "It was Pokey. A few of them started asking if they could pet him or walk him around the park themselves. They kneel beside him, the tough street hustler disappears, and it's just a boy and a dog. Some of them cry. I started sitting on a bench for an hour or two each day. Once they realized I wasn't trying to score, they would talk with me. Neil, you have no conception of how difficult their lives are."

"Probably not."

"Most of them were kicked out of their homes or ran away from some form of abuse. They sleep on the streets, as often as not. They're always hungry. Many of them are hooked on pills.

The police harass them, johns beat them, random people on the street spit at them or rob them. Most of them carry knives, but really, they're just frightened children in a world that doesn't have a place for them. I try to help."

"How?"

"Carefully. If they knew how much money I have, they'd be like a plague of locusts. I'll buy them meals. Pay for a flophouse room on a cold night. A few of them have told me their real names and where they're from, and I write their families to try to arrange a reconciliation. It generally doesn't work. Mostly, I just listen."

"All right, let's say I accept all that. What is it you need help with?"

Frank's grip on his glass tightened. "A few months ago, a new boy started hanging out in the park. I don't know his real name. He calls himself Alice. I think he's a little older than most of them, but he's very short, very slender. He has delicate features and long blond hair. I doubt he can afford hormone treatments—almost none of them can—but he's much more convincing than most of them at being a girl. He wears a dress sometimes. Did you know there's a law in this city that you can be arrested if you're not wearing three items of clothing that are, and I quote, appropriate to your gender?"

"Yes," I said. "It's so they can hassle people who might scare the tourists."

"I've seen Alice arrested twice for that. I had many long talks with him." He paused. "I suppose Alice would want me to say I had many long talks with *her*. She told me she was from Ohio, but she would never say anything else about her past, or how she got to New York. She could be as ferocious as any of them, as nasty, but there was more to her. She showed me poems she wrote, and I'm no expert, but I think they were good."

He smiled at the thought, then his expression turned grim. "The thing is, I haven't seen her in more than a week. Of course, they come and go all the time. You could guess she's sick, or that she got picked up on some more serious charge. But I think something else happened."

"And what's that?"

He rubbed his jaw. "Do you know the name Tony Duke?"

I sat back, surprised. "I do."

"What do you know about him?"

"I've seen him a few times. He works the door at the Stonewall Inn, which means he's connected. Almost all the gay bars in the city are run by the Mafia."

Frank nodded. "That's my understanding. I don't really know why."

"Legitimate business owners don't want to deal with raids and protests. Plus, gays are a captive audience. You can water down their drinks and treat them like shit. Where are they going to go? Another bar you own?"

"I'm sure that's all true," Frank said. "But the queens love the Stonewall. They tell me it's the only place in the city that allows men to dance with each other. The only place they can be themselves."

I didn't tell him I'd been on that dance floor a few times myself. The Stonewall was an absolute shithole, with no running water, no fire exits, filthy bathrooms, and staff that could be hostile. Police raids were common, though it was an open secret that the owners funneled hundreds of dollars a week into the local precinct to keep the raids brief. But I could understand the release that dark, cramped, exuberant space would offer to boys living the kinds of lives Frank had described. "The Stonewall has its good points," I said. "Tony Duke isn't one of them. He's a nasty piece of work. He likes hurting people who get out of line, and he decides what constitutes being out of line. And I've heard that he's blackmailed more than one customer. Some poor clown from Wall Street works up the courage to go to a place like the Stonewall. Next week Duke is in his office, saying what a shame it would be if his boss found out."

"I don't doubt it," Frank said. "He's also what the queens

call a chicken hawk. You understand the term?"

I nodded.

"About a month ago Alice started complaining about Duke. She said he was obsessed with her. He wouldn't leave her alone when she was in the bar. A couple of times he got her in a corner and started groping her. When she stopped going there, he started going to the park during the day, looking for her. He showed up once when she was talking to me. As soon as Alice saw him, she took off running. He went after her. She got away from him, but she was terrified. A few days later she was gone."

"Maybe she's just avoiding him." I was following Frank's lead in referring to Alice as *she*. It seemed to fit. "The park is right across the street from the Stonewall."

"Maybe," Frank said. "But I've talked to the other boys, and none of them have seen her either. She might be in jail or the hospital. Maybe she left the city. But I have an ugly feeling Duke is involved."

"You couldn't get the police interested?"

Frank made a bitter noise. "Of course not. I don't even know Alice's real name. I don't believe Tony Duke is a birth name either, do you?"

"Probably not."

"The policeman and detectives I talked to clearly believed I was infatuated with Alice and trying to get her away from a new boyfriend. I assure you, Neil, I have no romantic or sexual feelings for that poor child. I just want to know she's all right." Frank pulled out a roll of twenties. He counted out ten of them on the table between us. It was more money than I'd seen in months. "Will you try to find out?"

Back in the closet-sized room I was subletting, with the unfamiliar feeling of cash in my pocket, I stretched out on a bare mattress and thought. The obvious play was to surveil Duke's place, maybe even search it if I saw a chance, but I had no idea where he lived, and, thanks to Max, nobody who could find out was talking to me.

At six I had a security shift at a warehouse at the edge of the Village, one of the temp jobs keeping me afloat. At two in the morning, when it was over, I could go wait outside the Stonewall. Sooner or later Duke would come out and I could follow him.

Hell of a plan. Neil Fell, supersleuth.

I needed some sleep to be ready for a long night. Between thinking about Alice and the sweltering heat, rest refused to come. After half an hour I surrendered. I went to the shared phone in the hallway and dialed a number I didn't have to look up.

"Fell Investigations."

"Hi, Sophia," I said. "Can I talk to Max?"

Her voice dropped to a whisper. "Sorry, kid. He's not in."

"You mean not in for me."

"Have a good day, Neil. Take care of yourself."

She hung up. We'd been having the same conversation two or three times a week for a year now. I couldn't blame her for being bored with it.

By two on Saturday morning, the temperature had dropped a tenth of a degree or so. Before I was halfway to the Stonewall, my shirt was sticking to the layer of sweat on my back. New York gets ugly in that kind of heat. The streets were busy for that time of night, full of people wandering the sidewalks or sitting on steps, looking for the chance to put a finger in someone's chest and get something started.

I turned onto Christopher. A block ahead, the street between the Stonewall and the sliver of green space the city called Christopher Park was dense with milling knots of people. Their attention was focused on the bar side of the street, where a police patrol wagon was parked with a couple of cruisers. I slowed, scanning the crowd, trying to get a sense of what was going on.

A shirtless man in bell-bottoms came past me from the direction of the park. He banged two pieces of scrap lumber together, his head back, yelling to the sky. "Wake up, Village! Wake up, people! The revolution has come!"

Five or six men stood on the stoop of the building next door to the Stonewall. I recognized one of them, a college kid named Terry who clerked at the Oscar Wilde, the city's first gay bookshop. I climbed the steps and worked over to him. "Terry," I said. "What's going on?"

Terry was normally one of the most placid people I knew, but his jaw was set, and he was so tense that the muscles in his shoulders bulged against the fabric of his shirt. "Raid, man. There're a dozen pigs in the Stonewall. They just turned me loose."

"This time of night?" The payoffs the local precinct collected from the Stonewall's owners meant that raids usually happened soon after opening, allowing employees to be bailed out and confiscated liquor to be replaced before the profitable hours.

"Some inspector has a bug up his ass," Terry said. "They're letting people go a few at a time, deciding who to bust."

The crowd in the street was growing, people drawn in by the sense of something happening. Most were young and male. A solid half circle was forming around the police vehicles, edging in closer, receding a bit, then advancing a little more. The cops standing by the wagon had their nightsticks out. "Usually everybody just slinks away," I said.

"People are pissed," Terry said. "It's the second raid this week." He raised his voice to a shout. "Faggots pay taxes too, motherfuckers!"

I didn't see Tony Duke. If he was still inside, he was probably going to be spending the night behind bars, which didn't do me any good. I was about to ask Terry if he'd seen Duke when the door to the Stonewall opened and half a dozen kids came out. They were probably some of the street hustlers Frank Grierson knew, hovering on the boundary between adolescence and adulthood and finding their own edge between the sexes. A few were wearing blouses and wigs, and two carried purses. All wore makeup. They seemed taken aback by the crowd but recovered quickly. The tallest of them, a Puerto Rican with thick red lipstick, raised his hands above his head and strutted past the cops, twitching his ass. "Lily Law, you jealous of the queens!" he crowed. "You only wish you looked this good!"

The crowd whistled and applauded. The other queens followed his lead, sashaying and twirling their way into the pack. The last and smallest did a spin directly in front of one of the cops, ending by blowing a kiss in his face. The cop spat, put the tip of his nightstick against the boy's chest, and shoved him hard back into the waiting throng.

A low rumble of anger worked its way through the crowd. Before anything more could happen, the Stonewall door opened again. Six cops came out, leading between them five of the bar's employees. The fourth in line was Tony Duke, a stocky fireplug of a man, with a thick mustache and gray coming in at his temples. His face was twisted in a scowl.

At the sight of them, the crowd erupted in heated booing. "Lock those Mafia assholes up!" yelled somebody on the stoop just below me. Terry stepped up to the top step and raised both his fists. "Gay power!" he bellowed, in a voice I wouldn't have thought he could muster. A few people nearby took it up, and soon much of the crowd was chanting it, pumping their fists. "Gay power! Gay power!"

I couldn't tell if the cops or the Mafia members looked more alarmed. The cops began pushing Duke and the others into the patrol wagon. The young transvestite who had been shoved with a nightstick jumped forward, swinging his purse into the burly back of the cop who'd done it. The crowd cheered him on. The cop turned and raised his nightstick, but at that moment everybody in the street was distracted by a screech of rage that must have been heard blocks away.

"Jesus," Terry said reverently. "Look at that dyke fight."

Four cops had carried a woman out of the Stonewall. She

was a big woman with close-cropped hair, wearing jeans and a plaid shirt with most of the sleeves cut away. Even with a cop firmly clamped onto each arm and leg, she was writhing and twisting with everything she had, alternating piercing screams with furious curses. The cops fought her to a cruiser and shoved her into the back seat, one of them catching a kick straight to the face and falling back. They didn't realize that the door on the other side of the car was open. The woman popped out into the arms of two cops who had come running from the wagon. They tried to push her back toward the car and she swung her elbow viciously into one of their jaws. She looked out into the mob and yelled, "Why don't you guys *do something?*"

That was when the first bottle came arcing up into the air from somewhere in the middle of the street and bounced off the head of one of the cops. He stumbled backward, more surprised than hurt. Two more followed. Then, as if the woman's yell was a signal they'd been waiting for, the air was filled with bottles, rocks, and coins, showering down on the knot of cops near the vehicles. The crowd surged forward. Dozens of them surrounded the wagon and began rocking it back and forth.

All the cops in the street pulled into a circle, nightsticks waving, and retreated toward the heavy doors of the Stonewall. "Get that wagon out of here!" one of them yelled. The door in the side of the wagon was still open and the prisoners who had been shoved inside began tumbling out, into the frenzied crowd. Duke was among them. He stumbled, righted himself, and tried to push through in the direction of the park. I craned my neck, keeping him in sight as the street erupted into chaos. The wagon rumbled to life and began to move, people in front of it slowly making way as the last of the cops slipped inside the Stonewall, the big black door closing behind him. I knew the doors were heavy and well barred, and the windows to either side of it were covered in thick plywood and robustly braced. Barriers designed to slow cops down might save some cops' lives tonight. Fists and bottles battered against them, incoherent shouts of rage drowning out the stalwarts continuing with "gay power."

I turned back to the street and spotted Duke, holding his forearms up around his face and swaying back and forth like a boxer being pummeled. He stumbled forward as he reached the edge of the park. After a few feet, he collapsed onto a patch of grass.

I pushed my way down the stairs and into the street. In Germany, I was assigned to security at a Berlin Wall demonstration after the East Germans killed two people trying to cross. The anger and sorrow were palpable, but the protesters were orderly, their chants and signs directed at the indifferent concrete. This was nothing like that. Everyone seemed wild with fury, but at the same time joyful. I heard a lot of laughter along with the yells and the sound of approaching sirens. A knot of men pushed past, holding above their heads a parking meter that had been wrenched out of the ground. "Set fire to it!" somebody near me yelled. "Smoke the pigs out!"

I wanted to join them. I wanted to beat my fists against the doors. I imagined the cops inside, in the dark, listening to the fury outside, nervously resting their hands on their guns, wondering when the faggots had gotten so bold. It didn't matter that I'd been a kind of cop myself, that I'd wanted to be a crimefighter since I was born. The things cops did in the Stonewall had nothing to do with fighting crime.

The door boomed as the parking meter became a battering ram. I was stepping back toward the bar when I caught a glimpse of one of the street queens and thought of Alice. I turned myself around.

Tony Duke was still half sprawled on the grass in a patch of shadow, staring at the scene in the street. I crouched against a tree a dozen feet behind him.

The patrol wagon was gone. All along the block, people in upper windows looked down at what was happening. The crowd filled the street, fists pumping in the air, the "gay power" chant again going full force. A thin line of smoke was rising into the air from somewhere near the bar. A cab that had been trying to drive down the street had pulled over to the curb and the driver was slunk down low in his seat, unable to move. Tony Duke sat, watching the assault on his bar, and I wiped my hand across my forehead, slick with sweat, and watched him.

A line of cops came around the corner. They were wearing helmets and heavy vests, and they carried truncheons and had shotguns slung over their backs. The Tactical Patrol Force. They paused, forming a phalanx that stretched most of the way across Christopher Street, then began to advance slowly. As they came within reach of people, they began swinging their weapons. A boy who looked no more than fifteen fell, blood coating his face. Someone behind the line had a bullhorn. "Clear the streets! *Clear the streets!*"

Clumps of people broke and ran, some into the park, others directly away from the cops. Across the street, Terry and the people with him backed as deeply as they could into the doorway at the top of the stoop. Tony Duke pushed himself to his feet. I stood, getting ready to follow him.

In the middle of the cleared space, a few dozen feet in front of the TPF line, a dozen street queens stood in a group. I recognized the tall Puerto Rican who taunted "Lily Law," and the girl who hit a cop with her purse. In the harsh light of the streetlamps, they looked terrifyingly young and delicate, the biggest surely no more than one hundred twenty pounds. I waited for them to flee as the phalanx grew closer. Instead, they formed their own line, faced the oncoming cops, put their arms around each other's shoulders, and began a kick line, singing as loudly as they could.

We are the Stonewall girls!
We wear our hair in curls!
We don't wear underwear!
We show our pubic hair!

The cops stopped, looking at each other. The street queens started the chant again, their coordination getting better as they kicked their feet energetically into the air. One of the cops shook his head angrily and moved forward again, the others falling into step. The queens stood their ground until the cops were four or five feet away, then broke, scattering into the park or around the corner.

I could almost hear the cops sigh in relief, walking forward more quickly. They had just reached the door of the Stonewall when they became aware that the street was refilling behind them. The queens had run around the block and now, an even larger group, they faced the back of the TPF, remade their formation and began kicking. *We are the Stonewall girls!*

The cops spun with the air of an irritated bull being goaded. A couple broke ranks and charged the kick line, but, weighed down by their gear, they were left behind as the queens again scattered.

Another ragged group had returned to the corner the TPF line had originally been advancing upon. They began hurling rocks and bricks. Some of the cops turned back in that direction, others setting off to chase the elusive queens. The line was broken, to bursts of applause from some of the windows above.

Tony Duke shook his head, evidently disgusted. He walked across the park, away from the bar, passing within a few feet of me. I wanted to see how many times the queens could pull off their daring taunts, but again I thought of Alice. I let Duke get twenty feet ahead of me before I followed him. He stumbled frequently as he walked, rubbing the side of his head. I wondered if it was a cop who tagged him, or a Stonewall patron seizing a chance at revenge. Duke wouldn't have many friends on either side.

There were still a lot of people on the streets, many running to or from the shouts and sirens in front of the Stonewall. After a block, two police cruisers passed us, and a man walking on the other side of the street picked up a rock and hurled it at them. Duke paid no attention. He never looked around or up, focusing on his feet. I closed to ten feet behind him.

We'd gone three blocks when he climbed the steps of an apartment building and used a key on the front door. I hustled up and caught it before it could close. Duke still took no notice of me. Up close, I saw a ragged, bloody tear just behind his left ear. He went up the half flight of stairs just inside the building. A corridor ran toward the rear. Duke stopped at the second door on the left, apartment 2C. He was putting the key into the lock when I came up behind him, took his left arm, and twisted it up between his shoulder blades in a way that would send pain shooting from his wrist to his shoulder. Control grips are one of the first things they teach MPs.

"Inside or I break it," I said into his ear. He grunted, turned the key, and I pushed him through into the apartment, kicking the door closed behind me. Duke tried to break away. I kept up the pressure on his arm as I clamped my right forearm across his windpipe and squeezed. He clawed at the arm and then tried to reach around for my eyes, but he was already weak from the head wound. All I had to do was wait, thinking about the time I saw him break a glass against the head of a dancer at the Stonewall and break into laughter. After thirty seconds his arm dropped to his side. I gave him another thirty without air and eased him to the floor. He was breathing, but it would be a while before he did anything else.

We were in a dirty room with a few chairs, a couch, and a TV on a rickety stand. There was a small kitchen to the right. I went to the door in front of me and turned on the light. A naked man was stretched out on the bed. He was young and slightly built and so thin I could count his ribs. He had long blond hair and there were ugly purple bruises on his face and torso. His right arm was stretched up over his head and handcuffed to the metal frame.

I shook his shoulder. "Alice?" He stirred, his eyes flickering, but then lapsed back into stillness. I lifted one of his eyelids and saw a dilated pupil. I couldn't begin to guess what he'd been given to keep him quiet while Duke was out.

I returned to the outer room, reached for the wall phone, and hesitated. The cops in this precinct were busy and poorly disposed toward gays. I tried to imagine an explanation for Alice's state and Duke's injuries that didn't end with me spending the next few days as a guest of the city.

Duke's key ring was on the floor near his feet, a handcuff key on it. I unlocked Alice and then dragged Duke into the kitchen and cuffed his right hand to the refrigerator's door handle.

By the time I returned to the bedroom, Alice had turned onto her side and was weakly pawing at the mattress. I dug through Duke's closet hoping for a trench coat, but that wasn't his style. I managed to get Alice into a pair of shorts and wrapped a belt around her so they would stay up. I had to cut a new hole in the belt to get it tight enough. The shirt I put on her hung like a circus tent, and I had to loop the laces of Duke's tennis shoes around her ankles to be sure they would stay on. The whole time I was dressing Alice, she mumbled incoherently and tried to push me away.

There was no force to her at all.

"Okay, Alice," I said finally. "Let's give this a try." I lifted her to her feet. She swayed and would have fallen, but I wrapped my arm around her and waited. In a moment she stabilized. Her eyes flickered. I walked forward and she came along beside me. I was carrying her more than leading her, but I thought that to anybody who saw us, we'd just look like a drunk and a helpful friend.

I glanced at Duke as we went through the outer room. He hadn't moved, and I didn't care.

The four blocks to Frank Grierson's brownstone took us a little over half an hour. It was just past four in the morning when I leaned on his doorbell. I stayed on it until lights came on in the windows above. A minute later the door cracked open, and Grierson peered out underneath a security chain.

"Oh my," he said. The door closed and then opened all the way. "Come in, come in."

I was tired of half dragging Alice. I got one arm under her

knees and one under her shoulders, picked her up, and went in.

"There's a guest bedroom," Frank said. "It's the next flight up."

"Lead the way."

He started up the stairs. "What's wrong with her?"

"She's been beaten. He's got her on something, probably a heavy sedative."

Frank didn't say anything more. We went into the bedroom, and I set Alice in the middle of a heavy four poster. Frank hovered. "Should we call the police?"

"Do you think you'd have any more luck explaining this than you did before?"

"No," he said. "My sister is a nurse. She lives uptown. I'll call her."

"Good."

Frank went to the phone. I went into the hall to look down the stairs and be certain the front door was closed. There was a big soft couch out there. I sat, then stretched out, and that's the last thing I remember for a while.

Frank woke me a little after nine. He made a shushing gesture and led me downstairs to his kitchen, where he had eggs and bacon ready. I dug in gratefully.

"Joyce says that Alice should be all right," he told me. "The bruises are bad, but nothing is broken. She ate a little and she's sleeping off whatever he gave her. Of course, we don't know what the last several days were like for her."

"We can imagine," I said.

"Imagining isn't the same," Frank said.

The morning *Times* was on the table, and I glanced over the front page. Nothing about what had happened in the Village a few hours earlier. Maybe in the afternoon edition. The Mets and Yankees had both lost. NASA's final rocket tests had been successful. In a few weeks, men would be walking on the moon.

Maybe they'd like things better there.

"What will you do with her now?" I asked.

Frank was fussing with the dishes. He sat down. "She can stay here while she recovers," he said. "After that I don't know. Am I correct in assuming Tony Duke is still alive?"

"He's probably pretty pissed off," I said, "but he's not dead."

"Are you worried he'll come after you?"

"I've got no reason to think he knows who I am. He probably didn't even get a good look at me. But Alice he knows. She should leave the city when she can."

"I can help her with that," he said. "Do you want to stay until she's awake? I'm sure she'd like to thank you."

"I've got something I need to go do. But I'll check in with you soon."

When I was a kid, I thought my uncle Max was the bravest person on the planet. That was before I saw the Stonewall Girls singing about their pubic hair to fully armed riot police.

I went back to my place long enough to take a quick shower and grab clean clothes. I caught a bus to the Upper West Side, where Max had his office and, on the next block over, his apartment. He'd be in one or the other. I'd been avoiding the entire neighborhood for a year, but that was over. Today was the day he was going to either give me my job back or look me in the eye and tell me why not. Today was the day to find out how brave we both really were.

REVIVAL

John McFetridge

The American was in his thirties at least, looked like he wanted to get his hair cut. He said to me, "I bet you're glad you're not over there."

"Vietnam? I would be if I was American."

"It's easy to get out of."

"Easy to get out of the draft?"

"Yeah, easy. All you have to do is lie."

I thought, well there you go, but I didn't say anything.

Rodney, the guy I worked for and the one who set up this meeting, said, "If your man's in Toronto, Billy can find him."

The American said, "He's here."

"And you want to take him back," I said, "and show him how to lie to get out the draft?"

"We want to put him in prison for making bombs."

"That's what he does?"

"And he sets them off. In the last four months eight bombs have gone off in New York City alone. General Motors building, Standard Oil, Chase Manhattan bank."

I said, "You sure it's a radical? Could be a disgruntled customer."

The American took a photostat out of his briefcase, laid it on the desk, and said, "A letter they sent to the *New York Times*."

It was typed. The first sentence was, "The Establishment is in

243

for some big surprises if it thinks that kangaroo courts and death sentences can arrest a revolution." That's all I read. I said, "And the guy you're looking for is one of this gang?"

"Robert 'Bobby' Williamson, though he isn't using that name, of course. We don't know what name he's using."

"Doesn't matter," Rodney said. "Billy can find him. He finds kids all the time, isn't that right?"

I didn't like working for Rodney and I was sure as shit not going to do a sales job for his lame private eye racket. But I still had a possession with intent to traffic charge hanging over me, and Rodney may have been an ex-cop, but his partner was the still-working arresting officer, so I did what I had to do. "It's usually kids from small towns come to the big city looking for the hippie scene," I said, "and we find them." Their parents file missing persons reports, and the cops don't do anything. Rodney's partner, Sergeant Graham McCaskill, suggests they hire the M&P agency, and they never find out he's the M.

Rodney said, "We know the scene."

"I heard you're a regular *Mod Squad*."

"Not a squad," I said. "Just me."

The American took a photograph out of his briefcase and put it on top of the *New York Times* letter. "Bobby Williamson. Date of birth: September 25, 1947. Six feet tall, a hundred and seventy-five pounds. You can probably draw long hair and a scraggly beard on this to see what he looks like now." He looked up from the picture to me and said, "Or look in a mirror."

"He's in the Army?"

"He was. He's a deserter." He looked sideways at Rodney and said, "And now you guys let them in just like you let in draft dodgers."

"We do?"

"It was in the papers," I said. "Immigration isn't allowed to ask about military status."

"As of May of this year," the American said.

He looked like he was going to start a rant, so I said, "Have you got any idea where he is at all? Anyone he knows here? Any relatives or Army buddies or anything?"

"Nope."

"You must have informants in the anti-draft office, those guys on Baldwin Street, they have anything?"

Again, he looked at Rodney but not upset this time. "We don't have any operations in Canada. Everything is done through official channels."

Rodney said, "Which is why we're doing this."

I thought, well yeah, and we're being paid, but I didn't say anything.

The American said, "He's somewhere in Toronto, he's probably made a connection with the anti-draft bunch, that's a good place to start."

Rodney said, "Billy knows what he's doing."

"He better," the American said. "This guy is dangerous, and we need to find him pronto."

Rodney said, "How dangerous?"

"Just locate him, find out where he's staying, and call us." He looked at me and said, "Do not, under any circumstances, engage with him."

"That would cost you extra anyway." I picked up the photo, which looked like his military ID photo. It was true: put long hair on him and he looked like half a million guys at Woodstock. There were a few scars on his forehead, but they were faded and seemed a lot older than his draft notice. I said, "Was he in a car accident?"

"When he was a kid," the American said. "Probably when his brain got scrambled."

"You'd think that would be something the Army noticed before they taught him to make bombs."

"We're a little shorthanded," the American said, "with all these guys coming up here and all." He stood and said, "Call us as soon as you locate him. He is very dangerous." He walked out of the office.

Rodney turned to me. "You got a lot to learn about customer relations, kid."

"You believe him?"

"What do you mean?"

"That they don't have any operations in town?"

Rodney shrugged and said, "I don't know, and I don't care. McCaskill says they probably screwed up; they were supposed to be watching him and they lost him. They're desperate."

"And McCaskill saw a way to make a few bucks."

"They have it to spend. You know what they say about the Americans: over-sexed, over-paid, and over-here."

I said, "What?"

"Ask your father," Rodney said. "It's from the war. The real war, the one we were in."

I said I'd do that and picked up the photograph, the letter, and a few more pages the American had left for us. But I hadn't spoken to my father in a couple years and didn't plan to anytime soon.

The offices of Bartlett Promotions were in an old house just off the campus of the University of Toronto in the heart of the city. A short drive from M&P's offices down by police headquarters. I parked my Beetle and even put a dime in the meter. I was on an expense account.

There wasn't anything as formal as a receptionist, just a big open room and a bunch of desks, each one staffed by a young person talking on a telephone. I saw Robin at the same time she saw me, and she stood up and walked over quickly, saying, "What are you doing here?"

"He's not still mad at me, is he?"

"He's always going to be mad at you. What do you want?"

The walls of the office were covered in posters for rock bands that Johnny Bartlett had booked into the Rockpile: The Who, The Doors, John Mayall, Arthur Brown, Mothers of Invention,

Chuck Berry, Howlin' Wolf.

Robin pointed at a poster, a drawing of an air balloon with Led Zeppelin written on it and Edward Bear written on a flag dragging behind. "You should have been there. It was a great show."

"If it had been the Yardbirds maybe."

"Come on, buy me a coffee." She pushed open the door and I followed her out into the bright fall sunshine. The street was full of students still trying to figure out which building their classes were in. We walked half a block to a coffee shop and went inside.

The small shop had most of the same posters on the wall that Bartlett Promotions did and a few more for Hare Krishna meetings and some for folk singers and antiwar demonstrations.

Robin lit a cigarette and said, "So, who are you looking for now?"

"What makes you think I'm looking for someone?"

She made a face, tilted her head a little, exhaled smoke out of the side of her mouth.

"Hey, I wish I had a choice."

She said, "You have a choice," and it was my turn to make a face. She said, "All right, looking for runaway kids is better than being a snitch for a crooked cop."

"You could just say cop."

"Too bad he makes the big bucks, and you just get the crumbs."

I took the photo of Bobby Williamson out of my pocket and put it on the table.

Robin said, "This isn't some kid."

"He's a deserter."

She picked up the picture and said, "So they say."

"What's the name of that firebug, the guy who always wants to put on fireworks at the shows? Carl something, isn't it?" One of my stints in the Don Jail overlapped with one of his but I didn't really remember him beyond the fact he wanted to blow things up.

Robin took a drag on her smoke and said, "Carl Franklin."

"He had some dynamite, didn't he?"

Robin said, "I think he was selling that to some FLQ guys."

"Any idea where he is?"

"He was in the office yesterday. He's in the Vagabonds."

The motorcycle gang. I'd run into them a few times, usually at bars and coffee houses selling their shitty hash and speed. I said, "Why were the Vagabonds in the office?"

Robin leaned in and said, "Ticket sales are slow."

"They don't usually pay for tickets."

"Johnny put up a lot of money for this, he wants it to be big, huge, the best festival."

I said, "He knows Woodstock was a month ago, right?"

"He's thinking big, he's trying to make it historic, that's why he's calling it the Rock 'n' Roll Revival, like a religious thing. He's bringing the old and the new together, trying to bridge the generation gap. He's got Chuck Berry and Little Richard and Jerry Lee Lewis and Bo Diddley and Gene Vincent."

"Be bop a lula. Who's he got for new?"

"The Doors, Chicago, Alice Cooper."

"Who's she?"

"Not a she. That's the band's name, they're good."

"That's not much new."

"That's why he's getting Lennon."

"John Lennon?"

Robin took another drag on the smoke and let it out slow. "He told Vinnie it was for sure."

"He said he's getting the Beatles?"

"No," she said, "just Lennon."

"So, the Beatles are breaking up?"

"No way." She shook her head. "Lennon said he might do it and Johnny's put everything he's got on it. And more."

I said, "He took money from the Vagabonds?"

Robin took a last drag and stubbed out her smoke in the ashtray on the little table. "Lennon said he'd bring Eric Clapton."

Johnny Bartlett was a huckster like every other music promoter, but I didn't think he was crazy enough to borrow money from the Vagabonds.

I said, "Is Carl Franklin the sergeant at arms?"

Robin said, "I don't know, but I bet if you need to make a bomb, he could hook you up."

"My kind of people."

We stood up and walked out of the coffee house, and on the street, Robin said to me, "Why don't you just admit you like it?"

"Like what?"

"Playing private eye."

"I'm not playing."

She shook her head and gave me a quick hug. "If you need a ticket let me know, the Toronto Rock 'n' Roll Revival is going to be big."

The Vagabonds had a clubhouse on Gerrard in the east end. The houses on either side had been turned into businesses, a plumbing supply store and an appliance repair shop. When I pulled up in front in my Beetle, I could smell the barbecue, and I figured the neighbors would all tell me what great guys the Vagabonds were, always helping out and inviting people over for burgers and hot dogs.

As I walked up to the front door it opened. Vinnie stepped out and saw me. Didn't look like he was going to invite me in, but I wasn't a neighbor. He said, "The hell you want?"

"I heard you're in the rock 'n' roll business."

"You looking for tickets, you cheap bastard?"

"I heard they can't give them away."

"Wait till they announce John Lennon is coming."

"I hope he does come, Vinnie," I said. "And I hope it's a big success, I really do."

He looked at me for a moment as if trying to think of something to say. All he came up with was, "What do you want?"

"I'm looking for a guy."

"You won't find any fags here."

I wasn't sure that was a hundred percent true, but I said, "An American. Carl might know him; they have some interests in common."

Vinnie smiled a little and said, "McCaskill still owns your ass, doesn't he?"

"I'm working for him, yeah."

He stepped close enough for me to smell Export A cigarettes on his breath and said, "Lots of people thought you'd snitch. But I knew you'd never do that."

"You're a good judge of character."

He laughed. "You're something, Billy. I don't know what, but you're something."

"Is Carl here?"

He turned around and yelled, "Hey, Carl, get your ass out here," and then looked at me and said, "You don't get to go inside, no patch." He tapped his finger on my chest.

The door opened and Carl Franklin came out. The last time I'd seen him he was wearing a green army jacket and a bandanna but now he looked like all the other bikers in a leather vest and black T-shirt. And he'd pulled his long hair into a ponytail. He saw me and smiled and said, "Holy shit, Billy, haven't seen you since the Don. You finally going to join up?"

Vinnie was pissed off and said, "No, he isn't, that offer no longer stands."

"I do appreciate it," I said.

Carl said, "You did another six months after I got sprung, didn't you? Shit, I hate that jail, it's got ghosts."

I said, "Yeah, it does."

Vinnie started walking toward the bikes parked on what was once the front lawn and said, "Don't give him shit."

After he pulled out and drove off, Carl said, "You want a beer?" and I said I did.

Carl lifted the lid on a cooler and pulled out a pair of bottles.

I stepped up onto the deck and took a seat on one of the big living room chairs.

"You might want to reconsider," Carl said. "These guys have their shit together."

"Yeah, it looks like it."

"So, you looking for some supply? I hope you ain't bringing in your own, these guys won't like that."

"I'm not in that business," I said.

Carl laughed. "No? You find anything else makes as much money, you let me know."

"Right now, I'm looking for a guy, an American."

"You talk to them down on Baldwin, that's where all the draft dodgers are."

"This guy was in the Army. Made bombs."

Carl smiled a little and then drank some beer. "Americans love to blow shit up."

"He might be a radical now, looking to do some of that here."

"Here?" Carl looked surprised then reconsidered. "Like the US embassy, maybe?"

"Maybe, maybe the consulate building here in Toronto."

"Or maybe a bridge," Carl said. "Radicals love stuff that looks big."

I said, "There are no bridges in Toronto, that's one of the weirdest things about it."

"Bloor viaduct, but I get your point. Rainbow Bridge in Niagara Falls would be a big story; it would go international."

"Anybody talk to you about that?"

Carl drank some beer and considered it. "There's always someone talking about it."

"Anybody talking about it recently?"

"You know the picture place on Baldwin?"

"The gallery, yeah. Draft dodger runs it, right?"

"Not him," Carl said. "Girl who works there. She might have asked about something."

"Thanks, man, I appreciate it." I finished my beer and looked around for a place to put the bottle.

"Don't worry about it," Carl said. "We got guys called hang-arounds, they pick up all the shit." Then he laughed and said, "You really should think about joining up."

I dropped the empty on the floor and stood up. "I'll think about that."

"You can probably skip the hang-around part."

"These guys break rules like politicians."

"It's 'cause they have so many rules," Carl said. "More than the Army."

He was still smiling as I climbed into my Beetle and pulled away.

The Baldwin Street Gallery had a sign in the door that said it was closed, so I went next door to the Student Union for Peace Alliance. When I stepped inside it sounded as if there was a war going on in the back office—yelling, banging on the tables, people stomping around.

"You here to immigrate?"

I hadn't noticed the only person in the reception area, a young woman behind a desk.

"No, I was born here."

"Lucky you."

"You weren't?"

"No." She was wearing glasses and her long hair was in a ponytail. She was sitting in front of a typewriter. "There are women in the movement, too."

"I didn't think you could get drafted."

"We can't, but we can protest the war."

"But you don't have to come to Canada to do that."

She motioned over her shoulder to the inner office where the shouting was coming from. "That's what they're fighting about. The Marxists say they should stay in America and fight there."

"They'll go to jail, won't they?"

"That's what they say they should do, fill the prisons to overflowing with anti-draft protesters."

I said, "That seems easy to say from Canada."

"That's what the pacifists are saying."

"How many different groups are in there?"

She tilted her head and shrugged a little. "How many people are in there?"

"I thought no man was an island."

"Sounds like you haven't been in many planning meetings."

"I do try to avoid them."

"You came to the wrong place."

"The gallery was closed."

She said, "Oh, so you really weren't coming here?"

"I don't have anything against this place," I said. "But I'm looking for a woman who works in the gallery."

"Emily."

"Maybe."

"She's the only girl in there. Turns out photographers are as much of a boys' club as everybody else."

"Do you know when she'll be back?"

She walked back to the desk, pulled the piece of paper out of the typewriter, and said, "As soon as she puts this letter in an envelope."

I said, "Hello, Emily, my name is Billy."

"Hi, Billy. What can I do for you?"

She walked across the reception area, took an envelope from a pile of stationery, and folded the paper.

There was a loud shout from the back office that sounded like, "We're done here!"

I said, "Maybe I can walk back to the gallery with you?"

"Sure thing."

She led the way out the door, saying, "I do work here, too, and it's mostly typing. You'd be surprised how many letters a revolution needs to write."

She unlocked the gallery's door and stepped inside. The front room was small, and the white walls were covered with black-and-white photos in frames.

I said, "Which ones are yours?"

"The back wall." She pointed as she walked down a hall to an office.

The pictures on three of the walls were mostly musicians and fans at concerts, probably Woodstock. Emily's pictures were all at protests. I recognized a few of them from a couple years before, the big antiwar rally at City Hall on Canada's hundredth birthday, July 1, 1967. A lot of the pictures showed the signs people were carrying, almost all saying that US troops should get out of Vietnam. There were also a few pictures from smaller rallies in front of the US consulate on University Avenue in Toronto.

Emily came back into the room, and I said, "This was just a couple weeks ago."

"For people who couldn't make it to Woodstock."

I said, "That's what the Rock 'n' Roll Revival is for."

She stood beside me and said, "So, what do you want?"

"I'm looking for someone," I said.

"Who?"

I took the photo the American had given me out of my pocket and showed her.

"He's a deserter?"

"So I'm told."

"Why are you looking for him?"

"I have something he needs."

She looked at me and said, "What?"

"It's really for him. Something he's trying to do."

"What's that?"

I waited a beat and then said, "We're interested in more direct action."

"You and him?"

"That's right."

She glanced at the picture again and said, "He's not interested in direct action."

"Are you sure?"

"Yes."

"So, you know him?"

"I know him well enough to know that."

"Do you know where I can find him?"

She walked away from me toward the door of the gallery and said, "You should go now."

For a moment I didn't move. "We're on the same side here."

"No, we're not, you're a cop."

"No, I'm not."

"You're better at hiding it than most but I'm better at spotting it."

I said, "This guy is dangerous. His kind of direct action could get innocent people hurt. Or killed."

She smirked. "Innocent."

I looked away from her and toward the framed photos on the wall. One of the pictures wasn't from a protest; it looked like a ceremony, a lot of people standing in a circle around a young couple. In the small crowd outside the circle, I saw someone I recognized. Talking to the guy I was looking for.

"When was this taken?"

"You have to go now." As I walked past her, she pointed at the photo still in my hand and said, "Your bosses lied to you, he's not into direct action."

"What's he into?"

She shook her head. "Get out, narc."

I'd been called a lot worse, and I expected to be called a lot worse in the future.

Officially Rochdale College was a student-run, alternative-education co-op. But really it was an eighteen-story apartment building filled with U of T students and no rules. It had opened the year before and was already falling apart. In front of the building was a small concrete space that the architects probably figured would be used as an outdoor meeting place or be used for impromptu art exhibits or small concerts but was almost always filled with panhandlers and drug dealers.

My kind of people.

"Hey, Billy."

A girl was coming toward me, smiling. I said, "Hi, Sandy, how you doing?"

"Doing good."

I would have asked how high she was, but I didn't want to know.

She said, "You still got paid for finding me right, even though I came right back?"

"Yeah," I said, "I still got paid." She'd been easy to find, and her parents thought it was a great deal when they paid M&P, but it didn't come with a money-back guarantee any more than Sandy went back home with a guarantee that she'd stay in Sault Ste. Marie.

"So, you've got some money?"

I took a two-dollar bill out of my wallet and said, "Is Stringer around?"

"He was here."

I held the bill back. "Where is he now?"

"He's coming back."

"He is?"

She put her hand on her heart and said, "Promise." Then she squeezed her own boob and giggled and said, "I should be a go-go dancer."

I handed her the bill. "You should be a lot of things, Sandy."

She took my money and danced away, into the crowd.

A couple of girls had set up a folding table and were selling bowls of brown rice with vegetables, so I bought one and sat on a bench and waited. Sure enough, less than half an hour later, Jay Stringer showed up looking way too much like a salesman trying to be nice to everyone. He saw me and I waved him over. "If your product is good, you don't need to try so hard."

"Don't worry about my product." He was still smiling that phony smile, but it was clear he wasn't happy to see me. He said, "You know if you try to work here, I have to call Sam."

"You know I don't do that anymore."

"Oh yeah, you're looking for runaways now. You want to be a pimp you still have to talk to Sam."

"I'm looking for this guy." I held up the photo of the deserter.

"Never seen that guy in my life."

"There's a picture of you talking to him hanging on the wall at the Baldwin Street Gallery."

"Not me."

Behind him a couple of cops in short-sleeved shirts open at the collar made their way toward us, and the older one said, "You guys starting a union?"

Stringer said, "I don't even know this guy."

"I thought we told both of you to stay away from here."

I said, "Sergeant McCaskill asked us to do him a favor."

"Did he now?"

"Somebody's daughter ran away."

The younger cop said, "We can find her."

"This is somebody important who doesn't want an official police report."

"What's the name?" The young cop stepped closer to me, so I looked past him to the older one and said, "She sees you, she'll run. We'll find her and tell McCaskill you were very helpful."

The older cop said, "Okay, punk, you make sure he knows. I don't want to be walking this beat when winter comes."

I said, "He'll know."

The younger cop was still mad, but he followed the older one and walked away.

I looked at Stringer and said, "Where can I find this guy?"

"Why don't you actually become a cop; you already stink like a pig."

"Where?"

"He's got a room at the Waverly."

"He's doing all right."

"The product is good."

The Waverly Hotel was above the Silver Dollar bar on Spadina, just a few blocks further west along Bloor from Rochdale. I could've walked, but I drove my Beetle, parked a block from the hotel, sat in the Silver Dollar, and waited.

The country band was just finishing their first set when the guy in the photo came in. Bobby Williamson. He did have longer hair now and was wearing a leather jacket and jeans, but he still had the scars on his forehead. I watched him make two deals in ten minutes. Then I went to the pay phone and called Rodney and woke him up.

"I found him."

"Do not engage with him. Where are you?"

"He's not a mad bomber," I said. "He's just a dealer."

"You sure?"

"I know a deal when I see one go down."

"Yeah, I guess you do."

"Looks like the guys from the consulate lied to you."

Rodney said, "Where are you?"

"Waverly Hotel."

"He's there?"

"He is."

The phone went dead. I thought about waiting around and seeing who showed up, if it would be the Americans or McCaskill and a dozen Toronto cops or just McCaskill and Rodney, but I figured it could get ugly. This really looked like a deal that was way above my pay grade.

Walking out of the hotel I thought it was too bad the guy was just a dealer and not really a mad bomber. It would've felt good to have stopped someone from blowing up a bridge and killing a lot of innocent people. But I'm no hero.

Robin was right, though, I liked being a private eye.

Might have to take her up on that offer, see if John Lennon really shows up at the Toronto Rock 'n' Roll Revival.

DISORDERED

Jarrett Mazza

SIXTY MINUTES.

Sixty minutes is all that I have before I forget what I know and must return to the very beginning in order to remember.

A night of a full moon, such is also a time for trying to retrieve the contents of my letters, something else I plunged into the back of my fragile, increasingly *more* fragile mind. Able to retrieve a few details, certainly, mostly, it comes in parts—*tiny fragments I can only reassemble with enough diligence and effort.*

Diagnosed with Alzheimer's two years to the day, the last letter, that is the last one I can recall, forced me here, on the road, driving in the wake of night toward something I don't know unless I concentrate. Once the greatest detective, I need to remind myself that not everyone is as they seem, how the world isn't filled with perfect people, only perfect in some parts, and that mistakes that shouldn't have been made but were, *nonetheless.*

Still, tonight, I know where I'm going, yet not what brought me here...not *quite so.*

There aren't many who are like me, that is the men who were born with terrific minds, yet also some with a mind that rots a little more each day.

I wish had more time. Always, more time.

Son of a bitch...

I don't usually correspond with the killers I'm trying to find.

Every sick son of a bitch, I remind myself, is only a misunderstood, mislabeled sick *son of a bitch*, and someone who often has a story; a reason for why they are *what* they are.

Like my mind, people tend to lose things, and I'm the one who tries to remember what it is—remember so I can find my way back.

What is the difference between a police detective and a private detective?

A joke, spoken by my friend, also a detective, Brenda Song, a woman who stayed uniform because she said she needed to. Such changed when she was promoted and even more changed when she asked me to help her with a few murders happening in and around San Francisco.

I wore flip-flops, jeans, whenever I was with her.

Old friends.

One works for profit and the other works for justice?

Laughing, she was one of the finest officers I've ever had the privilege of working with, and said she needed someone who might spot things she didn't. I think she just wanted me close. In my life, Brenda Song, the captain of a county south of San Francisco, where I lived, and one who was in fact treating me to a beer whenever the topic emerged.

You feeling okay?

Never wanting to tell her the truth, I decided I would let her know when I had no other choice.

No, I always wanted to tell her, couldn't, because if she knew, she wouldn't need me, and if I wasn't needed, then there was no need to.

And now, filling the sky, a sprawling haze of light that engulfed the horizon, illuminating the fine ridges you can't see unless you try, I was on the road. Driving, while not permitted to because of my condition, I sucked on my cig as if it was the last I would ever taste.

I guess, in a way, it was.

The thick, fresh smoke stung my lungs as I inhaled, and feeling

the smoke, it burrowed deep inside, which was good. It distracted me.

Forty minutes was all I had, but then what was the point of
knowing if not to come to fully understand his motives, and finally unravel the reasons why.

"Why do you think he's doing this?"

Shrugging, I answered.

"Does he even need an answer?"

The process, or more accurate to say, the decay, began after I
received a letter.

Addressed to me, I asked why and then noticed the clues.
The life of a detective, always about asking questions, always
on the lookout for narrative and a complex web of lies, though
his was the same, from what I could remember.

You'll see why I do what I do.

A hot air assimilated in my lungs and concentrated to the
point I unleashed a throaty cough that scraped my esophagus,
upturning phlegm and flakes of ash. Gulping them down like
always, I looked up at the sky, it like a wall covered with a layer
of slick paint, the stars peppered the sky, not nearly enough as
what I saw earlier.

I try to see his face but am left only with his words.

Why?

Incapable of comprehending what would possess a father to
fatally burn his only child, of course, this was only the story
told, not one I could by any means validate.

The first conversation was a letter.

Writing it to me, only to me. With my name written in full on
the envelope and him addressing me the way, so few things did.

The first letter was in a manila envelope.

*In this world of utter despair, people stop and cry and plead
to understand why it's so unfair.*

*I have said goodbye to the world as it was and seek to shape
it in the way I wanted, and when people would ask why, I will
simply say...because.*

Those who change the world provide no reason for why they are what they are, their need for destruction...maleficence.

But then that's why I have chosen to write this letter to you and no one else.

You know you will not remember, and yet that compels you to see beyond yourself?

I promise that you will see what you could not before.

Trust me and you'll understand, why I am the future...the one you've been waiting for.

Keeping the letter, I told no one about. Even if I did, I wouldn't remember or know what to say.

Since when do killers write to their detectives?

Unless they wanted to be found, and by the only one who will not remember.

The sixties, a decade sparked by waves of cultural upheaval and many social norms that were challenged and turned. When it happened, everything we knew to be true had changed: music, fashion, the call to be something more. A time of enlightenment, of rebellion, a time where people made certain changes while fighting for something greater than themselves.

At least, that's how I chose to see it.

What did the decade ask of its people?

I imagined he, the one writing the letters, I figured we were the same, one with a proclivity for detail, a detective blessed and cursed with low latent inhibition and an escalating case of Alzheimer's worsening every day.

Too much at one time made me weak in the knees, dizzy.

The first thought I had after reading the letter was to tell Brenda. She was the only one with a mind that I felt was greater than mine. But, before I could form a proper response, I forgot the reasons why I was calling.

However, the letter, the words, were still there.

And, aside from the fact that each crime committed, each note uncovered was addressed to me. In each one, he insisted on constant yammering or unleashing his belittling, philosophical conundrums, all of which he thought I cared to hear.

Today, driving past a store that sold color televisions, I couldn't help but tilt my head and peer inside. The radio, still playing, I never bothered to change the station. It was the Beatles, playing one of their many adored songs about love. If only they knew what was happening, the monsters who walk among us...how come no one ever sings about that?

Finishing the cigarette, bits of tobacco sticking to my teeth, and imbedded between.

Licking them clean, I had what I had, and knew that in time I would learn more about who I was too.

No one knew about the letters, especially not that that person writing them was front and center for every major news story flooding the radio, the TV circuit. Wanting to tell Brenda, the pieces that were there, but even so, there was so much missing.

Pausing, extending the examination, remembering fragments of what I had: the letter, the riddles, the paraphiliac fantasies he likely had about each of his victims. Always mere seconds from knowing and forgetting, such was not a game I was willing to play as much as it was an attempt to see what will happen; how it would eventually end.

Every week he would send me another, another preview of something hidden, and a hint about what he was planning to do next. With some diligent note taking, immediately after, even doing this, still, I would forget.

Detective Henry Yu, one of the other detectives who worked alongside Brenda Song, in San Francisco, his definition of a decent greeting was to say that my reputation preceded me. Only talking about my younger days, when I solved a few missing-person cases and was told that I was the best.

I wish I could remember those days.

From the letter, I didn't notice at first, or maybe I couldn't remember, there was Ottendorf cipher built into it.

Under the light, some of letters brightened.

In this world of utter despair, people stop and cry and plead for why it's so unfair.

A long time ago, I said goodbye to the world as it was, and began to shape it in my way, and when people ask why I say...because. A great letter provides no reason for why they are the way that they are, their need for destruction, maleficence.

But then that's why I have chosen to write this next letter to you and no one else.

You see things as they are, all the things that have broken your memory.

I promise that you will see what you could not before.

Trust me and you'll understand, why I am the one you've been waiting for.

Only reading the letter once, the message emerged.

I took another one for you.

Of all the words written, only two resonated:

For you.

Most wouldn't write to someone like me unless they wanted to be tailed, surveilled, or remembered, and he knew I wouldn't do either. Few knew of my growing condition, though he did. A private eye, once a damn good thinker who kept damn good notes, before this, most of my job was me, talking to divorced Hollywood housewives who believed their husbands were engaging in lascivious activity with housemaids, which was, for the most part, true, but also, a failure to admit that they married assholes and should have chosen better. For this guy, I knew it was never about murder, leaving a trail, or anything else that these cunning predators of the new era were only just starting to become.

While I liked puzzles, liked clues, I hated more to forget.

The bodies, only two, the first of which I discovered hanging upside down in a vacant garage two blocks from the nearest subway station.

The face, burnt, the fingers appeared shredded.

No way of properly identifying.

There was a note found on the body. Brenda handed it to me.

See the dead, look ahead, you depend on only what needs to be said, for there is a truth here that cannot be put to rest.

Squinting, the note was only a warning.

"Weird one, huh?"

He didn't want me to call the police. If I did, he would only kill someone else.

Sipping scotch, just to take the edge off, it helped me to remember the way I wanted to.

Forget now, forgetting almost all the time.

He wanted to interact with someone capable of following him into the confines of his breaking mind. He wanted me to see his crimes escalating, and currently, such a purpose was to indicate something bigger.

When doing any of my investigations before my memory began to fade, it was helpful for me to conduct conversations as if I were the suspect.

Helped with remembering as well.

"Sending good men to find the bad ones and then making arrests, putting them behind bars while all the while the world rots from the outside."

While it was being sealed, I recalled a little of Brenda and my last conversation.

"And is that the purpose of these riddles and rhymes, to what, keep us guessing even though we have you to do that for us?"

Again, I couldn't tell her.

"What he seeks to do will do more than just provide clarity, maybe he's trying to help us see something."

Thinking again about the cipher, I looked again at the messages when I returned to my apartment.

Purpose?

Continuing to play, the incessant repetition of songs that were always about the same fucking thing, a world full love, of peace, if only they knew...

Always with a new song and was just to navigate the letter.

Complex, relentless, but then that was his game.

Puzzles and problems, puzzles and problems.

"You want to solve it, you have to be looking for the solution, not the reason."

These words my words, not Brenda's, and she didn't know what I was looking for.

More songs followed:

"Light My Fire,"

"If I was to say to you"

"Living in the Past.

"Happy and I'm smiling."

A new song sung while going over his letter, for the fifth, possibly the tenth, or fifteenth time.

In addition to the note, there was a symbol.

Subtle, initially, this was not the first time I was seeing it.

A crisscross, a circle with a line drawn through the side.

Later, I received a call. It was from Brenda.

"Another body."

Being called in, I saw her, with the other police, all crowded around something I couldn't see. Heading in, dipping under the tape, I moved in, and Brenda stepped aside and allowed me to see.

With arms spread cruciformly, the victim was there, facedown, with knife wounds along the neck. Counting seven, she was likely dead after two, and still the killer persisted.

Spotting a squiggling line with a loop around the woman's left side, there was a symbol, and Brenda raised her hand and pointed.

"Never seen this before."

At the scene, Brenda, not telling her of the code recovered in the letter, something I could only barely remember. This I had forgotten, yet it was something I could also remember, *vaguely.*

There was a symbol.

A Leo.

Mine.

Not telling the local police, without my pad, I could only barely recall what was, or what might see in the days that followed. Whenever the word "fed" was mentioned, he didn't necessarily mean FBI, although these days Hoover's elite investigation unit was primarily interested in tracking politicians, *celebrities.*

Lugging the body, the victim, identified as prostitute Michelle Mathers, it was a name given by my close friend, Wade Henretty, a Black man who, though not a detective, worked as a forensic photographer.

He knew more about how to look at clues than half the people employed at the precinct.

He informed me that the symbols were Zodiac, which I knew, but could not remember.

Lost, there was nothing new to place or nothing not to, other than to wait.

"Wait until when?"

Frustrated, my fight, not with Wade, never was, the idea that, unlike my law enforcement buddies, who were not really buddies, I had to wait if I was to unlock the truth.

Three days later, another body. Unlike the others, this one was found in a chair, tied by the arms and the wrist, and through the skull, a smoking hole, and a phrase carved into the stomach.

What you think you know you will not believe.

You're preparing for a future that, even now, you know you cannot see.

Below the words, the carving; a letter…K.

I thought about taking it to Brenda Song. She didn't have a clue what she saw.

Still, I wanted to tell her.

Many mistook her for Korean, though her ascension to one of the lead detectives in law enforcement in just one district in the great city of San Francisco was the result of her diligent mind. It was also the fact that, prior to her promotion, she oversaw the arrest of three criminals operating an illegal gambling outfit outside Santana Row.

Gazing at the body, there was another symbol, and so another clue, the other reason why I was brought here. Squinting, trying to remember, another Zodiac sign, though I didn't say I had seen it before or how, with each letter, another clue was given to the victims; clues that were scattered about my consciousness, like spilled cereal.

"You're the brilliant detective, I think you're in a better position to answer than I am."

Always flattered by how much Brenda thought I was the man I once was; she had a way of commending me that kept me focused, maintained my proclivity for ensuring how the details remained at the forefront of every one of my investigations.

This exchange, solely between us, once the crime scene was cleared, Brenda and I were by the car, sharing a cigarette, and looking up at the God damn, most beautiful sky I had seen in a long time.

"Thanks for coming in."

"No problem."

"So, you think this is the *same* guy?"

Pinching the cigarette, still trying to remember.

Maybe.

I didn't say.

Watching me all the time, he had to be considering how he knew my routine so well.

An outsider who spied, surveilled, with each night, before bed, after scavenging my mind for answers, I would go to the roof, and look up at the sky.

With those recovered, Brenda was tracing the footsteps of each of the victims. The ones so far were nameless, came from broken homes. The morality scale that was once used to measure people based on how they obeyed the institutions that governed them, though not obsolete, was becoming less impactful, less indicative of who people were, at least it was around here.

Trying to remember, the notes sprawled across my desk: names, photos, reports, all of it connected by string, crossed along the pictures and roped around the pegs beneath them.

Pieces I could remember, pieces I couldn't.

Even now, I could see them all, the faces, and asking myself what connected them.

What was the *connection*? What was the *narrative*?

Scanning all the faces stored somewhere in my memory, such was not something that could escape anyone. Of course, detectives are always on the lookout for narrative because narrative pertains to motive and motive pertains to reason, and once you find the reason, then you can stop them.

The next day, another clue, this one left in my mailbox, with spaces between, left to read along with a new letter. His riddles, not designed to provide clues, rather to taunt, torture, and to remind me how I wasn't the man I used to be.

A watchmaker following the ticks of a clock, why on Earth do you continue to roam and cluck, when the journey toward the end begins at a quarter past dawn?

The last clue?

With a time and a location, I could remember what I read last, but not much else.

Racing down the CA 130, the address, barely able to recall, the dawn now transforming into the night, he had selected his locations based on those that embodied such changes.

Alameda Valley, the reveal, suddenly I saw it, came in the same way as the others.

Appearing again in my consciousness, the clues, highlighted in each of his letters, bringing it to the light, the details returned to me.

I could see more of the details.

What is it that you are now?

Are you all a detective or all a man who cannot see beyond these fortuitous frowns?

Of those who look at him each day and cannot seem to remember the reasons for why it is they're down to play?

I know you will never remember this soon-to-be-over game.

Now that you have answered the call, do you vanish not knowing what's all mean?

Soon you see I am the key to all things.

You'll know why it is I who gave birth to the twenty-first century.

In the various places, more letters that, once retrieved, translated to this place.

You're the only one who sees.

Gripping the wheel, sixty minutes, old man.

Sixty minutes is all you have, and then you'll never see it again.

Checking my watch, forty minutes disappeared in a flash, and the valley I was in now was but a ceaseless canyon, a desolate park. In the wake of the night, such a location *should* be vacant, and was now so dark it would be like journeying through a flourishing abyss.

Bringing the car to the park, trudging across fat pockets of greenery, brushing aside whatever bushes, or small assortment of plants stood in the way, the light caught two figures on the ground.

You'll see.

Shaking my head, his voice continued to rattle, burrowing deeper and deeper, like feet digging into mushy soil.

I bumped into one of the trees and hunkered down to catch my breath.

"No."

Sinking deeper into the mossy ground, the bodies of the girls, still warm; their faces stung the tips of my fingers as I reached out to touch. Perforated by stab wounds, all inflicted throughout, to feel them now was only to admit that they were slain in cold blood. I never cried when I saw the dead. If you weep for those you've lost, every night will be as sleepless as those you fear when trying to rest.

Making the call, the park was sealed, not by Brenda.

This wasn't her scene.

How did I get here? How long was I driving?

Resting near a squad of patrol cars, the sun-parched landscape became but another scene that needed to be siphoned, and the bodies, two children, Deborah Furlong and Kathy Snoozy. Both were around the ages of fourteen and fifteen, and Brenda, arriving shortly after, she followed when she was told by the neighboring precinct, and yet, she showed as soon as she heard I was present.

The police, swarming the grooves of the hills, they later notified the families before they rolled the victims off into a pair of stark ambulances.

"May I ask what brought you here, to the park?"

Sitting on the edge of the smallest hill, a snooty cop with the curved nose insisted on asking me redundant questions as he aimed his flashlight in my face.

"I'm not a suspect, asshole."

Condescending, I disclosed how I was given a tip from someone who said to come here, didn't say who. My reputation protected me, I thought.

"Who? Give us a name!"

Shaking my head, couldn't remember.

Eyes shut, the conversations shared with the maniac surfaced in mere fragments, and I couldn't put them together, and it was like I was listening to another bad song, one of the many coined during this time. And yet, each one, supposedly housed its own message, I couldn't help but wonder if that was where the idea came from: listening to too many songs and reading too many books.

You'll see.

Brenda, next to the provoking fucking cop who insisted on reminding me of the sixty minutes that had passed, it was too late to make any difference.

Dave Toschi was his name.

This was his scene.

"He killed them! He fucking killed them!"

"Yeah," said Brenda. "I know."

Not the only detective present at the crime scene, with word for the main investigator, she was here because she felt she was tracking the same killer. I had yet to tell her if she was or wasn't. *Of course not.*

"We will find him," she said. "With your help, we'll find him sooner."

Standing up, and then nodding, I wiped my face clean of the sweat that glazed my cheeks. Rarely did I sweat, and yet now, I was covered.

I couldn't remember.

In 1969, a string of murders relentlessly accumulated in the sunny state of California, each one initiated and designed by one man.

Holding the newspaper, the front page was occupied with a sketch of a man in black, a symbol etched in his chest, showing him like he was some classic comic book villain. I never told anyone what he had given to me, except for his last letter, which was hardly a pattern, but farewell to all the time spent.

Sometimes, Brenda would call, ask me to look at some things.

Holding out my hand, looking to the first letter that followed the first victim, I read, and inferred meaning, and heard his voice nudging my consciousness, poking at my stability.

Karl Werner, who confessed to the murders of Deborah Furlong and Kathy Snoozy, and at the trial, Brenda, in attendance, she was there next to me, had been the whole time.

"Got 'em."

"Got who?"

On the phone, later, she mentioned a suspect.

Mr. Werner, who was the only suspect when he was arrested, confessed to only one of the crimes. When asked about the others, Werner confessed to none.

His voice, unfamiliar, déjà vu, when I heard him, I could swear...

Knowing the letters meant nothing if I couldn't view the signs that began at the beginning, in the end, he was just another killer, no mark on history, no name to be remembered.

"Do you think he's still out there?"

Brenda, following the case but not working on it outright, we met again for coffee, and still, she didn't know.

"I'm sure they'll find him sooner or later."

"Do you still have those letters?"

Last question she asked me before I finished drinking.

"I don't know," I said, holding my mug, seeing more fragments, the pieces, the symbol, the name...

"I am trying so hard to remember."

Photo Credit Amber Bracken

MICHAEL BRACKEN is the author of several books, including the private eye novel *All White Girls*, and more than twelve hundred short stories in several genres. His short crime fiction has appeared in *Alfred Hitchcock's Mystery Magazine, Ellery Queen's Mystery Magazine, Espionage Magazine, Mike Shayne Mystery Magazine, The Best American Mystery Stories 2018, The Mysterious Bookshop Presents The Best Mystery Stories of the Year 2021,* and in many other anthologies and periodicals. A recipient of the Edward D. Hoch Memorial Golden Derringer Award for lifetime achievement in short mystery fiction, Bracken has received two Derringer Awards and been shortlisted for two others. Additionally, Bracken is editor of *Black Cat Mystery Magazine* and has edited several anthologies, including the Anthony Award-nominated *The Eyes of Texas: Private Eyes from the Panhandle to the Piney Woods* and the *Mickey Finn* series. Born in 1957, he experienced the sixties through the eyes of a child and still remembers stringing his own love beads.

ABOUT THE CONTRIBUTORS

MICHAEL CHANDOS is a Colorado Licensed Private Investigator and the Macavity Award-nominated author of stories published in *Black Coffee*, *Shotgun Honey*, *Stories in the Near Future*, *Stories from the World of Tomorrow*, and *The Eyes of Texas: Private Eyes from the Panhandle to the Piney Woods*.

WIL A. EMERSON was raised on the other side of Eight Mile Road, Detroit city limits. She's a three-time Derringer Award nominee, an award winner in Bould Anthology Award 2020, and her work has appeared in numerous anthologies.

JEFF ESTERHOLM was the little kid you may have noticed standing on a dock at a Wisconsin lake in the mid-sixties, wearing a Beatles wig and playing kick-ass air guitar. Now he writes short stories, which have appeared in Akashic Books' *Mondays are Murder*, *Rock and a Hard Place Magazine*, *Shotgun Honey*, and *Tough*, among other publications. In 2013, he received the Sternig Award for Short Fiction from the Council for Wisconsin Writers.

JOHN M. FLOYD's short stories have appeared in *Alfred Hitchcock's Mystery Magazine*, *Ellery Queen's Mystery Magazine*, *Strand Magazine*, *The Saturday Evening Post*, *Best American Mystery Stories*, and many other publications. A former Air Force captain and IBM systems engineer, John is also an Edgar finalist, a Shamus Award winner, a four-time Derringer Award winner, a three-time Pushcart Prize nominee, and the author of eight books. As a college student, he spent the summer of 1967 working in Flint, Michigan.

NILS GILBERTSON is a crime and mystery writer and practicing attorney. Although a more recent UC Berkeley graduate, he has long been interested in the Free Speech Movement that defined campus culture in the 1960s. His short stories have appeared in *Mystery Magazine, Mickey Finn: 21st Century Noir Vols. 2 & 3, Rock and a Hard Place Magazine, Pulp Modern,* and others. You can find him on Twitter @NilsGilbertson and reach him at nilspgilbertson@gmail.com.

WENDY HARRISON is a retired Florida prosecutor who spent the early sixties in Greenwich Village, listening to jazz and watching people storm out of Lenny Bruce gigs. In the late sixties, she marched in anti-Vietnam War parades down Broadway. She does remember the sixties even though she really was there. Her stories have been published in numerous anthologies, including *Peace, Love & Crime, Autumn Noir, CRIMEUCOPIA: Tales from the Front Porch*, and *Death of a Bad Neighbour*.

DAVID H. HENDRICKSON has published seven novels, including *Cracking the Ice* and *Offside*, which have been adopted for high school student required reading. His short fiction has appeared in *Best American Mystery Stories, Ellery Queen's Mystery Magazine, Mickey Finn: 21st Century Noir*, and *Pulphouse*. He is a multi-finalist for and winner of the Derringer Award. He has released four short story collections. He spent much of the sixties battling with his parents over rock and roll, the Devil's music.

GAY TOLTL KINMAN has nine award nominations for her writing. The author of twelve novels, eight short story collections, and twenty plays collected in *The Play's the Thing*, her work has appeared in several magazines, anthologies, professional journals, newspapers, and books, including Mystery Writers of America's *How to Write a Mystery*. She co-edited two non-fiction books, has library and law degrees, and once checked out a book titled *The Sixties*.

LYNN MAPLES is a former award-winning journalist and marketing professional. Writing is his escape from the daily grind of web copy, marketing campaigns, and the nine-to-five hustle. He's been published in several mystery and crime anthologies. He lives in Memphis, Tennessee, the home of the blues and the King of Rock and Roll. It is also a city steeped in racial injustice that still echoes down the alleys and pathways walked by those determined to make a difference.

JARRETT MAZZA is a graduate of Goddard College's MFA in Creative Writing Program and The Humber School for Writers. He has been published extensively online and in print, was an Honourable Mention for the Freda Waldon Award for Fiction, and was featured in an anthology shortlisted for an Indie Book Award. Everything he learned from the sixties he learned from his mother and *Once Upon a Time in Hollywood*.

JOHN MCFETRIDGE was seven years old in 1967 when the world came to his hometown of Montreal for Expo 67 and seventeen when the world came back for the 1976 Summer Olympics. He's been stuck there ever since.

ROBERT PETYO grew up in the sixties and remembers his older sister going nuts when they watched the Beatles on *The Ed Sullivan Show*. He is a Derringer Award finalist whose stories have appeared in small press magazines and anthologies, most recently in *Hardboiled, Flash Bang Mysteries, The Black Beacon Book of Mystery, We're All Animals Under the Skin,*

Asinine Assassins, Careless Love, Now There Was a Story, Whodunit, and *Mickey Finn: 21st Century Noir.*

GRAHAM POWELL is the author of numerous short stories published in *Black Cat Mystery Magazine, Fedora III, The Eyes of Texas,* and many other publications. He remembers the sixties, so he must not have been there.

BEV VINCENT (BevVincent.com) is the author of *The Road to the Dark Tower* and *Stephen King: A Complete Exploration of His Work, Life, and Influences,* and more than one hundred twenty short stories, including appearances in *Ellery Queen's Mystery Magazine, Alfred Hitchcock's Mystery Magazine,* and *Black Cat Mystery Magazine.* His work has been nominated for the Stoker, Edgar, Ignotus, and ITW Thriller Awards. He was born at the tail end of the baby boom in the early 1960s.

JOSEPH S. WALKER, born five months into the seventies, began a lifelong fascination with the sixties through afternoon reruns of *The Monkees.* His stories have appeared in *Alfred Hitchcock's Mystery Magazine, Ellery Queen's Mystery Magazine, Mystery Tribune,* and many other magazines and anthologies. He has been nominated for the Edgar Award and the Derringer Award and has won the Bill Crider Prize for Short Fiction. He also won the Al Blanchard Award in 2019 and 2021.

STACY WOODSON (StacyWoodson.com) is a US Army veteran, and memories of her time in the military are often a source of inspiration for her stories. She made her crime fiction debut in *Ellery Queen's Mystery Magazine*'s Department of First Stories and won the 2018 Readers Award. Since her debut, she has placed stories in several anthologies and publications. In 2021, she won the Derringer Award. A lover of history, she learned about the sixties from books, documentaries, and her father—a Vietnam veteran who volunteered to serve.

BOOKS

On the following pages are a few
more great titles from the
Down & Out Books publishing family.

For a complete list of books and to
sign up for our newsletter,
go to DownAndOutBooks.com.

27 Days
A Nick Crane Thriller
Patrick H. Moore

Down & Out Books
February 2023
978-1-64396-298-6

27 Days is a topical political thriller in which veteran Los Angeles PI Nick Crane races against time to save his partner Bobby Moore, who has been abducted by a powerful right wing domestic terrorist named Marguerite Ferguson.

If Nick doesn't surrender to Marguerite within twenty-seven days, Bobby Moore will be sent to Scorpion Prison in Egypt where he will be tortured and killed.

Quietly Into the Night
Vincent Zandri

Down & Out Books
February 2023
978-1-64396-299-3

A bestselling author wakes up on a train and has no idea how he got there. When he finds himself accused of throwing a fellow author off the balcony of a New York City high-rise apartment building, he now must battle not only memory loss, but he must also fight for his very life.

From *New York Times* and *USA Today* bestselling Thriller and Shamus Award-winning author Vincent Zandri comes a novel of deception, murder, and double-crosses that only Alfred Hitchcock could concoct.

Yesterday Rising
Three Crime Novellas
Stephen Burdick

Down & Out Books
February 2023
978-1-64396-301-3

Joe Hampton seems destined to continue living a life of solving crimes—a life from which he officially retired. The old itch won't let him rest, and he can't resist the need to help his friends Detective Carly Truffant and Detective David Sizemore as they go about uncovering the truth surrounding the mysteries that arise.

"An authentic police voice. It's like going on a ride-along."
—Colin Campbell, author of the Jim Grant Thrillers

Drums, Guns 'n' Money
A Lou Crasher Thriller
Jonathan J. Brown

Down & Out Books
March 2023
978-1-64396-305-1

Rock drummer turned amateur P.I. Lou Crasher has just found his good friend Trix Rockland murdered. Forming an odd partnership with attractive detective Tanaka, the two launch go at the list of suspects. The case begins at L.A.'s rock scene and moves into illegal incarceration, and possibly the for-profit prison system.

"*Drums, Guns 'n' Money* is a jazzy up tempo mystery that kicks like a snare roll. Jonathan Brown brings his musicality to this down and dirty crime story. Loved it!"
—SA Cosby, bestselling author of *Razorblade Tears*